Grant Wolves Series

Early Grave
Shallow Grave
Grave Threat
Grave Legacy
Grave Origins
Grave Rites

Secondhand Magic Series

Null Witch
Hollow Witch
Witch Hunt

Standalone Books

Ghost Magnet

Anthologies

Undead Tales
Dark Shadows 2
Before, During, and After

WITCH HUNT

SECONDHAND MAGIC #3

LORI DRAKE

Published by Clockwork Cactus Press

PO Box 1874

Leander, TX 78646 USA

WITCH HUNT (SECONDHAND MAGIC #3)

ISBN-13: 978-1-955545-02-0

Cover by Christian Bentulan

Edited by Rebecca Hodgkins

Proofread by AE McKenna

For Sandi Lawson

In loving memory.

1

The *whump* of the warehouse door being breached was quieter than I expected in the crisp pre-dawn air. My heart thumped rapidly in anticipation as I held my position at the back of the line, feeling exposed despite the bulky Kevlar vest strapped to my torso. Large block letters across the front read CONSULTANT, as if that might stay the itchy trigger finger of a perp willing to do serious time for shooting a cop.

Tink, tink, tink, BOOM, BOOM, BOOM.

The flashbang went off, the line pushed forward, and I followed, the caboose on this little law enforcement train. It was pitch dark inside but for the beams of barrel-mounted flashlights, shouts of "Police! Put your hands up!" echoing off the ceiling of the cavernous building. The air smelled like sawdust and motor oil, and I wondered what this place had been, once upon a time.

Shaking off the thought, I turned my attention to my real job: keeping an eye out for magical threats, though I wasn't expecting any. But the whole point of my presence on this raid was to give me practice, so I did my duty diligently. The exterior of the building had been free of wards, as had the doors. I'd checked those out before we breached.

Now I scanned the darkness for any visible traces of magic as we moved between the pallets stacked fifteen-plus feet high on either side. The knowledge that there wasn't much I could do if I *did* discover a magic threat lingered like a bad odor. I had a couple of charms on me, but they were utilitarian at best. I missed my warded trench coat keenly. It was against regulation to wear the coat over my vest, and the coat was too bulky to wear the vest over it. If I encountered a magic threat, well, I had two options: warn the officers ahead of me or intercept the spell—if I happened to be in position to do so.

Having no weapon to point around, I panned my flashlight along the sides and upper edges of the pallets as we continued forward. The corridor was too narrow and the stacks too high for me to see over the top edge, but the print on the side of the stacked sacks on the pallets was legible even through the layers of industrial plastic wrap. Sand and salt, the sort used to de-ice roads in winter. Nothing exciting.

We emptied out of the corridor and into an open space at the center of the cavernous room, surrounded by towering pallets of plastic-wrapped sacks. In the very center sat a giant cargo crate. "FRAGILE" was stamped in red letters on the side facing us, easily read by the light of the dozen or so flashlights pointed at it.

"We've reached the center," a voice said over the earpiece tucked in my left ear. "No contact."

"Davenport?" Mike asked over the comms.

I stepped aside for a better view and squinted at the crate from about fifteen away. "Looks clean from this angle, but I can't say for sure. Get me closer?"

The group inched forward, flashlights panning once

more, all eyes and ears on high alert. The cops must've been feeling the same apprehension that I was. It was too quiet. We should've encountered someone by now. The intel had said the warehouse was guarded night and day, but we hadn't seen a living soul, inside or out.

The group stopped about ten feet away from the box, and I wiggled my way through to the front. I made a full circuit of the shoulder-high box but found no hint of magic on the outside.

"No wards, no traps," I concluded, though I hadn't expected to find anything. "Anyone bring a crowbar?"

The officers all looked amongst themselves, but a crowbar wasn't included on the standard raid kit.

"There's one in the truck," someone said.

"Go get it," Mike replied. Technically, he didn't need to be involved in this raid either. Narcotics raids were nothing new to him, given his background in that department. I suspected he was there to supervise me and keep me out of trouble, but whatever. He was my partner. It'd be weirder if he *wasn't* there.

We waited while someone fetched the crowbar, the only sounds the occasional creak of an equipment harness or shuffling feet on the bare concrete floor. There was no conversation, just tense silence. Heavy, hasty footsteps heralded the arrival of the officer with the crowbar. Mike appeared at my elbow and caught my arm, gently drawing me back from the crate. I shot him a questioning look, but he just guided me back behind the SWAT team. I rolled my eyes and tugged my arm from his grip but stood where he'd put me. At least he hung back with me while the guy with the crowbar worked to open the crate.

As I stood there waiting, craning my neck to try and peer over the shoulders of the guys in front of me, a tingle at the edge of my perception made me freeze. Then it was gone. Had I imagined it? I looked around, peering into the dark shadows between the tall, stacked pallets.

Mike bumped my arm with his, drawing my attention. It was his turn to fire off a questioning look. I held up an index finger and closed my eyes, shutting out visual stimulus for a moment to focus on my other senses—in particular, my magic perception.

Witches can perceive magic in several ways. The first, most obviously, is with our eyes. But our "magic sense" goes beyond that, and mine's always been sharper than most. When I'm in the presence of another witch, I know it, even when they're not actively using magic. I can feel it tugging at the edge of my consciousness like a forgotten word on the tip of your tongue or a face you can't quite put a name to. I used to think all witches could sense the latent magic in each other, but no . . . apparently that's just me. My awareness of magic has sharpened even further since my conduit powers awakened. It used to be, I had to be within ten feet or so of a witch to sense their magic. That had at least doubled over the last couple of months. Hell, I'd even detected the magic in a fetus still in its mother's womb. I drew on that heightened awareness now, extending it as far as I could in every direction.

There! Yes. There was definitely a witch in range. Behind me, to the left, and . . . up? My eyes snapped open as I realized our error. Sure, we'd panned our flashlights up the stacks, but we couldn't actually see across the tops of the pallets from the floor. The stacks were easily fifteen feet high, the aisles between them narrow, and the space in the center not wide enough to see far over the tops of the ones on the opposite side. All they'd had to do was keep far enough back to not be spotted, be silent, and wait. I flicked my flashlight off and grabbed Mike's arm, gesturing up at the stacks with the darkened device.

His eyes met mine, silent communication flaring between us. He glanced up at the stacks, then back at me, lifting both brows. I nodded emphatically.

"Movement sighted up top," he said into the comm, and as one, the dozen or so SWAT guys pivoted to face the pallets instead of the crate and turned their barrel-mounted flashlights up. Even the guy working the crowbar froze.

"Police! Come out with your hands up!" someone shouted.

"Suck my balls, pigs!" came a shout from above.

A few flashlights changed direction, trying to locate the source of the shout, but I kept my focus where it was. I could still sense the witch up there, and the hairs on the back of my neck stood up as they crept closer. The sound of metal skidding across concrete came from several directions, and I jumped back as something bumped up against my shoe, bumping into one of the SWAT guys. He pushed me away reflexively, and I managed to keep my balance but lost my flashlight in the process. It hit the floor and skittered away into the darkness.

Before I could decide whether to go after it or rely on my backup light charm, all hell broke loose. The metal canisters that'd been rolled across the floor began to hiss and belch smoke, prompting cries of "Smoke!" and efforts to kick them back out to the edges of the room. Then the hair on the back of my neck stood up as magic flared above me. My eyes snapped upward, and I caught a brief glimpse of a figure wreathed in golden energy before a spell went flying over my head. I ducked instinctively, though it missed me by a country mile, and spun to see it land across the lid of the giant crate. To what purpose, I couldn't tell. Chaos surrounded me as a series of noisy cracks from above sent all of us scattering for cover—only there wasn't any. It was a shooting gallery. Even those who, like me, managed to retreat into the narrow corridors between the stacks found little respite. I stumbled over the body of a fallen officer sprawled across the aisle and barely managed to catch myself on the nearest pallet.

"Ow! Watch it, will you?" he groused.

"Sorry!" I said quietly and stooped to collect his gun. Waste not, want not. It was a compact assault rifle of some sort, and it felt weird in my hands. I'd never fired anything but pistols, but I figured pointing it and pulling the trigger was the way to go. I panned the beam of the barrel-mounted flashlight down the aisle, then up. Spotting no enemies, I turned to look back toward the crate just in time for a sharp whistle to pierce the air from over my head.

I peeked around a corner into the center of the room. Whatever spell had been cast was gone, and now the lid was being pushed off from inside. Six shadowy figures popped out amongst the smoke and began firing pistols at the retreating SWAT team.

Crack, crack, crack.

I retreated farther into the stacks, ducking around a corner to get out of line of sight and pressing my back to the wall of winterization supplies. My heart pounded against my ribcage. The witch had stopped actively casting, but they hadn't moved. I could still sense them above and behind me. I pushed off the wall and spun, shining the flashlight up the side. The way the stack was wrapped in plastic left little in the way of handholds for climbing. Still, I had to get up there somehow. Or get them down. Maybe I could shove my fingers into the plastic and use it as a hand-hold? Would it hold my weight? With my luck, I'd get halfway up and it'd rip, spilling me back down onto the unforgiving concrete.

I was still contemplating my options when someone came barreling around the corner. I turned and fired instinctively, but the shot went wide.

"Jesus, Davenport!" Mike grabbed the barrel of the gun and pushed it toward the floor. "Don't you think—"

I clamped a hand over his mouth and motioned upward with a jerk of my chin. "Witch up there," I said in a harsh whisper. "Did you see any way up?"

He glanced up, shook his head, and peeled my fingers off his face. "There has to be one somewhere."

I couldn't fault his logic, but I'd seen a witch climb a wall like Spider-Man more than once. Hell, they could've levitated their people up there if they were strong enough. Magic was good for a lot of things, and I didn't want to waste time looking for a ladder that might not exist. "Gimme a boost."

"I can't boost you that high."

"Do you have a better idea?"

He ran his eyes upward again, peering into the darkness overhead. I followed suit, hoping to find some sort of catwalk we might gain access to. But all I saw was the underside of the industrial aluminum roof and the sprinkler system's network of pipes and spigots. The idea must've struck Mike at the same moment it did me, because when I grabbed his arm and his eyes lowered to mine, he wore a wicked grin.

"Got a lighter?" I asked.

He nodded, and we retreated to the edge of the building, away from the firefight taking place at the center, and worked our way along the perimeter until we found a trash barrel stuffed with assorted packing materials. Thirty seconds later, we had its contents alight, smoke billowing up into the rafters. It didn't take long at all for the fire alarm to trigger, flooding the cavernous space with its harsh, grating bleats.

We high-fived and retreated from the scene of the crime, so to speak, making our way back to the row where I'd last sensed the witch. Along the way, the sprinklers went off, showering the space with cold water and making the concrete floor regrettably slick, but our gambit paid off. The showering water hindered the enemy's visibility as much as ours, and though we couldn't yet get up to the ones up top, they couldn't easily get down to us either.

Or, at least most of them couldn't. The hair on my arms stood on end as magic surged nearby, and I looked up in time to see a golden-ringed figure leap over the edge of the pallet. They hovered in the air briefly and fired off a fast and dirty spell in my direction. The air rippled between us as it rapidly closed on me, but I threw up a hand and "caught" it, grounding it safely into the concrete below my feet. The witch's eyes widened in the light cast by the flashlight on my weapon as she dropped to the floor, slowing her fall enough with a quick featherfall spell to land safely, but water still splashed beneath her boots on impact.

She shook off her astonishment, replacing it with a cocky smile. "So you're the city's witch I've heard so much about," she said, placing her fists on her fatigue-covered hips. She wore a tactical harness much like the ones our SWAT team wore, along with a military-style billed cap that shielded her eyes from the artificial rain shower. The glow around her flared brighter. "Ready to dance?"

"Uhhh, sure." I fired off a three-round burst, but she threw up a shield of air and the rounds splattered harm-lessly against it. The next spell she threw at me yanked the gun from my hands and tossed it away with a clatter. Yeah, this definitely wasn't good. I hadn't gone into this expecting a magic duel. If I had, I would've tried harder to fit my vest over my warded trench coat.

The witch hesitated, probably confused why I didn't light up and throw down. The fire alarm continued to blare, but the cracks that sounded between its wails reminded me that there was still a firefight going on, so we had to make this fast.

"You got this?" Mike asked.

Though I hated to admit it, I knew my limits. "Nope." Without the protection of my coat against offensive magic or a weapon, I was going to have to ground what I could, dodge what I couldn't, and hope Mike could get the drop on her. Unless, of course, I could get close enough to drain her magic. But that was a card I wasn't ready to play. The fewer people who knew about that, the better.

I didn't dare take my eyes from the enemy witch, but I caught Mike's nod out of the corner of my eye. "Helen Keller?" he asked, referring to a trick we'd worked out for taking hostile witches into custody. Since I couldn't bind a witch's magic, we had two options to stop them from slinging spells at us if they weren't inclined to stop on their own: render them unconscious or blind them. You can probably guess which one was the Helen Keller.

"Yup." We'd both taken to carrying strips of cloth into the field long enough to use as an expedited blindfold, but I hadn't brought mine with me—talk about getting caught with my pants around my ankles. I hoped Mike asking meant he'd brought his. Knowing him, he had. My partner was the ultimate Boy Scout.

The exchange only took a few seconds, but the witch wasn't about to stand there and let us strategize. She spun together another spell and tossed it at our feet. I had to give it to her, she adapted quickly. Once she saw me intercept a spell, she stopped lobbing them at me and started targeting things around me instead. I shoved Mike to get him moving and jumped back as the water on the concrete floor froze, ice crystals forming and spreading rapidly until a large swath of the path at the edge of the building was completely covered in a solid sheet of frozen water. With the water still raining down from above, it wouldn't remain frozen for long, but for now, it was too slick to cross.

I grabbed Mike's arm and pulled him into one of the narrow gaps between the towering pallets. I still had one edge on the witch, and that was that she didn't know I could sense her movements. She'd expect us to go around the pallet we'd ducked behind to get to her, and indeed I felt her move to intercept us, but instead, I drew Mike farther down the aisle until we came to a major intersection. I nudged him around the corner to the right and motioned for him to wait there, then crossed to the other side and walked a few paces down the aisle, waiting for the witch to come out from between the pallets. When she did, I spun and dashed back to the intersection, turning left to break her line of sight again.

Then I waited.

I couldn't hear her footsteps over the racket, but I felt her approaching at a sprint as if there were a magnet in my chest and she was a pole, the magic in her a near tangible thing. I met Mike's eyes from across the aisle and curled my hands into fists, making a motion like tugging something taut between them. He reached into his pocket, but that was all I had time to see before the witch came barreling around the corner. I triggered my light charm—a vintage poison ring I wore with the hidden compartment facing inward—with a flick of my thumb and flared open my fingers, hitting the witch square in the face with a bright beam of light.

She flung up her hands and cried out, skidding to a stop, and I grabbed her wrists. A struggle ensued as Mike shot across the aisle behind her with his makeshift blindfold in hand. She balled her hands into fists and yanked them straight down, breaking my hold, then threw a shoulder against my chest that sent me staggering backward. My feet slid out from under me, and I hit the floor with a splash, pain shooting straight up my spine from my tailbone. Mike tried to get the blindfold over her eyes, but she spun and elbowed him in the side, then brought her fist up in an uppercut that would've rocked his world if he hadn't jerked back at the last minute. Even blinded, she was a force to be reckoned with, and we only had a few more seconds before her eyes adjusted again.

I scrambled to my feet and charged, wrapping both arms around her and taking her down. We hit the floor with a mutual grunt, and with Mike's help, I was able to get her pinned, blindfolded, and cuffed.

Before we could pat ourselves on the back for a job—well, done, the lights came on, the sprinklers shut off, and the alarm went silent. I leaned against the nearest pallet to catch my breath, ears ringing, blinking rapidly in the suddenly bright light.

"Exercise complete." The device in my ear vibrated with the Lieutenant's low rumbling bass. "Debriefing in one hour. Get your asses back to the station."

I looked over at Mike. "Did we win?"

He shrugged and took out his keys, unlocking the cuffs binding the witch's wrists behind her back. She rolled over and sat up, pulling the blindfold off her head and shooting me a glare. Her hat had gotten knocked off in the tussle, and her wet, short blond hair was plastered to her head.

"What the hell was that?" she demanded. "Why didn't you fight me?"

"We did, that's how you ended up cuffed and blindfolded," I said.

Her eyes narrowed. "You know what I mean."

I did know what she meant. She wanted to know why I hadn't fought her with magic, and I wasn't sure how to answer without telling her I didn't have any. Standing now, Mike offered me a hand and I grabbed it, hauling myself to my feet with a wince. I'd be sitting gingerly for a couple of days. "I don't think we've been properly introduced." I shook my wet hand out, then offered it to her.

She slapped a wet palm against mine and used it to pull herself up. "Kara Seaver. I know who you are, Davenport." She eyed me once more, her features a study in disappointment. "I expected more."

I shrugged an insincere apology as officers from both the city's team and the state's team began to wander past us on the way to the exit, both sides sporting splotches of paint from simulated weapons fire. They laughed and joked with each other as they went, in stark contrast to the chill in the air radiating from Kara.

I understood why she was pissed. I mean, she'd come at me with her best and, with Mike's help, I'd blinded her and put her in cuffs without casting a single spell. Sure, I'd sucked one of her spells out of the air, and she'd probably be thinking about that for a long while, but hopefully she'd just conclude I'd used a charm or a clever counterspell.

"I wasn't aware the State Police had a witch on staff," Mike said.

"Surprise," Kara said, flaring her fingers, but her jazz

hands game was weak. Her heart wasn't in it. Perhaps an olive branch was in order.

"Those were some good moves. Maybe we can get together sometime and talk tactics."

"Yeah, maybe, sometime." Judging by her tone, that sometime could be anytime between never and never. But after a moment, she shook herself. "I'm sorry. I'm kind of a sore loser. It's a flaw."

"If it helps, I'm pretty sure your team won and that's largely thanks to you," I said.

As if on cue, one of the staters passing by paused and smacked the arm of the SWAT guy next to him. "There she is, our very own ace in the hole! Come on, Seaver! You're drinking for free tonight."

She hesitated a moment, then stooped to snatch her hat from the floor. "See you around, Davenport." It sounded like a promise. She wrung her hat out, then slapped it on her head and stalked off to rejoin her team.

I watched her go, then glanced at Mike. "To the Batmobile?"

He chuckled and nodded. As we followed the others toward the exit he commented, "You handled yourself well."

"It was rude of them to not give us a heads up they had a witch."

"It was realistic. We won't always know. We have to be ready for anything."

I sighed. "I can't go on every raid."

"No one's asking you to."

"I know, but when I don't, the only way they can stop a witch is with a bullet. Hell, it was my first instinct when I had that gun in my hand."

"Hey." He caught my arm and drew me to a stop. "First off, this was a training exercise and it was a paintball gun. I doubt you would've been so quick to fire if it had been live ammo. Hell, you weren't supposed to have a gun at all. Second, magic can be as deadly a weapon as a gun, so if a witch starts slinging spells at cops, don't you think they're within their rights to return fire?"

I didn't have a good answer for that. I wanted to say no, but I also got where he was coming from. Humans were defenseless against magic. That's what made it so difficult for police departments to catch and detain witch suspects. "I guess that depends on the lethality of the spell. The bottom line is, we need smarter tactics, better tools, and more training. And more witches."

"I don't disagree. And we'll work on that together, okay? But for now, we just took down a well-trained witch with a blindfold, a light charm, and a can-do attitude. Let's celebrate that win."

I let a smile creep onto my lips. "That was pretty cool."

He slung an arm around my shoulders and we continued toward the exit, but all the way back to the station I couldn't quite shake the thoughts that'd been simmering in the back of my mind for the last few weeks. Was Magic Crimes doing the witch community a disservice, for all our good intentions, by insulating the force as a whole from having to learn how to deal with witches in a safe, humane manner?

2

Cleanup and debriefing after we got back to the station took longer than I'd anticipated. By the time I left the police station, it was almost eleven and I was running late for my brunch date. Squinting in the sunlight, I started across the parking lot to my car but froze when I spotted the black Escalade parked a few spaces down from my little red Corolla.

Adrian Volkov. The Circle representative had been shadowing me for over a week, ever since I threw him out of my apartment after he informed me of the ridiculous investigation I was under thanks to my mother's meddling.

Ridiculous! But also terrifying.

Bad things happened to witches who falsely claimed to be Circle witches. I wasn't about to become another statistic. Especially when I hadn't done what I was accused of.

I marched up to the idling SUV, approaching the driver's side. The tinted window rolled down with a quiet hum.

"Good morning, Ms. Davenport." His tone was cordial, if formal, and thick with his Slavic accent. I noted the uncharacteristic shadow along his jaw and less-than-perfect hair with petty satisfaction. My early morning departure—a deviation from my normal schedule—must've interrupted his morning routine. Poor baby.

"Has anyone ever told you, you have more balls than brains?"

A dark brow inched upward. "I—"

"There's a word for men who sit around in cars outside a woman's workplace, who trail them around town and stick their nose where it doesn't belong."

"Investigator?"

"Stalker. Unless you're a cop or a licensed PI. Are you a licensed PI?" I gave him a chance to shake his head before barreling on. "I didn't think so. Now, you sound new to this country, so for your benefit, I'll point out that this"—I gestured at the building—"is a police station." Yeah, I know. Not my finest moment. But the guy was really getting on my nerves by then. "Do you want to know why I'm not in there filing a restraining order right now?"

"By all means," he said with a tolerant, borderline patronizing, air.

"Because I don't want trouble with the Circle!" I also didn't want my co-workers involved in whatever this was. But I couldn't tell him that, not without undermining the threat. "So I'm going to give you one warning. Stop following me, or I'll do whatever I need to do to make you stop."

He studied me for a moment with piercing green eyes, expression unreadable. I met his gaze and lifted my chin, holding firm in my challenge.

"There's no need to go to such lengths, Ms. Davenport," he said calmly. "All you need to do is prove to me that you're a witch, and my business here will be concluded."

"I don't have to prove anything to anyone. I'm not a Circle witch. I've never claimed to be a Circle witch."

"You are a registered practitioner in the state of New Mexico?"

"Yes, but—"

"And you are Emily Davenport, daughter of William and Camille of the Davenport Coven?"

"I've never claimed to be a member of the Davenport Coven. Check my registration. No coven listed. I don't care what my mother has told you, I—"

"So, you don't deny that you are Emily Davenport, daughter of William and Camille?"

"As much as I'd like to, no."

"And there lies the crux of the issue. You claim to be a Davenport witch. According to William and Camille, their daughter is a null."

My hands tightened into fists at my sides, and I clenched my teeth shut to keep the truth on the tip of my tongue. Inside, I seethed. My mother had sicced this hound on me because she thought I was masquerading as a witch. The truth was so much more complicated than that, and as much as I didn't want my mother—or the Circle—all up in my business, revealing myself as a Conduit would ensure just that. It was a lost talent, and I didn't want to end up as anyone's lab rat or prized show dog. I just wanted to be left alone.

"You have three options," he said after several tense moments of silence. "One, prove to me beyond a shadow of a doubt that you are a witch. Two, withdraw your name from the state registry and abandon all claims to being a witch. Or three, return to Salt Lake City for a tribunal."

A tribunal was the Circle's version of a trial, and they were . . . less than gentle . . . when it came to extracting answers from the accused. Let's just say that innocent until proven guilty wasn't exactly their creed. My heart hammered against my ribcage, the anxious flutter of a trapped animal that doesn't know which way to run. My mouth went dry. I had to peel my tongue off the roof of it to reply, but I was anything but cowed.

"Listen up, because I'm only going to say this one more time. I am not a Circle witch. I have never claimed to be a Circle witch. I am not a member of the Davenport Coven, nor have I ever claimed to be a member of the Davenport Coven. I am a Davenport, yes, and I use my knowledge of magic to help the police solve magic-related crimes. Registering with the state was a condition of my employment."

"So, they require all their magic experts to register as witches, even when they're not?" Again, he arched a brow. I wanted to slap him. He was just too smart.

"Stop following me, or I'll file a restraining order. I'm serious. This is the twenty-first century, and I'm a US citizen. Your organization has no authority over me."

He inclined his head, the soul of politeness. "You have seven days to comply. Good day, Ms. Davenport."

I stood rooted in place, glaring at him in silence while he rolled up the window, put the car into gear, and pulled out of the parking place. Then I watched him drive off, thoughts whirling in my head and emotions swirling in my heart. He was gone, but for how long?

Seven days. Shit. It took me longer than that to decide how much to get trimmed off at the salon.

What was I going to do? Withdrawing from the registry —if that were even possible—would mean giving up my consultancy with the SFPD. Right now, that was my sole source of income. I couldn't prove that I was a witch without revealing my Conduit status, and that would open a whole can of worms I wasn't ready for. The possible consequences might be worse than facing a tribunal—which would probably get the truth out of me anyway, a lot less pleasantly.

Of course, I could follow through on that restraining order, but that would send Mike through the roof. My partner had a protective streak a mile wide, and as much as I appreciated it, I didn't want or need him to ride to my rescue.

There had to be a better solution. I just had to figure it out.

In seven days.

Shit.

3

Saturday brunch at the Tin Whistle Cafe wasn't quite as brisk as Sunday brunch, but that meant the line was only halfway to the door instead of out the door. As I moseyed to the back of the line, I scanned the dining room for my group and smiled as Matt caught my eye and waved. The movement prompted the others to look my way, and I waved at them all while I waited my turn.

My brother was there, of course. This was his farewell brunch, of sorts, since he was starting at the police academy on Monday. Everything had happened so quickly after he sent in his application. But he'd gotten his application submitted and passed his entrance exams—barely—in the nick of time to join the six-month session that was about to begin. If he'd taken any longer, he would've had to wait for the next session, which would be months away. Beside him sat his friend Tracy, though she was quickly becoming a friend of mine as well. Across from them sat my BFF Matt and the empty chair that was probably mine.

There was another empty chair at the end of the table, though, with a mug and plate in front of it. Mike must've beaten me there, which wasn't surprising since I'd been held up on the way. The rich aroma of freshly ground coffee and sizzling bacon soothed any lingering irritation from my confrontation with Deputy Archon Volkov, and I pushed the whole situation out of my mind while I turned my attention to the colorful, hand-written menu board over the register. Not that I didn't know it by heart, but sometimes a girl just likes to browse.

After placing my order, I wandered through the wide-open dining area with my number on a stick, admiring the newest pieces of local art on display. One of them, an oil on canvas desert landscape with rich colors and angular lines, reminded me of a particular firefighter's work. Sure enough, I recognized the signature in the corner, even from afar. I saw it every day on my wall at home, after all.

Turning my attention to the long wooden table my friends were clustered around, I flashed an apologetic smile. "Sorry I'm late, things ran—" I blinked, because the empty seat at the end of the table was empty no more, and the man sitting in it wasn't Mike. "—long." I darted a glance at my brother, who sat there looking far too innocent. Also, smug. Until that moment, I wouldn't have thought it possible to appear both at once. "What an unexpected surprise! It's nice to see you, John."

The aforementioned firefighter flashed his pearly whites and lifted his mug in salute, drawing my attention to his muscular forearm, laid bare by his rolled-up sleeve. I'd never considered myself a forearm girl. Glutes were more my thing. But there we are, and there I was, trying valiantly not to drool.

I slid into the empty chair next to Matt and set the tall table number in front of me like a shield. "No sign of Mike yet?"

"He had to cancel," Dan said. "Something came up. We're going to have drinks later instead."

Weird. Mike hadn't said anything to me about not being able to make it. Had that something come up after I left? Was it related to a case? No, he would've called me if it were that. I checked my phone just in case I'd missed a call or message. Nope.

"Sorry we didn't wait for you," Matt said, prompting me to scan the mostly empty plates on the table.

"It's okay. I'm starving, though. I haven't had anything but coffee, and I was up before dawn." I unrolled my silverware and used my fork to help myself to some of the leftover migas on Matt's plate since it was closest and he wouldn't care. In fact, he nudged it toward me in open invitation.

"How did it go?" Dan leaned forward, eyes alight with interest. "Did you put the smackdown on some staters?"

"Not exactly," I said around a mouthful of egg, corn tortilla strips, and cheese. The tortilla strips were rubbery, but the flavors still danced on my tongue. I tore off a piece of leftover flour tortilla to go with it. "But it was good experience." For Tracy, Matt, and John's benefit, I added, "I participated in a training raid with Narcotics today. The State Police played the part of the bad guys."

"Does that mean you'll be going on real raids?" Matt asked, eyebrows drawing together in obvious concern.

I pushed his plate back in front of him, content to wait for my own now that I'd had a bite. Nothing like cold eggs, congealed cheese, and rubbery tortilla strips to keep the appetite at bay. "Occasionally. Probably not Narcotics ones, unless it's related to a Magic Crimes case. Or a witch is believed to be involved. But enough about me. Today is all about you." I pointed finger guns at my brother.

He smirked, sitting back in his chair again. "Like every day isn't about me . . ."

That's my brother. Narcissistic and self-aware to the point of hilarity. Once we all stopped laughing long enough to draw breath, the conversation continued, bouncing around the table like we were all old friends despite the fact that, of the five of us, only Matt and I actually were. Before long, Matt and Tracy were deep in conversation about cryptocurrency while Dan looked like he might break a sweat just trying to keep up.

"Blockchains and mining?" Dan said. "Sounds more like prisoners on day work for good behavior. Are you sure this is all legal?"

When my plate of huevos rancheros was set in front of me, I fell upon it like the ravenous beast that I was. Just with slightly better table manners and a minimum of growling. I'd really wanted the blue corn cinnamon pancakes but talked myself into something with a little more protein. I wasn't disappointed. The eggs were cooked to perfection, with firm whites and runny yolks that combined with the red chile sauce into a scrumptious delight on a fried corn tortilla.

I may have moaned. Maybe that's why John's eyes held a glint of amusement when I looked up to find him watching me while the conversation flowed around us. Convinced my lips must be ringed with sauce, I licked them self-consciously and watched in an uneasy mix of titillation and horror when John's eyes lowered to my mouth. What was wrong with me? I looked away and brought my napkin up hastily to blot my lips.

"We have a lot of leftovers," Dan said after a moment, probably desperate for a subject change. "Maybe we should pack up a doggie bag for your creeper, Em."

I stared at him blankly for a moment before my brain caught up. "Ha-ha, very funny."

"Creeper?" John asked, frowning.

While I was busy glaring at my brother, Matt stepped in. "Emily's family hired an investigator to look into her activities."

Dan laughed. "That's one way of putting it."

Matt gave Dan a look that shut him up faster than any of mine ever had. I marveled for a moment, then returned my napkin to my lap with a resigned sigh. "Long story short, my mom found out I registered as a witch, and she wants me to stop 'pretending' to be a Davenport witch."

"Ahh." John cupped his coffee mug with both hands, leaning his sexy forearms on the table. "Sicced the Circle on you?"

Silence blanketed the table as we all stared at him.

He chuckled. "What? I don't live in a cave. I know the Davenports are a Circle coven."

I don't know why that shocked me as much as it did. I mean, John had been present the night my conduit powers manifested for the first time. He'd taken me to meet Kassidy, who'd told me what I was, and he'd let me experiment on him more than once. He knew I wasn't a normal witch, knew that my family thought I was a null, and knew I was a Davenport. That name held weight in the witch community. Still, the depth of his insight surprised me.

"Great, so we're all on the same page," Dan said. "Mommy Dearest is shitting kittens, and rather than confront Em herself, she loosed the Circle's hounds on her."

"She did send a letter," I said, but certainly not in her defense.

Dan snorted. ". . . telling you that she was onto you, and

since you obviously hadn't heeded her warnings, you had to answer to a higher authority."

"Yeah. Whatever. The Circle has no authority over me."

"I doubt the Circle would agree," John said.

"Yeah, that's the impression I get." I poked at my food, dragging a piece of potato through the cooling puddle of sauce. "I threatened to file a restraining order against the guy, but I think he knew I was bluffing."

"Why were you bluffing?" Matt asked. "That sounds like a great idea."

"Because the Circle doesn't like it when mundane authorities interfere in witch affairs," Tracy said. "They've been the self-appointed magic police on this continent for centuries."

"Bingo." And my family had a long history with the Circle—they were one of the founding covens. Hell, my uncle sat on the Council of Covens, the Circle's ruling body. "Anyway, he told me I have seven days."

"To?" John asked.

"To prove I'm a witch or renounce any claim to being a witch and remove myself from the witch registry." I felt the warm weight of Matt's hand on my back, rubbing in soothing circles. I craved the comfort but made myself pull away.

He gave me a curious glance as he withdrew his hand. "And if you don't?"

"Tribunal," Dan, Tracy, and I said in unison.

John shook his head, mumbling something that sounded like, "And they call our ways barbaric."

I was about to reply when a throat cleared nearby, drawing everyone's attention to a Hispanic man standing a few feet away from the table. I hadn't seen Hector since his trip to the ER a couple of weeks ago in the wake of several slurs aimed at Tracy and an altercation with Dan's fist. His nose was healing nicely. Mostly straight, even.

"Hey, Hector," Tracy said. "How's it going?"

Hector pointedly ignored his recent ex-girlfriend, his dark eyes focused on me. "Emily. I need to speak with you." He jerked his head toward the nearby patio door and took a few steps in that direction.

Curious, I pushed back my chair and set my napkin down on the table, meeting Tracy's eyes and shrugging in answer to the question in them.

"If I'm not back in five minutes, send help," I joked before following Hector outside.

4

I had no clue why Hector might want to talk to me. Our paths had crossed a few times, but never casually. At best, we were not-quite-hostile acquaintances. Whatever it was, it must've been serious for him to approach me when Dan and Tracy were around. I had no doubt that he blamed Dan for Tracy breaking things off with him, though according to her Hector's toxic masculinity was to blame.

He stood on the patio waiting for me, his hands shoved in his pants pockets. The patio was mostly empty, the late-February weather still being a little on the chilly side for outdoor dining most days. The few brave souls that'd opted to sit on the patio under the big metal heaters still had their jackets on. My own arms prickled with gooseflesh as soon as they came into contact with the chilly air. Hopefully, whatever Hector wanted wouldn't take long.

"Okay, you've got my attention. What's up?"

"You still looking for information about that new drug? The one that's killing witches."

He'd had my attention. Now he had my interest. Still, I

tried to play it cool. It wouldn't do to appear too thirsty for information. "Yeah, sure. Whatever you've got."

"They call it 'fairy dust.'"

I waited a few seconds for him to continue, but he didn't. Was that it? I tried to keep the disappointment from my voice, not wanting to discourage him from coming to me in the future. "That matches up with what I've learned since we spoke. Good to know we're on the right track. Anything else?"

"Yeah." He shifted his weight between his feet, glancing around before leaning toward me a little. "There's a punk dealing it at Ragle Park. Skinny white kid, long brown hair, skater type. Name's Alvin."

Now that was valuable information. I took out my phone to jot that down. "Ragle Park. Alvin. Skater kid. Okay, that's helpful. Anything else?"

"He's been dealing it to high school kids."

I thought about the kid who'd died on my watch—one of the last patients I'd seen before I was fired from my job at St. Vincent's. My blood ran cold. It's not that I didn't know teenagers were taking it, but knowing that someone was hanging out at a local park, specifically dealing to them? That was another matter entirely.

"Very good to know," I said. "If you know someone who has taken it, I'd really like to talk to—"

"No." He straightened and backed up a step. "It's performance-enhancing. But only for witches. That's all I know."

"Performance-enhancing how? Strength? Endurance? Speed?"

"Yes. All of that."

"But only for witches." Baffling. Witch physiology wasn't significantly different from human physiology. It was difficult to imagine any drug having a different effect on a witch than it did on a human.

He nodded. "That's what I've heard. Apparently, the Santa Fe High baseball team is looking really good this year. But you didn't hear that from me. Actually, you didn't hear any of this from me."

I winced inwardly. Anonymous tips aren't great when it comes to building a case because it's difficult to determine their credibility, and unless you have other evidence that supports the tip, it might not be actionable. It'd be better if I could get him on board as a confidential informant. "This is one of those awkward 'I'm not a cop' moments, I'm afraid. I'll need to give your name to my partner, and he may need to speak with you himself. But he can redact your name as far as the record is concerned, so you'll remain anonymous except to him and me. And I'm certainly not going to tell anyone." I mimed locking my lips and throwing away the key and hoped he wouldn't push back. Given our history, the odds weren't great.

He hesitated a moment, then gave a terse nod. "Alright."

"Thank you. This is really helpful." I tucked my phone back in my pocket, relief over his unexpected agreement filling me. "We'll be in touch. And if you come across anything else, you know how to reach me."

"Just get that punk off the streets before someone else gets hurt."

He stepped around me, headed for the door before I could question him further. Not that I had much to ask, but I was curious who he knew that'd gotten hurt. Someone's kid, perhaps. Hector may have been an asshole, but he wasn't completely heartless. Apparently.

I followed him back inside, but he turned and headed

for the exit without another word, so I moseyed back to the table.

"What was that about?" Tracy asked.

"Work-related," I said, hoping to leave it at that.

Dan looked like he might press me, but Matt swooped in like a hero . . . and brought up another sore subject. "Speaking of work, have you had any luck finding an attorney for your case against the hospital?"

Sighing, I reached for my water. "Not yet. Honestly, I've been thinking about what you told me weeks ago, about going to HR and threatening to sue for discrimination. Maybe just the threat will get me somewhere."

"Have you tried any of the legal aid or legal referral services?" Tracy asked.

"Yeah, they're all willing to talk to me about it, but they won't actually represent me without being under contract, and that requires a retainer."

Tracy looked thoughtful for a moment, then snapped her fingers. "You should reach out to the American Witch League. I bet this is just the sort of thing they'd be interested in. They've got contacts and lawyers that would probably do it pro bono."

"I don't think they have an office in Santa Fe," John said. "Closest one would be in Albuquerque, probably."

"Everything from the consultation to the filing can probably be done online," Matt said. "They'd just have to come out here for the court date." He turned to me. "Your laptop should be fully capable. It's got a built-in camera and microphone. I'll make sure you have the programs installed that you might need."

My eyes began to sting as tears welled up. I swallowed and blinked a few times in an effort to keep them at bay. I'd spent so many years holding everyone at arm's length, not daring to really make friends, that I'd lost sight of just how valuable they could be.

"Okay," I said, once I could trust my voice not to waver. "That's a good idea. Thanks, you guys. I'll look into that."

Matt took out his phone. "There's probably a contact form on their website . . ."

"Later," I said with a laugh. "I'll look into it later. For now, I'd just like to enjoy a little more time socializing."

Dan's eyes drifted toward the exit Hector had recently left through, his expression thoughtful.

"Tracy, have you found a new coven yet?" Hopefully, I could distract my brother before he decided to try interrogating me about Hector's work-related visit.

Tracy rubbed the back of her neck and grimaced. "Not yet. I know I need to, I just . . . It's hard."

"May I ask why you're looking for a new coven?" John asked.

"Bad breakup," Tracy said. "My ex is the leader of my coven, and that makes things awkward. To say the least."

Dan leaned back and threw an arm over the back of his chair, smirking. "Her ex was the little ray of sunshine that just came to see Em."

"Ah. Does he work for the police department too?"

I couldn't not laugh at that, but I kept it to a minimum. "No, he just . . ." Shit. He wouldn't be a confidential informant if I went blabbing about him giving me work-related info. "He wanted to talk to me about something work-related. I'm the only witch on the SFPD payroll. Though, I did find out this morning that the State Police have a new recruit who is a practitioner."

"Oh really?" Dan eyed me with newfound interest. "Not gunning for your job, is he?"

I shook my head. "She. But probably not. She's still got

that fresh out of the academy smell." And swagger. But I kept that to myself. "The State Police consider themselves a cut above city law enforcement. Maybe they are." I shrugged. "I don't have much experience with them. But they're definitely more . . . regimented, I guess is a good word. Their academy is more like boot camp."

"All academies are like boot camp," Dan said. "But at least the one I'm going to doesn't require you to shave your head." He brushed his hand lightly over his precious hair.

"I dunno, I think you'd look cute with a little fade or buzz," Tracy said, lips quirking in a playful smile.

Dan tilted his head, eyeing her. "Yeah, no. Not even for you, babydoll."

Tracy snickered. "Anyway, Em . . . want to interview covens with me? I could use a friend. And you're looking too, right?"

I hedged. "Eh . . . I don't know. Been thinking about it, but it's complicated."

"Maybe joining a coven is just what you need to do to get the Circle off your back," Matt said. "After all, if you're publicly a member of another coven, they can't claim you're pretending to be a Circle witch."

I stared at my bestie for a long moment, blinking slowly. "That couldn't work. Could it?"

"It might," Dan said. "Can't hurt to try."

I ran my thumb along the outside of my water glass, dragging a line through the condensation as I thought about it. Could it hurt to try? "Well, either way." I met Tracy's eyes. "I'd be happy to tag along with you for moral support."

"More like immoral support," Dan said.

"Yeah, that's more your area than mine, Danny."

That sparked another round of laughter, and the conversation moved on. But Matt's suggestion stuck with me even after we all bid each other farewell and went our separate ways. Could it really be that easy? Could I join a coven and negate my mother's charges against me without having to reveal my Conduit status to the Circle, or would it just entangle an innocent group of witches in my bullshit circumstances?

I didn't know the answer, but I could at least mull over the question.

5

Flush with new intel I was dying to share, I sent Mike a text as soon as I left the Tin Whistle, and he invited me to drop by his house. I'd been curious about what had come up that kept him from brunch, but knowing that he was hanging out at home a couple of hours later made me even more curious.

The sun was high overhead when I parked by the curb out front. There was an unfamiliar car parked behind Mike's Cherokee in the driveway, a sleek black muscle car with a wide orange stripe down the hood and matching pin-striping along the sides. A custom license plate read, "CUFF EM."

Unexpected company would explain why he'd bailed on brunch, but I hated to interrupt. What's more, I couldn't really talk about Hector's tip in front of his guest—or guests. But he had invited me, so he didn't mind me dropping by. And even if we couldn't chat about the case, I was curious enough about his company to get out of the car and head for the front door.

Mike answered the door in a Broncos T-shirt and cargo

shorts, his feet bare and a beer in his hand. "Hey there! Come on in."

I lingered on the doorstep, torn between good manners and nosey curiosity. "I'm sorry, I didn't realize you had company. I hate to impose."

"It's fine. No one important."

"I heard that!" a male voice called from somewhere inside.

Mike merely smirked and waved me in, so I crossed the threshold and looked around while Mike shut the door and locked it.

"Want a beer?" he asked, wandering toward the kitchen.

"No thanks, but water would be great."

I removed my shoes and left them by the others in the entryway, noting the extra pair of sneakers sitting beside the small pile of Mike's shoes, then padded across the pale carpet in his wake and into the tiled kitchen. That was where I found, presumably, the owner of the voice and shoes sitting at the dining table, upon which was an open file folder and various documents spread around.

It took me a moment to recognize the man out of context. I'd seen him around the station and at the training exercise that morning, but we'd never been formally introduced. His dark hair was buzzed down to a uniform quarter inch of stubble. Dark eyes sat beneath bushy dark brows, the beginnings of crow's feet at the corners, and his smooth cheeks bore faint laugh lines that deepened as he smiled at me.

"Ah, the infamous Emily Davenport. Finally, we meet!" He stood, and I marked him as a shade under six feet as he stepped closer to offer me a handshake. "Xavier Suarez, Narcotics."

I shook his hand firmly, brows lifting. "Pleasure to meet you. But infamous?"

"Ignore him," Mike said, offering a bottle of water. "He's prone to exaggeration. Especially around women."

"Well, I was about to say that I'd heard nothing but good things about you, but now that wouldn't sound sincere." Xavier returned to his seat, grinning.

I chuckled and eyed Mike as I took the bottle, which was cool and beaded with condensation. "Hopefully it was mostly good, at least."

"Oh yeah, mostly." Xavier's eyes twinkled as he took a swig of his beer.

Mike cleared his throat. "We were just going over the fairy dust case. Xavier's going to be working with us."

"Why's this the first I'm hearing about it?" If I sounded a little peevish, it's because I was.

"Because I just found out after the training exercise, and I didn't want to keep you from your brother's brunch."

"Oh. Okay, then. Thanks." I twisted the cap off my water, taking a sip while Mike pulled out a third chair and sat across from Xavier, leaving me the one between them. I sat.

My eyes roamed the paperwork littering the table. We'd spent the last week and change combing through reports and conducting interviews, looking for cases that might have something to do with our mystery drug. That was how we'd learned its street name, but not much else besides overdose symptoms and a growing body count. We had no idea who was manufacturing it or distributing it, and there were no samples in evidence that we could find.

"I hope you like a challenge, Xavier," I said.

"It ain't much, but we've started with less. Right, Esco?" He grinned across the table at Mike, and my eyes bounced between them. It took me a moment, but I figured it out.

"You were partners," I said.

"She's sharp. I can see why you like her."

Mike chuckled but nodded, lifting his beer in salute before taking a sip. "One of the reasons I keep her around."

"Hello? Sitting right here." I resisted the urge to roll my eyes at the two of them, instead turning to the reason I'd come by in the first place. "I've got a lead on a dealer."

Mike didn't move, but his full attention shifted to me. "What've you got?"

"A source who wants to remain anonymous—" I held up a finger when Mike opened his mouth to interrupt. "—but he's agreed to speak to you, so you can onboard him as a CI. He says there's a skater kid named Alvin dealing it at Ragle park."

Xavier groaned and pinched the bridge of his nose. "Dammit, Alvin."

"You know him?" I asked.

"Yeah. This'll be his third strike. But maybe we can use that to our advantage."

Mike made an agreeable noise, but that still left me in the dark.

"How?"

"Offer to let it slide if he cooperates and gives up his supplier," Mike said.

"Alvin's a little fish," Xavier said. "He's no criminal mastermind, he just moves the goods."

I folded my arms across my chest. "Well, he's dealing to teenagers. He deserves that third strike if you ask me."

"What else did you find out?" Mike asked, as if sensing there was more.

"It's performance-enhancing, but only for witches."

Xavier accepted this with a nod, but Mike frowned and

held up a hand. "Wait, only for witches? How is that even possible?"

"That, I don't know. But I know a few doctors. I'll follow up. Anyway, my source hinted that if we want to look for possible buyers, we check out the Santa Fe High baseball team."

Xavier whistled. "That's bad news. I'll have to reach out to the coach, and I guess we'd better pick up Alvin."

"Yeah. If we're lucky, he'll have some on him," Mike said.

"That'd be phenomenal." My mind raced with possibilities. We could finally get a chemical analysis of the drug, maybe get a jump on how to counteract it. Save lives. "When can we do this? I mean, I imagine you two are going to need some coffee first."

"We're both still on our first," Mike said. "It's no big deal."

Xavier glanced at his watch. "Shit, I need to get going. This afternoon is bad for me. I told the missus I'd be back by one. She's working this afternoon, so I'm on kid duty."

"Oh, okay. Well, I'm sure Mike and I can handle it on our own."

Mike went suspiciously quiet, and when I looked his way, he sighed. "I don't think that's a good idea."

"What? Why not?"

"Aaaand that's my cue." Xavier drained the last of his beer in a couple of gulps and walked the empty over to the recycle bin, moving around the kitchen with unmistakable familiarity. "Text me later, Esco. I'm free tomorrow any time after eleven. Nice to meet you, Emily."

"You too." My response was automatic. The truth was a bit murkier. He seemed nice enough, but his history with Mike and their easy friendship put me on edge.

Mike and I sat quietly until the front door closed behind Xavier.

"Why don't you want me to come with you to talk to the dealer?"

"I told you." Mike pushed to his feet. "I don't think it's a good idea."

"But why? I'm your partner. I've gone with you before."

"And the last time we went to visit someone with a record, an SoH skinhead almost pumped you full of birdshot. This Alvin kid may be a punk, but the people he works for aren't." He picked up his half-empty bottle and moseyed over to the sink.

The memory of that terrifying day was fresh, but not fresh enough to dissuade me entirely. "Come on, Mike. You can't shut me out. I'm still your partner."

He took a long final pull on his beer before pouring the rest out, staring out the window over the sink. "This is different. I wasn't expecting that to turn into a shoot-out."

"And this time you are?"

"It's a hell of a lot more likely. Like Xavi said, he's on his third strike. He'll be twitchy."

"Then it's even more important that I be there. I'm your partner. I watch your back, you watch mine."

Turning back around, he leaned against the sink and eyed me from afar. I met his gaze evenly, unwilling to back down.

After a prolonged staredown, he sighed. "You can ride along, but you have to wait in the car."

"I'll wear a vest."

"Damn right you will, but you'll still be in the car."

I narrowed my eyes at him. "You can't wrap me in bubble wrap, Mike. We've talked about this. I'll wear a vest, but I'm not waiting in the car. I can bring my gun if you're that worried about me."

"No gun. You're a consultant, not a police officer. Carrying a gun in the course of your duties . . . blurs the lines. Also, you're a terrible shot, and I don't want to have to worry about you shooting me or Xavi by accident."

"I'm not that bad, yeesh. I've been putting in range time like you insisted." I hadn't really expected him to say yes to the gun, but did you notice how he dropped the wait-in-the-car thing? That's the art of negotiation right there. "So, I'll meet you two at the station tomorrow around 11:30? With vest but without gun."

"Fine," he muttered, dropping his bottle into the recycling bin.

It was a weak victory, but I'd take it.

6

I'd told Mike and Xavier that I knew a few doctors I could tap for information, and that was certainly true. However, there was only one whose number I had among my personal contacts, and that was Dr. Russell Carson. Russ worked a lot of night shifts in the ER, so I waited until late in the day to give him a call. As it turned out, he was currently on days and I was overdue for a coffee date with his wife, so I didn't put up much of a protest when he invited me to their house to have our chat over dinner. It helped that they were phenomenal cooks, and I was in no position to turn down a free meal.

I'd only been to their house once, but I remembered it well. It was a beautiful home in a gated community nestled in the foothills on the east side of the city, though why anyone needed the extra security of a perimeter wall around a community in this area, I'd never know. New Mexicans are fond of walls and fences. You'll find one around pretty much any single-family residence, and not just around the back. Their perimeters extend around the edges of the property to the sidewalk in front. They even put gates at the foot of their driveways, despite the fact that, for most, it means having to get out of their car to open it before they can park. If good fences make good neighbors, New Mexicans are the best.

Russell and Suzi didn't have to get out of their car to open their gate. It was a high-tech deal with a callbox at the foot of the driveway. I rang the house, waved to the camera, and the gate swung open to admit me. As I pulled up the long driveway that curled around the side of the house, I admired the structure in the orange-tinted light of the setting sun. It was a large adobe home built on a hill, so it was only one story but that story was spread across two "steps" in the side of the hill. A round room jutted out over the "first floor" with tall narrow windows. I'd wondered what was in that room ever since my first visit, but I'd forgotten to ask. Whatever it was, I was sure it had a spectacular view.

I parked outside the three-car garage before trekking along the brick path to the back door—only strangers came in the front, Suzi had said on my previous visit, friends and family came in the back—crossing the back patio with a bottle of wine tucked under my arm. My mother had taught me better than to show up at someone's house for dinner without a gift of some sort. With my limited budget, I'd had to settle for digging a bottle out of the back of the pantry that Matt or I had purchased at a nearby winery at some point. I'd been saving it for a special occasion. This would have to do.

I could see my hosts moving around in the kitchen through the window in the back door as I approached, Russell manning the stove while Suzi stood at the island counter, chopping vegetables and tossing them into a big wooden bowl. I knocked, waving when they both looked over, and Suzi smiled brightly and gestured for me to let myself in.

Heavenly aromas greeted me when I opened the door, smacking me in the face like a hunger-inducing breeze. I detected notes of cumin, onion, garlic, and of course chile as I quickly scooted inside and shut the door behind me to keep the smells—and the warm air—from escaping.

"I don't know what's for dinner, but it smells amazing."

Suzi put down the knife and rounded the counter for a hug, a bright smile on her face. "Nothing fancy. Enchiladas, rice, and salad."

I gave her a warm squeeze and then held out the wine bottle. "Glad I went with red, then. Thanks for having—oh shit, I totally forgot." I pulled my hand back, clutching the bottle against my chest. "You can't drink."

Suzi laughed, eyes twinkling as she reached out to gently pry the bottle from my fingers. "I appreciate the thought. You'll just have to enjoy it for me."

"I don't drink when I'm driving, so I guess Russ will have to enjoy it for both of us."

The man in question came around the island, wiping his hands with a dishtowel. He took the bottle from Suzi and turned it so he could see the label. "Is this from that place out on the way to Taos?"

"Yup," I said, still mentally kicking myself for bringing a bottle of wine to visit a pregnant woman. "Don't worry, I didn't make a special trip. I've been saving it for a special occasion. Why don't you just hold onto it for another time?"

"If you insist. It's good to see you, Emily." Russell leaned in to give me a one-armed hug before retreating to tuck the bottle into the wine rack with the other bottles gathering dust for now.

While they went back to finishing up, I perched on a

stool and made small talk. When everything was ready, we migrated to the already set dining table in the breakfast area —friends and family also didn't use the formal dining room, I guess—and their "nothing special" turned out to be pretty amazing, so I was too busy stuffing my face to broach a serious subject. The enchiladas featured corn tortillas wrapped around fork-tender shredded pork with onions and green chile and smothered in a tart tomatillo sauce. And cheese. Lots of cheese. I ate three and briefly considered licking my plate clean. Instead, I leaned back in my chair and patted my "food baby."

"That was amazing. If that's your idea of nothing special, call me when you go all-out."

They laughed, and amusement lingered in Suzi's eyes as she dabbed her mouth with her napkin and set it on the table beside her own empty plate. "You caught us on a good day. We love to cook, but on workdays, we don't have time to slow roast a pork shoulder. Off days? Anything is fair game."

"I've got a friend who swears by his pressure cooker. It's electric, so it doesn't heat the kitchen up, and it produces a tender cut of meat in a fraction of the time." I'll give you one guess who that friend was. Yup, Matt. Some days I thought he loved that damn thing more than me, and that was *before* we broke up.

"We've thought about getting one of those," Russell said. "But I dunno. Call me old-fashioned, I guess."

"You're not *that* old-fashioned," Suzi said. "We do have a slow cooker."

Russell chuckled. "Slow cookers have been around long enough to be considered old-fashioned, babe."

I knew better than to get in the middle of that debate, so I scooted my chair back and collected my plate but Suzi hopped up when I did. "I'll take care of that, Emily. Please, sit. You're our guest."

"I don't mind, really." I reached for Russell's plate, but Suzi snatched it up.

"I insist," she said. "Besides, didn't you have something you wanted to talk to Russ about? I'll just drop these in the sink and put on a pot of decaf. Did you save room for dessert? We've got some leftover berry crumble in the fridge I could heat up." She held a hand out for my plate.

I handed over my plate reluctantly and resumed my seat. "I never say no to dessert. But just a little bit, please. If I'd known dessert was on the table, I would've tried to save more room."

"Sure thing. Honey, do you want some?"

"Yes, please." Russell leaned an elbow on the table and looked over at me curiously. "So, what was it you wanted to talk about? You said you had some questions about witch physiology?"

"Yeah. I mean, I know they—er, we—are pretty much the same as humans. Same internal organs, basic biology." It would've been really hard for us to hide in the modern age, if not.

"I would argue that witches are humans, but not all humans are witches."

I blinked slowly. When had I started thinking about witches—myself included—as inhuman? That was unnerving, but Russell's correction at least confirmed I'd come to the right person. "Right. Thanks for that. Anyway, what I'm specifically curious about is the effect of drugs on witches. Do you know of any drugs that affect witches in different ways than they're supposed to?"

"Drugs as in pharmaceuticals, or street drugs?"

"Yes."

He made a thoughtful noise and leaned back in his chair. For a few seconds, the only sound in the room was Suzi rinsing dishes at the sink. "Hmm. Well, I guess the answer is the same either way: no, not that I'm aware of. But it hasn't been long since witches went public, so it's possible that things we once thought were individual variances— someone responding differently to a course of treatment for no obvious reason—may not have been. There's a lot of catch-up to do, and it's only been a couple of years. Why do you ask?"

"You know how we've been seeing those weird cases in the ER where the patient presents with opioid overdose symptoms, then goes crazy after it's reversed?"

"Ugh." He made a face. "Yeah. I've treated three of those this week. One of them put an orderly in traction."

My stomach swooped. "Oh jeez, that sucks. Which one?"

"Oscar."

"Jesus, really? He's a big guy."

"Yeah, the guy popped his restraints and went after him like he was on speed."

"Maybe he was. Or something like it."

"He's lucky Oscar's too nice to press charges. Says he can't hold the guy accountable for what he did when he was off his rocker."

That explained why I hadn't heard about it before now. A witch assaulting someone, with or without magic, would've gone straight to Magic Crimes. "That really sucks. Please give him my best wishes next time you see him."

"You could always drop by yourself, you know. They haven't barred you from the building."

"Yet." I chuckled, but the joke fell flat. "Anyway, I've been trying to track down whatever it is they're OD'ing on, and I've recently learned that it's performance-enhancing. But the weird thing is, it only seems to affect witches. Or, at least every case I saw in the ER involved a witch. Hence the question."

"Interesting. I guess I wouldn't know someone was a witch if they weren't registered and didn't start throwing magic around. I just assumed it was a mix." Russell rubbed his chin, his expression thoughtful. "Yeah, I dunno. I mean, it's not out of the question. Witch physiology is a popular subject in medical journals right now, but the research has been largely inconclusive, and studies take time. In my experience, the medications I prescribe seem to work the same way on witches as they do on everyone else. With the notable exception of sedatives on those OD'ing witches. It's like the naloxone triggers a flood of psychotropic adrenaline, and it takes enough sedative to take down someone twice their size to put them under, which definitely isn't normal. Witches usually go down like everyone else."

"Psychotropic adrenaline. That's an interesting way of putting it. Not inaccurate, though. Do you remember anything about any bloodwork that may have been done on them? HIPAA makes it really hard for us to get medical data on anyone living, and I can't remember the names of the ones who died on my watch."

Russell frowned. "Don't think of it like that, Em. You know better. Those deaths weren't your fault."

I blinked again. God, my head was a messy place. "Yeah, yeah, of course." I reached for my water glass, wondering if I really believed it. "Anyway, short of ordering every autopsy result for the last two months and going through them all looking for a familiar face, I'm kind of spinning my wheels on that front."

"I can get you some names for ones that didn't make it recently. I just need to go through my cases for the last couple of weeks to find them. But now that you mention it, there was something weird about the bloodwork."

I perked up at that. "Oh?"

"Yeah, each one tested positive for an opioid, which we'd expect, but—"

A noisy crash from the other side of the room made us both jump and twist to see what had happened. Suzi stood in front of the refrigerator, her back to us and the door still open. Whatever had hit the floor was on the other side of the island, so I couldn't see it. But I was less concerned about that than about Suzi, who just stood there stock still holding the door open.

Russell shot to his feet, and I caught a quiet "Not again" fall from his lips as he hurried across the room, only to stop short a few feet from his wife. "Shit. Em, do you still have your shoes on?"

I rose, darting a glance around the kitchen. "Yeah, where's the broom?"

"Come over here. Quickly."

When I rounded the island, I saw the mess, the shattered glass dish and leftover berry crumble all over the floor at Suzi's feet. Her white socks were dotted with red and purple splatters. I hoped none of it was blood.

"I've got to get my shoes. Can you go stand behind her and make sure she doesn't fall?"

"Fall? What's going on?" I asked, even as I moved into position behind my friend. "Suzi? Are you okay?" I touched her shoulder, but the moment I did a *ZAP* of magic crackled between my fingers and her skin. ". . . the hell?" I looked for Russell but he was gone, presumably off in search of his shoes.

It was then that I realized the faint hint of magic I'd sensed in her a couple of weeks ago had grown significantly.

How hadn't I noticed that when she'd hugged me earlier? Though Suzi herself had no magic, the child she was carrying did. I'd sensed it before she'd had a chance to share the good news with anyone—not even Russell. But that tiny kernel had grown exponentially, even though the bun was under three months in the oven. I had no idea if that was normal since it was the first time I'd ever knowingly sensed magic in a fetus, but I was pretty sure whatever was going on now wasn't.

Before I could put much more thought into it, her knees buckled and I hooked my arms under hers instinctively, bracing for another charge that never came as I stumbled backward with her until my hips hit the island. I held her up as best I could considering she was completely dead weight, limp in my arms. The close contact allowed me to sense the retreat of the magic within her as it shrank back down to a less noticeable level.

Fortunately, Russell reappeared swiftly to scoop her up in his arms, relieving me of the burden and turning without a word to carry her out of the kitchen. I followed, so many questions spinning in my head that not one of them could land on my tongue for long. He eased her down on the sofa, tucking a pillow beneath her head and then kneeling on the floor beside her, fingers resting over the pulse point on her wrist. He was the picture of calm now that his medical training had kicked in and Suzi was no longer zoned out and surrounded by broken glass.

"Russ? What's going on? Is she okay?" I moved to the end of the sofa and carefully peeled her socks off. The skin beneath was unbroken, much to my relief.

"Yeah." He glanced at me and smiled faintly. "Thanks for your help."

"This isn't the first time this has happened, is it?"

"No." He brushed her hair back from her face with his free hand, looking down at her with tender concern. "It started happening last week. I had her checked out thoroughly after the first time. It's nothing medical. We think it's the baby."

I agreed with them, given what I'd witnessed. But they couldn't sense the waxing and waning of the magic within her the way I could. "Why?"

"Because her visions usually come when she's asleep."

I dropped Suzi's inside-out socks on the coffee table and sank heavily into a nearby chair. It was no secret, at least not between the three of us, that Suzi had a psychic twinkle. It manifested as eerily prophetic, though at times difficult to interpret, dreams. But waking visions? That was uncharted territory. "Shit. Have you considered seeing a specialist?"

"Her OB says everything is fine."

"Sure, medically."

He looked up at me sharply. "What are you saying?"

"Don't panic. I'm just saying that she's got a magic bun in the oven. Is her OB a witch?"

"You think something's wrong with the baby?" His features tightened as blood drained from his face.

"I didn't say that! But I think you're right, that whatever is happening to her is linked to the baby's magic. It was . . . I dunno, stronger while she was in the trance, and it reacted when I touched her." My fingers still tingled a bit with the memory of the electric-like zap of energy.

"Reacted how?"

"Protectively. Have you ever touched her during an episode? I mean, before she passes out."

"Yes."

"Did you get a zap?"

He shook his head.

"Interesting. So, either it recognized you as safe or it only reacted because I'm a witch."

I mulled this over for a few seconds, but then Suzi stirred with a groan and lifted a hand to her temple. "Did anyone get the license plate on that—Emily!" She bolted upright, eyes wide and scanning the room until she found me.

"I'm here. Russell filled me in about the waking visions. How are you feeling?"

"Lie back down, sweetheart?" Russell urged, but Suzi shook her head and turned to sit on the sofa, leaning back. Her eyes never left me, and unease began to gather in my stomach.

"Did you see something about me?" I asked.

She nodded, her naturally fair skin a few shades paler than usual. Russell shifted from the floor to the couch, settling beside her and enfolding one of her hands in both of his. Her behavior did little to soothe the growing itch between my shoulder blades. Whatever she'd seen, it'd rattled her. I elected not to press, uncertain if I even wanted to know. The last time she'd had a vision about me, I'd ended up imprisoned and used as a magic battery. Her vision had been fairly vague, so it's not like foreknowledge had done me any favors.

"You were surrounded by a ring of fire in the eye of a—I don't know how else to describe it—a storm of magic," she said eventually. "I think you will face a difficult choice soon, and no matter how scary it seems outside the eye of the storm, the safety of the eye is an illusion because the fire is closing in."

I swallowed and nodded, immediately thinking of Adrian Volkov. A ring of fire—a *circle* of fire, closing in on me. Was that what Suzi's vision was about? Or was an even more dire decision in my near future?

"Well," I said, "that doesn't seem too bad. I mean, I'm unlikely to end up surrounded by a literal ring of fire in the eye of a magic storm. I face difficult decisions all the time. I'll be okay."

She offered me a weak smile, not seeming terribly comforted by my attempt at reassurance. "That's the pesky thing about fire. Whether you stay put or try to cross, you're liable to get burned."

7

I didn't stay much longer after Suzi's episode, but I did promise to reach out to a witch I'd met in nursing school who'd been planning to go into obstetrics. I was pretty sure I still had an email address for her somewhere, and if not, I could probably find her through the UNM alumni directory. As it turned out, I did have her email address, so I shot her a note before I went to bed.

It wasn't until much later, as I was drifting on the edge of sleep, that my unfinished conversation with Russell resurfaced. What had he been about to tell me about the blood work before Suzi's vision interrupted? I rolled over and sent him a text, then went to sleep.

The next morning, I had his reply.

The level of opioid present wasn't high enough for an overdose. There was another chemical compound present, but it was unidentifiable. The coroner may have access to different databases. I'll get you those names today.

I sent him back a thank you before rolling out of bed and getting my day started in earnest.

To his credit, Mike didn't try to shut me out of the outing

we'd planned. He, Xavier, and I met at the station around noon but passed a completely unremarkable Sunday afternoon at the park. Alvin was a no-show, and the address on his driver's license was out of date, so we made plans to reconvene the next morning. On the upside, Russell came through with a few names of deceased witches. I passed them to Mike so he could put in the request for autopsy records. Then I spent the evening composing an e-mail to the AWL—with Dan's help/interference—to see if they might be able to help with my case against the hospital. I wasn't sure it'd do me any good, but it couldn't hurt to try.

Monday morning, I donned my vest once more—though it took me a few minutes to find another blouse loose enough to wear over it—and joined the stakeout-already-in-progress after dropping Dan off at the academy and picking up coffee and breakfast burritos. I had no idea if they'd eaten, but I hadn't, and it's never a good idea to show up to a stakeout with food unless there's enough to share. Trust me on this one.

"Did I miss anything?" I asked, sliding into the back seat of Mike's department-issued unmarked sedan.

Mike caught my gaze in the rearview mirror. "Not a thing. How'd the drop-off go?"

"I was so proud I could burst." Sarcasm runs strong in my family. But it wasn't entirely untrue. I was proud of him for following through, for giving it a try. I'd be even prouder if he didn't wash out of the program. "I could tell he was nervous, but you know how he is. All enthusiasm and bravado."

Mike chuckled but nodded. "Looking forward to having your place to yourself again?"

I passed the coffee forward. "Damn right I am."

"You live with your brother?" Xavier said, taking one of the cups.

"He recently relocated from Boston. Long story. You need sugar or cream?"

Xavier waved them both off but thanked me for the coffee, using it to top off the contents of his insulated travel mug. The burritos were passed out next, and the car fell silent but for the regular chatter of the police radio and the occasional crinkle of aluminum foil. I kept an eye out the window while I ate, but aside from a few morning joggers, the park was quiet. Xavier had shown us Alvin's mug shot the day before, so I had a better idea of who we were looking for besides a "long-haired skater punk."

Hours passed. There was considerably less traffic in the park than there had been the previous day, probably on account of it being a weekday. We took turns getting out to stretch our legs and get a drink of water or use the facilities. Naturally, I was answering the call of nature and getting in a round of one of those addictive phone puzzle games when a text from Mike popped up.

He's here. Northwest corner. We're heading over.

I almost dropped my phone in my haste to grab toilet paper, and I'll admit I didn't give my hand washing the full twenty seconds, but soap and water did pass over them before I hurried out of the ladies' room . . . and came to an abrupt halt just outside.

Which way was northwest?

I did my best to orient myself based on the position of the early afternoon sun and soon spotted Mike and Xavier strolling down one of the paths. They didn't exactly blend in at the park in their collared shirts, ties, and sport jackets. I wasn't much better in my blouse, slacks, and long trench coat. But it was what it was. We weren't supposed to be undercover, after all.

I set an intercept course and strolled away from the restrooms, scanning ahead of me in search of the dealer. I spotted him leaning against a fence by one of the ballfields mere seconds before he noticed Mike and Xavier coming his way. He turned and strode for the main path, dropped his skateboard, hopped on, and headed off in the opposite direction—putting him directly in my path.

Mike and Xavier picked up the pace, jogging after him. I met Mike's eyes from afar. He scowled at me and shook his head. Alvin continued toward me at a brisk pace, rapidly closing the distance with the noisy rattle of wheels on concrete. He glanced over his shoulder, saw Mike and Xavier in pursuit, and pumped his foot against the ground a few times to pick up speed. I took out my phone, pretending to be absorbed in what was on the screen, but stuck my foot out when Alvin rolled past. He tripped, let out a surprised yelp, and went sprawling on the path, landing in an ungraceful heap. His skateboard veered off the path and landed in the grass.

"Oh my god, I'm so sorry! Are you okay?" I hurried to his side as he scrambled to his feet, but the delay was just enough for Mike and Xavier to catch up.

"Hey, Al, where you goin' in such a hurry?" Xavier asked.

"Away from you!" Alvin said, throwing up his scraped and bloodied hands. The motion caused his jacket to hang open, and he was not visibly armed. "I don't want no trouble, man!"

Xavier chuckled and scratched along his clean-shaven jaw. "Seems to me that only men up to no good have a reason to run from the law. Isn't that so, Esco?"

"Can't think of another reason," Mike said without

missing a beat. The whole exchange had a familiarity to it, like watching a carefully choreographed dance. "Should we take him in?"

Alvin dropped his hands and lifted his chin, but his eyes darted this way and that. "It ain't illegal to hang out in a park!"

I know I should've been focused on the matter at hand, but I couldn't stop thinking about the lacerations on the young man's hands. I pulled a half-empty pack of tissues from my coat pocket and held one out to Alvin. If I'd had antiseptic, I would've offered that too. "Here. For your hands."

Alvin glanced at the tissue, then at me, and scowled. "You tripped me, bitch!" His indignation didn't stop him from snatching the tissue and dabbing at the bloody cuts, wincing in the process.

"You're lucky she did," Xavier said. "If we'd caught up to you first, you'd already be in cuffs. Third strike, Al . . ."

Alvin recoiled so fast he almost tripped over his own feet. "You don't got nothin' on me, cop! It ain't illegal to be in a damn park."

"No," Mike said, "but it's mighty suspicious for a grown man to be hanging out in one by himself in the middle of the day."

"Unless . . . You're not some kind of pedo, are you Al?" Xavier asked.

Alvin's eyes widened. "Fuck off, man! I was meeting someone!"

"We know about the fairy dust," I said, tired of the cat and mouse and hoping to speed things along.

The skater froze, staring at me like he'd only just figured out that I was with the cops. I could practically see the gears turning behind his eyes as he calculated his options. Everything that happened next seemed to happen all at once. He reached behind his back, and Mike grabbed my arm and shoved me behind him while Xavier drew his pistol from his shoulder rig. The next thing I knew, Xavier and Alvin were squaring off, guns drawn. Alvin must've had one tucked in his belt behind his back.

"Drop the gun and put your hands in the air," Xavier said, all teasing melting from his voice in a heartbeat.

Heart racing, I peeked around Mike's shoulder, unhappy about being shoved behind him and of rather mixed feelings about using him as a shield. But he'd volunteered, and it was what it was for the moment.

Alvin's hand shook as he held the gun in a one-handed grip, sideways like he'd probably seen thugs do on TV. His accuracy would be shit, but at close range, he didn't need much. "I ain't goin' to jail!"

"Maybe you should've thought of that before you pulled a gun on two police officers," Mike said. I cleared my throat, and he added, "And a police consultant."

"It's not too late, Al. Drop the gun, and we can talk," Xavier said, taking a few slow steps to the side to separate himself from Mike and me, making it harder for Alvin to keep an eye—and the gun—on all of us at once.

One of the park dwellers had finally noticed the stand-off. I heard murmuring behind me, then someone screamed, and Alvin's itchy trigger finger twitched. The gun went off with a noisy bang. Mike launched himself at the perp, knocking his gun arm aside and taking him to the ground. Xavier remained standing in place, his gun trained on both of them.

My heart beating furiously in my chest, I checked myself for perforations, then looked around, trying to see where the bullet had gone. Fortunately, it didn't seem to have hit anyone. But the park was clearing out fast, parents clutching screaming children as they booked it far away from the scene as swiftly as possible.

My relief was short-lived, giving way to an adrenaline crash that left my hands shaking and my stomach woozy. The fight didn't go out of Alvin until Mike had him in cuffs. While Xavier informed him of his rights, Mike hauled the kid to his feet and met my eyes, one hand firmly holding onto Alvin's arm while he tossed me his keys. "Call this in before the department swarms. Shots fired, no injuries, gunman in custody."

I nodded and hurried off with keys in hand to do just that, grateful for a task to focus on and envious of Mike and Xavier's ability to handle the situation like it was just another day at the office. For them, I suppose it was. Heck, Mike had anticipated it and tried to keep me from coming along. I didn't regret pressing the issue. If I was going to continue working with the cops, I was going to have to get used to having a gun pointed at me now and then.

Let's just say I'd have ample opportunity to practice that week and leave it at that.

8

An hour later, I stood in the observation room adjacent to an interrogation room, watching through the one-way mirror as Mike and Xavier worked Alvin over like a well-oiled interrogation machine. The kid had clammed up as soon as the cuffs were on him, refusing to talk. But he hadn't requested an attorney either. Until that happened, we were free to continue leaning on him for answers. Or, rather, they were.

Did I resent being sidelined? Hell yeah. I knew that three-on-one were bad odds when you wanted answers—the more a perp feels ganged up on, the less likely they are to give in. But *I* was Mike's partner, dammit. This was *our* case. Observing the ease with which Mike and Xavier worked together was just salt in the wound. I probably should've taken notes, but the green-eyed monster was in full effect.

They'd found a significant sample of the drug—or *a* drug, at least—when they searched him, so it wasn't like they had nothing on him. I hadn't laid eyes on it myself before it was checked into evidence, but Mike had told me the white powder was portioned into individual baggies, obviously for sale. Still, the kid wouldn't talk. He just sat there, shoulders slumped and hair hanging in his face, staring at the table.

After a solid twenty minutes, Xavier's voice began to rise until he pushed back his chair and stood in a sudden burst of movement that Alvin shrank away from.

"This is a waste of time. I'm done," Xavier said.

Mike looked up at him, a vertical line appearing between his brows. "Chill, man."

"Don't tell me to chill! This little shit is dealing to teenagers, and he fired a gun in a park. He could've hit a kid! He deserves what he's got coming to him, no matter what he might tell us. I'm done with his stonewall bullshit. I'm going to go see if county can take him tonight."

As he turned on his heel and stalked out, yanking the door shut behind him, Mike sighed and shot Alvin a sympathetic glance. The kid was shaking in his seat, staring at the door, clearly unnerved at the prospect of being transferred. Meanwhile, I scratched my head—figuratively—wondering why Alvin would go to the county lockup before his arraignment which, given that it was already after five o'clock, wouldn't be until the next day.

"Sorry, he can be a bit of a hothead," Mike said. "But I guess I don't have to tell you that. You've dealt with him before."

Alvin's eyes darted between Mike and the door, and he dipped his chin in a slight nod. It was the most communication they'd gotten out of him since they sat down. Xavier's tantrum may have actually done him a favor.

The observation room door opened, and I turned to see none other than Xavier step inside. He nodded to me, closed the door, and walked over to stand beside me with his arms folded across his broad chest. He seemed perfectly calm, at odds with his storming out of the other room a few moments ago. Had it been an act?

I shifted my attention back to the interrogation room, where Mike stood and took off his suit coat, hung it on his chair, then walked around to the other side of the table to lean against it casually beside Alvin.

"I know you're scared, Alvin. I know you didn't mean to fire that gun. That doesn't change the fact that you did, but you and I both know you didn't intend to hurt anyone. You were just backed into a corner, and you did what anyone with two strikes would do. You panicked. You can't undo what you've done, and you're going to serve some time for it. But if you cooperate with me now, I can file minimal charges —possession and discharging a firearm in a public place— rather than possession with intent to distribute and attempted murder of a police officer. And the more you cooperate, the easier a time you're going to have with the DA."

Myriad emotions played across Alvin's face. Anxiety, fear, trepidation . . . He licked his lips, eyes darting to the door and back to Mike.

"C-can you keep me out of county?" Alvin asked. It was the first time he'd opened his mouth since the cuffs went on.

Movement out of the corner of my eye caught my attention. Xavier held a fist out to me. Smirking, I bumped it with my own.

"What's the big deal about county?" I asked quietly.

"Alvin's big brother is there."

"Simon? Or Theodore?"

He snorted. "Dale. He's a guard, though. Not an inmate. Al's gonna catch hell when he gets there."

Meanwhile, Mike kept Alvin talking. Now that he'd

started, he didn't seem to know how to stop. He admitted to dealing fairy dust. He gave up his contact in the supply chain and the time and location of the next drop. Unfortunately, he didn't know where it was being manufactured or really anything else about it. He'd tried it once, curious what the big deal about it was, but all he'd gotten was a headache. That at least confirmed our intel that it only worked on witches.

"I've never had a chance to watch him work like this," I remarked after a while. "He's good."

"One of the best," Xavier agreed. "We miss him in Narcotics, but you gotta respect it when a man answers a higher calling."

"You make it sound like he joined the clergy."

"May as well have. You know how he is about his work— or you'll figure it out, eventually. It's practically his religion. Marissa used to call it the Church of Law."

Mention of Mike's former partner drew my interest further from the interview on the other side of the glass. I did my best to play it cool. "Marissa . . . his old partner, right? The magic consultant?"

"Among other things."

"Other things?" I glanced at him, but his focus remained forward, his mouth shut. Like he'd realized he'd let slip something he maybe shouldn't have. I let it go, but it nibbled at the back of my mind like a squirrel with a nut. What other things might she have been? I mean, there was the obvious. Were they lovers? I recalled the empty second key hook on the wall inside his front door and that her death had hit him hard. "He doesn't talk about her much. What was she like?"

He thought about that for a long moment, during which I wondered if he was going to answer at all.

"Kind," he said. "I always thought she was too soft for police work. In the end, I guess I was right."

I cringed inwardly. Given the fact that she'd ended her life, he wasn't wrong. But it was still harsh. "Must suck, being right all the time."

He laughed and shoved my shoulder hard enough that I stumbled a step to the side. "Stop making me like you, Davenport."

I didn't want him to like me. Mostly, I wanted him off my case and out of my way. Telling him that might've helped squelch any budding bromance, but I got the feeling that even if I didn't necessarily want to trip over myself to get on his good side, I wouldn't like being on his bad side.

9

It was weird coming home to an empty apartment that evening. I mean, it's not like I'd never come home to an empty house while Dan had been surfing my couch, but there's a difference between living with someone and living alone. The place has a different feel to it. Like once someone has lived in that space for a while, their absence is felt differently than if they're just out at the grocery store. It reminded me a little of how the place had felt when Matt moved out, though with less heartache. It made me think of Mike and his empty key hook again, too.

Telling myself that in absolutely no way did I miss my meddlesome brother, I busied myself with cleaning up the mess Hurricane Dan had left in his wake. I felt a little better once the spare bedding was put away and his suitcase was stashed in the back of my closet, but the place still felt . . . empty, even with my cat Barrington meatloafed on the back of the sofa, tracking my movements with his mismatched eyes while somehow simultaneously seeming to ignore me whenever I glanced in his direction.

"Dammit, Em, you spent ten years without him. You can

spend six months. If he even makes it that long," I told myself, shaking my head in despair. I was being ridiculous, that's what. My wastrel brother had been nothing but a thorn in my side since he'd shown up in town two and a half months back. And if I kept telling myself that, I might just believe it. The truth was, we'd become closer than we'd ever been. Closer than I'd ever been with *any* of my siblings, for that matter. Sure, he was annoying. But he was my brother. Family. And, for a change, I was glad for that.

An unexpected knock on my door had never been more welcome. I bolted to answer it in record time, then blinked at the unexpected sight on my doorstep. What were Matt and Tracy doing here, much less together?

"Surprise!" they said in unison, smiling brightly.

Matt held up a plastic bag stuffed with takeout. "We brought Thai."

"And wine!" Tracy held up a bottle.

I stepped aside and motioned them in, pleased by the surprise visit but also bewildered to find my new friend and long-time bestie in cahoots. Tracy scooted past me through the doorway, but Matt paused and leaned down to kiss my forehead in passing. A whiff of his familiar cologne brought with it a wash of memories in that way scents do, sharp but fleeting. Normally I associate Matt's cologne with comfort and love, and being wrapped in one of his hugs is like being swaddled in a human blanket. But as close to the surface as the memory of him moving out was, all I could think about was how I'd had to replace a couple of sets of sheets that just would not let go of that familiar smell no matter how many times I washed them.

At least I wouldn't have to worry about that this time.

"Not that I don't mind the surprise visit, but what's this all about?" I asked as I shut the door, then wandered over to the coffee table where Tracy was already pulling takeout containers out of the plastic bag.

"We just thought we could make your nest feel a little less empty tonight," Matt called over his shoulder on his way to the kitchen. Barrington trotted after him, meowing until I heard the telltale rattle of the can of cat treats.

"He's my brother, not my kid." It was a weak protest at best. After all, they were right. My nest did feel a little empty. "And he'll probably be back, when he—" I hesitated, not wanting to talk too much shit about him in front of Tracy. "—finishes."

Tracy made a noise that was part chuckle and part snort. "I give him a sixty percent chance of making it to graduation."

"Sixty is probably generous," Matt called from the kitchen.

"Okay, if we're being honest, forty at best." I grabbed a pillow from the couch and dropped it on the floor, then settled on it with my legs folded beneath the coffee table. "But I should probably hope for better odds, considering he's paying my rent next month."

"That reminds me, did you reach out to the AWL yet?" Tracy asked.

"Yeah, I sent them an email last night. For the record, stakeouts are boring." I grabbed one of the to-go containers and opened it, exposing a mouth-watering noodle dish with thin-sliced vegetables and what looked like chicken. Condensation rolled down the top of the lid as steam wafted out to tickle my nostrils with the dish's aromatic scent. "Which one's mine?"

Matt came out of the kitchen carrying plates, silverware, and wine glasses. "Whatever you want. We just got a few different things and figured we could do it family style. I did get one pad thai shrimp, though."

"Because you love me." He knew full well that was my go-to. I made grabby hands for a plate until he passed me one, then I started filling it with a scoop of this and a scoop of that.

"How's the case going?" Matt asked once we were all served and settling in to eat.

"Better," I said between bites. "We're finally starting to make some progress after weeks of chasing phantoms. We picked up a guy who's been dealing the stuff, and he gave us a sample for the lab to analyze and another lead to follow up on. So that's great." I couldn't help but think about the conversation I'd had with Xavier in the observation room, and my eyes drifted to the side table across the room whose drawer contained my illicit copy of the Gentry case file.

"But?" Matt said, clearly picking up on something.

"Mike's old partner from Narcotics is helping us out on the case, and he let something slip today . . . I think he was implying something was going on between Mike and my predecessor."

"Oooo I love a good kiki. Spill that tea, girl!" Tracy said, setting her fork down and reaching for her wine.

I chuckled. "There's nothing to spill, really. You've now heard everything I've got."

"This would be the one who killed herself?" Matt asked.

"Allegedly." I speared a piece of shrimp and lifted it, turning my fork and studying the color of the spices wrapped around the pink and white flesh. "Mike told me once that it didn't sit right with him. I found a copy of her file in his desk recently and . . ."

"And what?" Tracy asked.

Good question. Why was I so fixated on this? Okay,

maybe fixated was a strong word. I'd barely spared the woman a second thought until I came across her file, and in a moment of weakness while I was worried about my own working relationship with my partner, I'd swiped it, read it, and made a copy before slipping it back in his desk before he noticed it was gone. Since then, I'd taken it out now and then and poked through it, studying page after page of additional notes in Mike's familiar handwriting, hoping to see something he hadn't—or had, given that he hadn't quite been able to put it behind him.

"And I looked through it. There's not much there, to be honest. At least not where the official investigation was concerned. It was a fairly open and shut suicide. There was even a note. But Mike had added pages of notes to his copy, things that didn't make it into the official report."

"Anything that suggested a relationship?" Matt asked.

"Well, there weren't hearts drawn in the margins or anything." I suppressed the urge to roll my eyes. Barely. "But no, not really. Most of his notes read like case notes usually do. Detached. Professional. But he wasn't satisfied with the results of the official investigation. Maybe that alone should say something. He's got good—no, terrific instincts."

"You do too," Matt said. "You just second-guess yourself too much."

Dismissing him with a shrug, I drizzled peanut sauce on my chicken satay and began to eat it right off the skewer.

"Hmm." Tracy twirled some noodles around her fork. "Losing someone you care about can cloud a person's judgment. I mean, there's probably a reason why someone else did the official investigation."

"Speaking of, was it someone you know?" Matt asked.

"The officer of record? In passing. Lupe Ortiz. I think I met her at the first happy hour I went to, but I don't remember if she was at the other one." The ladies of the SFPD were an interesting group, and I'd been faithfully attending their Tuesday night happy hours since I'd been invited a couple of weeks ago.

"The next one is tomorrow night, right?" Leave it to Matt to remember minute details of my schedule. "Maybe you could broach the subject with her."

"Hmm. I dunno. I mean, what am I gonna say? Hey, remember the last Magic Crimes consultant, the one who offed herself? Are you sure you didn't let a killer go free?"

Matt snorted. "Well, you started off good."

"You wouldn't want to approach her directly unless you want her to know you read the case file," Tracy said.

I mulled this over for a moment over a sip of wine, absently shooing Barrington away from the food-laden coffee table. It's not like the case file was classified or anything. Anyone with access to the database—which I had —could read it. The only times the officer of record would be notified were if the file was re-opened, amended, or printed. I hadn't done any of these things, since I'd just photocopied Mike's copy. But that brought an interesting question to mind. Ortiz had to know Mike had printed out a copy. Had she said anything to him about it?

"There's nothing wrong with reading a case file, but you're not wrong," I said. "Maybe it's best to just ask about Marissa in general and see if she volunteers anything. Heck, the other ladies might have something to share."

"Maybe she attended their ladies' nights," Matt suggested.

"Good point. Yeah, I can ask around about her, just say I'm curious about my predecessor. That's normal, right?"

"Totally," Matt and Tracy said in unison, then pointed at each other and said, "Jinx!" at the same time and laughed.

The topic of Marissa Gentry fell by the wayside after that, which suited me just fine. I had a bit of thinking to do about that one before I took any further action. It could be argued that I'd already done too much. At least Matt hadn't made judgy eyes at me when I admitted to keeping a copy of the case file.

"Oh, I almost forgot!" Tracy said as they prepared to depart a few hours later. She grabbed her purse and rummaged around in it, producing a sandwich baggie with something metallic inside. "Heads up."

She tossed it and I caught it, peering at the contents curiously while they were still in the bag. It looked like a bracelet made of old coins. I opened the bag and took it out, and the magic contained within it made the metal warm against my skin rather than cool. Sigils were etched on the backs of the coins, which were threaded on a stretchy cord.

"That's, uh, pretty," Matt said in a voice that said the opposite.

Tracy chuckled and elbowed him. "It's not supposed to be pretty. It's a shield charm to protect you from stray bullets. Or accurate ones, for that matter. Dan thought of it after you two had that dust-up with the Pueblo witch. He's been working on it ever since, but he had trouble with the on-off mechanism for someone without magic. It's easier when there's a physical mechanism, like with your ring."

I turned the bracelet inside out to better study the sigils. They looked like a twist on classic air shield sigils, and I wondered exactly how Dan had tweaked them. "So, I should only put it on when I'm expecting trouble."

"I said *he* had trouble with the trigger mechanism. He left it with me to fiddle with while he's busy with Hell Week. I cracked it this afternoon." She grinned.

Chuckling, I slipped the bracelet over my hand. The

elastic band was tight enough that it hugged my wrist but not so tight that it pinched or cut off circulation. "How does the trigger work?"

Tracy moved closer to me and reached for the bracelet, turning it until one of the coins, whose edges had been painted red, was on top. "The sigils have to be in contact with your skin for the shield to work. This coin here is the trigger. You tap it once to turn it on, tap it again to turn it off. If you've got long fingers and you're flexible enough, you might be able to wear the trigger coin on the inside of your wrist and tap it one-handed. But it should also work if you tap it against bare skin anywhere, it doesn't have to be a finger." She stepped back, her hand dropping away. "Go ahead and try it."

I did so, touching the trigger with a fingertip. The bracelet pulsed with energy, and a faint sheen of golden magic flowed out of it in both directions, covering my hand and speeding up my arm, leaving faintly tingling skin in its wake. I felt it travel across my shoulders, over my head, then down my chest until my entire body was covered, the shield standing out a fraction of an inch from my skin everywhere —just enough not to separate my clothes from my body. I blinked, heart stuttering in my chest. This wasn't at all what I'd expected.

"Is it working?" Matt asked, telling me that the spell's effect was invisible to the mundane eye.

"Yeah," I said. "This is . . . wow. I thought it'd be a bubble or something. I've seen Dan make impenetrable air shields before, but this is like a magic suit." I moved my arms and legs a bit. I could feel the shield flexing around me, but it didn't hinder my movements. Not wanting to deplete it, I tapped the coin to turn it back off. The shield faded from around me. "And this will stop a bullet?"

"Dan thinks so. We didn't have a gun to test it, but I whacked him with a frying pan."

"I bet that was satisfying," Matt remarked.

Tracy smirked. "Might have been more so if it hadn't been my favorite one. Dented the damn thing."

"Wow." I traced the edge of one of the coins with my thumb, wishing I'd had this during the standoff with Alvin earlier. "How long will it last?"

"A few hours, tops, so don't leave it on all the time. Also, it'll deplete faster if it actually has to deflect bullets—or anything else, for that matter. Blades, clubs, frying pans. It should take a few hits, but don't stand in a shooting gallery."

I chuckled. "I'd like to think I have a strong enough self-preservation instinct not to try that."

"Me too," Matt muttered, wrapping an arm around my shoulders and giving me a squeeze. "Sorry we can't stay longer, but I have work in the morning and I have to drop Tracy off on the way home."

I turned toward Matt, giving him a hug first and then hugging Tracy as well. "Thank you both for coming. It was just what I needed tonight."

Thanks to Matt's over-ordering, I ended up with enough leftovers in the fridge to last me several days. No doubt he'd done that on purpose since I kept turning down his offers to help me out financially. My situation wasn't that dire. I'd only been semi-unemployed for a couple of weeks, and I'd been carefully minding my spending so I didn't go through my savings too quickly. My consultant's wages would help with that, and Dan having a salary would also help a ton—however long that lasted. Hopefully, I had a ways to go before I had to decide which option was less nauseating: accepting money from my ex or tapping into the account where my parents had been depositing my "allowance" for the last ten years. I hadn't touched their money once since I left home; not needing it was a point of pride, and considering the mess they'd gotten me into with the Circle, it'd be a cold day in hell before I'd touch it now.

The Circle. Ugh. Long after Matt and Tracy left that night, I lay in bed staring at the ceiling, suffering from too many thoughts and not enough wine. The last thing I remember thinking before I finally drifted off was, "Thank god I don't have anywhere to be first thing in the morning."

You can probably guess what happened next.

10

A gaggle of noisy ducks woke me up at 7:30 the next morning, or at least that's what I thought at first. I flailed a bit, practically feeling flapping wings against my face as I bolted upright, blinking to find myself alone in my bedroom, the barest hint of morning sun visible around the edges of the blackout curtains. It took me a few seconds to trace the racket to my phone, and I growled as I swiped it from the nightstand. Every now and then, Matt got his hands on my phone and changed my ringtone. He must've done it last night while I was in the bathroom or otherwise distracted. Usually, he changed it to some embarrassing pop song or another, but this time? Ducks.

I was so annoyed that I answered the unknown number rather than declining.

"May I speak to Emily Davenport, please?"

"Speaking."

"Hi Ms. Davenport, this is Gordon McAllister with the American Witch League. I hope I'm not catching you at a bad time."

I nearly laughed at the audacity of the man. A bad time?

I looked at the clock again to make sure it was really 7:30 a.m. It was 7:31 by then, but still. A bit early for a—Wait, did he say American Witch League? I bit back the sarcastic response on the tip of my tongue. "It's fine. Um, what's up?"

"Oh, good. I wanted to let you know we received your email and set up a time when we can discuss your situation in more detail."

Hope flared in my chest. "Really? Oh, that'd be great. My schedule is pretty flexible. When did you have in mind?"

"Are you available this morning, say around 9 a.m.?"

I consulted the clock again. Seriously? "Um, yeah . . . But I'm not sure if I can make it to Albuquerque by then. It's an hour drive, and—"

"Oh, don't worry about that. We'll come to you. Are you familiar with the Tin Whistle Cafe?"

I blinked. They wanted to meet at my favorite eatery in town? "Yeah."

"Excellent. Come hungry, breakfast is on us. It's the least we can do for making this so last-minute."

I pinched my arm just in case I was still asleep and this was some strange mix of fantasy and nightmare. Nope. "Okay. I'll, uh, see you soon. Drive safe."

He chuckled. "I'll try. See you soon."

The phone beeped in my ear as the call ended, and I lowered it to peer at the screen, tapping to bring up my recent calls just to make sure that had actually happened. Then I rolled out of bed and got my ass in gear because I had just enough time to get in a run and a shower before I had to leave. And if I was going to have those blue corn cinnamon pancakes this time, my aforementioned ass would thank me for that run later.

By nine o'clock, I had ordered my pancakes and stood with number in hand, surveying the packed dining room and facing the sudden realization that I had no idea what Gordon McAllister looked like. My phone pinged as a text message came in from an unknown number.

Hey, it's Gordon. Back left corner.

I glanced up from my phone and flicked my eyes between the corners of the room. His left or my left? Or left from the front? Or from the counter? I was mentally cursing the lack of specificity when I noticed an unfamiliar man looking in my direction and waving his phone. He smiled as he caught my eye, and I smiled back and headed in that direction. He wasn't alone at the table; two other men in suits craned their necks to peer in my direction.

The man who'd been waving his phone stood as I drew closer. "Emily?"

"Guilty as charged. You must be Mr. McAllister." I offered a hand, and he clasped it firmly and gave it a shake.

Gordon McAllister was an older guy, probably fifty-something, bald up top with a ring of close-cropped graying brown hair around the bottom and probably the lightest blue eyes I'd ever seen outside of Hollywood. He was also a witch, something I'd expected given the organization he worked for, as were the other two men at the table.

When he finished shaking my hand, Gordon motioned at the number in my other hand and tsked. "I told you, breakfast was on me."

"Force of habit. It's okay, don't worry about it."

"No, no, I insist." Leaning over, he caught the edge of the receipt pinched between my fingers and the wooden block at the bottom of the number stand and plucked it free. "Timothy?"

The youngest man at the table stood swiftly. "On it." He took the receipt from Gordon and headed off to the counter with it.

I winced inwardly at the headache it'd be for the staff to reverse the charge and redo it but was frugal enough to not put up a fight. I was on a tighter budget now with less room for eating out than I'd had a few weeks ago. "Thanks."

"I suppose I should make introductions. You've met my assistant, Timothy. Well, sort of." He chuckled, then motioned at the remaining man at the table. "This is Kenneth Waters, an attorney who does some work for us now and then."

"Ken, please," the man said, standing to offer me a handshake as well. He looked to be a bit closer to my age, maybe a little older, a Black man with close-cropped hair and warm brown eyes.

It struck me as odd, briefly, that Gordon had called me himself rather than having his assistant do it. But maybe that was just his style. I shrugged it off and shook the attorney's hand, smiling politely. "Nice to meet you, Ken."

Gordon motioned to the table, and Ken pulled out a chair for me before settling back into his own. I sat, placing my number on the table and my purse on the floor between my feet. "I hope the drive wasn't too bad. I really appreciate you coming out to meet with me. We probably could've done this over the phone or online . . ."

Gordon waved the notion off. "Call me old-fashioned, but I prefer to meet face to face." There was a pause, but neither Ken nor I rose to the challenge. Gordon laughed, pressing a hand to his stomach. "Lighten up, you two. Anywho, I was deeply troubled by your email. Witches in this country face more than enough social prejudice. We can't let that carry over to our institutions. Being a witch shouldn't factor into employment decisions, but the sad truth is, it does too often. You said you were terminated because you failed to disclose your witch status when you were hired?"

Terminated. That sounded so much worse than fired. My throat went dry, but I swallowed and nodded. "Yeah. They said it had something to do with liability insurance, that I was in breach of contract."

Gordon thumped a fist on the table, rattling its contents. "Hogwash. That's just a convenient excuse. Right, Kenneth?"

Ken was engaged in mopping up a little coffee that'd sloshed out of his cup off the table with a napkin, but he glanced up at the question. "Sometimes it is. But depending on the circumstances, she may indeed be in breach of contract."

"Requiring a witch to disclose their practitioner status as a condition of employment ought to be illegal," Gordon said.

"There's been a box on every employment application I've ever filled out," I said. "Witch or not, check yes or no."

Ken set the now-brownish napkin aside and picked up his coffee mug. "Ought to be illegal and actually illegal are two very different things as far as the law is concerned, I'm afraid."

My stomach sank. "So, I don't have a case?"

"We wouldn't be here if we didn't think there was hope, dear," Gordon said, reaching across the table to lay his hand atop mine. Given that we'd just met, it was a gesture that should've felt less comforting than it did. But there was a paternal sort of warmth to Gordon that might've come across as patronizing if it didn't seem so genuine.

Timothy reappeared and presented me with a voided receipt and my cinnamon latte, then slid back into his chair and produced a tablet from somewhere beneath the table and began to take notes. Or maybe he was checking

Gordon's email or Amazon's Deal of the Day. It's not like I
could see from the other side of the table.

"Okay, well, hope is good I guess?" I eyed Ken, but he
either had a heck of a poker face or didn't share Gordon's
optimism.

"Other than the checkbox on the employment application, were you presented with any supplemental documents
asking you to certify your witch or non-witch status?" Ken
asked.

"I don't remember. This was seven years ago. Maybe
there was another checkbox on the health insurance enroll-
ment. But I don't remember any supplemental documents."

"See, Kenneth?" Gordon said. "Hope."

Ken inclined his head, but neither confirmed nor denied
said hope. Instead, he looked me in the eye and asked the
million-dollar question. "Why didn't you check the witch
box?"

I held his gaze for a moment, then looked down at my
latte and lifted it for a sip. I didn't want to open up about
being a Conduit, but I knew that not believing myself to be a
witch at the time I made the disclosure mattered. Or should,
at least. "I never manifested any magical talent until a few
months ago. I spent most of my life thinking I was a null."

No one said anything after that. I risked a glance up and
found all three men staring at me. Timothy's mouth formed
a small 'o' of surprise. Ken's gaze was thoughtful, while
Gordon's brow furrowed in confusion.

"But you're . . . of the Boston Davenports, yes?" Gordon
asked.

"Much to my mother's dismay." I managed a faint smile,
then hastily added, "But for the record, I am not a Circle
witch." It seemed prudent to start tacking that on.

"Your magic didn't . . . How is that even possible?"

Timothy asked, drawing a sharp look from his boss. He cleared his throat. "Excuse me. I mean, I've heard of late bloomers, but ..."

I couldn't keep the smirk from my lips. "I know, I'm a bit old for a magical adolescent."

Gordon sat back in his chair, stroking his clean-shaven jaw. "Interesting."

My eyes wandered to Ken, who still had that thoughtful look in his eyes. But after a moment, he cracked a smile. "Now that is what I call hope."

Relief surged through my veins and I chuckled as I took another small sip of my coffee, this time actually tasting it. "Glad you think so."

"You're registered now, yes?" Ken asked.

"Yeah. I work with the police, actually. Part-time. Magic Crimes Consultant."

Ken's smile broadened. "Even better. Yeah, I can work with this."

"Really? That's a relief. I mean, we might not even need to go to court. The threat of a lawsuit might be enough to get the hospital to cave, maybe?"

I got nothing but metaphorical chirping crickets for several seconds before a runner appeared at our table with a tray full of food. "Who had the blue corn cinnamon cakes?"

I raised my hand, and he placed a plate full of goodies in front of me before passing out the rest. The awkward silence lingered even after he collected our numbers from the table and headed back to the kitchen. Timothy had scooted his tablet as far to the right as he could to make room for his skillet breakfast. I could practically hear Matt lecturing about hot cast iron in proximity to electronics in my head, but it wasn't any of my business. The ongoing pause in the conversation, on the other hand, was my business. Both Ken and Gordon were frustratingly preoccupied with their plates.

"Sorry, did I not say that out loud?" I asked, unrolling my silverware with a more forceful snap of the thick napkin than necessary.

"No, no you did," Gordon said while shaking more salt on his hash browns than a man his age probably should. "Have you heard of Vernon and Tammy Mayhew?"

"No . . ."

"What about Michael and Matilda Jones?"

I glanced at Timothy and Ken, but both were focused on their plates. "No. Should I be?"

"What about Richard and Mildred Loving?"

That rang a bell in the back of my mind. A very quiet one. Something about the last name. "Yes. No. Wait. Loving . . . As in Loving vs Virginia, the civil rights case that ruled bans on interracial marriage unconstitutional?"

"Bingo." He "rewarded" me with an orange twist from the garnish on his plate, balancing it on the edge of mine. "Interracial couples existed long before them, of course, but most are all but lost to the annals of history. Victims of bad timing, more than anything else. But everyone remembers the Lovings."

"What do landmark civil rights cases have to do with . . . oh." I sat back in my chair, the stack of steaming pancakes in front of me all but forgotten.

Muttering, Ken pulled out his wallet and passed a twenty across the table to Gordon. Gordon said nothing, just smiled and tucked it away in a pocket, but his pale blue eyes sparkled with triumph. I narrowed my eyes at Ken who ignored me in favor of his Eggs Benedict. I couldn't entirely blame him. The Tin Whistle's green chile hollandaise is to die for.

"Now you understand, my dear. This case has legs. It could secure the rights of all witches for decades to come."

"How? My situation is rather unique."

"The specifics are, admittedly," Gordon said. "But pre-employment inquiries about practitioner status should be just as taboo as ones about race are. Otherwise, there's no way to guarantee that there aren't discriminatory hiring practices going on. It's time someone pushed the courts to establish a precedent."

"I'm pretty sure I've had to check a race box on every application I've ever filled out too."

"It's always in a section marked optional, with a disclaimer about the entity being an equal opportunity employer," Ken said, finally breaking his silence.

"Eat up, dear, your pancakes are getting cold," Gordon said, motioning at my plate with his fork.

I didn't like being told what to do, but I'd been daydreaming about those pancakes ever since those damn ducks woke me up this morning. And he was right. They were cooling, and cold pancakes were a crying shame. I spread the half-melted butter on the top around, then drizzled some syrup on top of the stack and watched it drip over the edges of the blue-tinted golden cakes while I thought over what they'd said.

Witches had the same civil rights as everyone else in the United States—in theory. That didn't mean no one pushed the envelope. I'd experienced the prejudice, the discrimination firsthand on multiple occasions, and I'd only been a registered practitioner for a couple of months. But did I want to be the poster child for witch rights? All I really wanted was to be left alone.

Well, and my job back. I wanted that too.

As I savored the first sweet bite of my breakfast, I looked

up from my plate and found Gordon watching me with a smile. The others were focused on their own plates.

"Good?" he asked.

"Mm-hm."

"Look, I know you're probably thinking 'why me,' but—"

"Nah. I'm pretty sure I know why me."

He inclined his head. "Oh?"

I swiped a bite-sized piece of sausage through the syrup on my plate. "It's because I'm a young white woman. Unthreatening. Palatable. Though I suspect my name has something to do with it as well. It's quite a coup, having a wrongfully terminated Davenport witch fall in your lap."

Timothy's head came up, his eyes bouncing between me and Gordon.

Gordon just smiled and shrugged. "I've never been one to look a gift horse in the mouth. Though I'm curious why you felt the need to reach out to us. Your family must have counsel on retainer."

"I'm a grown woman. I don't want or need my parents to solve my problems." It was true, but I also had no desire to rehash my family history with these virtual strangers. "Look, I'm in a difficult situation here. I want my job back, but I'm not sure I want to become the public face of witch rights in New Mexico."

"Why not? Do you think you're the only one who faces these struggles?"

"No, of course not. I just—I don't want to be in the spotlight."

He didn't answer right away, but I could feel his eyes on me. I focused on my breakfast, almost as uncomfortable under his gaze as I was with the thought of being at the center of a media superstorm.

"Why do you want to be a nurse, Miss Davenport?" he asked eventually.

"Emily," I corrected automatically, glancing up from my plate once more. "I don't know. Because I'm good at it?"

"But you chose the path before you became good at it. It required considerable education and training. Why that, and not, oh, I don't know, Library Science?"

"Because I like helping people," I said, but it was a standard answer. The truth went deeper than that. I liked being needed, to be completely honest.

"Just think of how many more people you could help by ensuring witch rights aren't curtailed by the narrow-minded opposition to them."

"That's not the same thing." But even as I protested, I felt the hook burrow beneath my skin.

"Perhaps not. But it's still a very important thing, and an opportunity like this one doesn't come along every day. Wouldn't you like to show those hospital administrators what a bad idea it was to kick this anthill?"

I thought about how it had felt to have the rug yanked out from under me, even if it was partially my own fault. I thought about the shame, the grief that'd overwhelmed me. It was easy to be angry at the hospital administrators, but there was still a part of me that legitimately worried what sort of trickle-down effect an expensive lawsuit might have on the hospital. Would there be budget cuts involved? Layoffs? How would it affect patient care? St. Vincent's wasn't the only hospital in Santa Fe, but it did offer some services and specialties not available anywhere else in the region, and it was a lot more accessible to the surrounding communities than driving all the way to Albuquerque.

I met Gordon's eyes. "Can we at least try the strong-arm approach? See how they respond, and escalate from there as needed? It's not just the hospital that'll pay for a lawsuit, you know?"

"I'm sorry, Miss Davenport, but I need to think about what's best for the movement. We need to press the courts to set precedents if we're going to get anywhere. Kenneth here has agreed to take your case pro bono as part of his work with the AWL, but as VP of the New Mexico chapter, I'm going to have to insist that a suit be filed."

All or nothing. Great. "Can I have a few days to think about it?"

He smiled, shedding his serious demeanor in an instant. "Of course, my dear. For now, let's enjoy this marvelous breakfast."

I wish I could say I enjoyed those cinnamon blue corn pancakes as much as I'd expected to, but I only ate a few more bites on account of my churning stomach. The rest ended up in a Styrofoam container, where it'd join the Thai leftovers in my fridge. I'd never tried reheating pancakes that had already been syrup'd before, but I certainly planned on it.

As we made ready to depart, Ken lingered at the table while Gordon used the restroom and Timothy went to fetch the car.

"I'm sorry about Gordon," he said. "He's always focused on the big picture. I think sometimes he forgets about the little things along the way being just as important."

I shrugged, fiddling with the strap of my purse. "It is what it is, I suppose."

"Just so you know, there's a non-zero chance the hospital will want to settle out of court. You'd be my client, not the AWL, so it'd be your call. No matter what Gordon says."

"Really? Okay, I guess that gives me something to think about. Thanks, Kenneth."

"Ken," he said, then added with a roll of his eyes. "Only Gordon calls me Kenneth."

I took my leave before Gordon returned. It was cowardly of me, maybe even rude, but I didn't want to make an on-the-spot decision I might regret.

11

I was so preoccupied with my legal dilemma, I barely remembered driving to the station afterward. Once I got there, I threw myself into my work. The drop we planned to crash wasn't until the next day, so Mike and I kept exploring other avenues of investigation while the interloper was, thankfully, preoccupied with his Narcotics caseload. Alvin had been arraigned that morning and managed to arrange bail before he could be transferred to county. That meant his brother the prison guard wouldn't find out he was in trouble when Alvin showed up at his workplace, but I doubted the news of his arrest was a bullet the kid would be able to dodge for long.

I sat in on an interview with one of the witch athletes from the high school and his parents, but we didn't break any new ground. The fifteen-year-old admitted to using, that he'd heard about fairy dust from another kid on the team and had bought it from Alvin. The DA would be interested in hearing that, but given that we'd caught Alvin with the drug on him, portioned for sale, she already had a pretty solid case. Mike put the fear of the law in the teen, who was only a few weeks shy of being eligible to be prosecuted as an adult. Hopefully, he was scared straight. But given the look in his father's eyes, I had a feeling he'd be grounded until graduation anyway.

Mid-afternoon, the coroner's office came through on the autopsy reports for the three witches whose names Russell had given me. The tox screens run by their lab were as inconclusive as the hospital's had been. One thing did jump out at me, though. Each witch had died with an opioid in their system and, as Russ had noticed, a low enough dose that it couldn't be considered an overdose. But what struck me was that the particular opioid was different for each one. Oxycodone, codeine, and methadone. I wasn't sure what to make of that, whether we were dealing with multiple batches of fairy dust in circulation cooked with whatever opioid they could come up with or if the victims had also taken an opioid alongside it. Could what we thought was an overdose have been a drug interaction?

I spent the rest of the afternoon in research mode, parked at the end of Mike's desk with the department laptop I'd been assigned to use while I was on the clock. Only full-time consultants got desks of their own, apparently, and though I surely could've used the money, asking to go full-time when I was still trying to get my job back at the hospital seemed like misrepresenting myself.

I was nose-deep in a medical journal when snapping fingers jolted me from my fugue. Frowning, I leaned back in my chair and looked up at Mike who stood beside me, putting on his coat.

"Call out?" I asked, preparing to rise.

"Quittin' time—for both of us. You're going to grow a

hunchback if you sit like that much longer. Get out of here, Em."

Now that he mentioned it, there was a bit of a burn behind my shoulders. I glanced at my watch and blinked. "Five-thirty already?" The last time I'd looked it'd been around three.

"Everything okay? You've been quiet today."

"Yeah, fine." I stood and stretched. Something in my back popped in a good way, and the burning in my shoulders eased.

"Come on, I'll walk you out."

I bent to log out of the computer, then retrieved my purse and coat before heading for the employee parking lot with him. We parted ways at my car, and as he walked away he called over his shoulder, "Say hi to the girls for me."

"Will do!" I'd all but forgotten about the happy hour, so it was a good thing he mentioned it. It probably should've surprised me that he remembered, but he was a details guy. It served us both well in our work.

My phone rang right as I chucked my purse into the passenger seat, prompting me to clamber in hastily after it in a bid to grab my phone before the call went to voicemail. I glimpsed John's name on the screen as I hit the button.

"Hey John, what's up?" My stomach, unused to him calling out of the blue, braced for bad news. It was just that kind of month.

"Hi there. I hope I'm not catching you at a bad time."

I shut the car door, at least stopping the chilly breeze from blowing into the car if not actually raising the temperature in the cabin. "Nah. I was just on my way to this happy hour thing. Ladies' night. What's up?"

"Oh, I won't keep you long then. I just wanted to see how

you were doing. You seemed stressed on Sunday, and with good reason. How are things going?"

My heart warmed at that. When was the last time someone other than Matt had called me out of the blue just to see how I was doing? I couldn't remember. "They're going. Hang on a sec, I need to start the car and put you on speaker." I did just that, and while I got on the road, I told him about my meeting with the AWL and the pressure they'd put on me to go to trial in exchange for their help.

"Free is rarely free, is it?" he said. "Did you agree?"

"Not yet. I'm thinking about it. I mean, I'd like to settle out of court. I just want my job back. But one thing they did give me was perspective. I'm certainly not the only witch this has happened to, but maybe—just maybe—I could be the last."

"There's nothing wrong with wanting something better for your people."

I chuckled. My people. That still felt weird. "Yeah, but to circle back to the cost of 'free,' if everything goes according to their plan, this would be a very public trial. My name and photo would be all over the media . . ." Just the thought of it made me want to slip on dark sunglasses and a ball cap.

"Giving up your privacy isn't an insignificant concern. Especially given the harassment you went through earlier this month."

"Yeah, no kidding. Wait, how'd you know about that?" The witch-haters had really come out of the woodwork after I registered, though I didn't remember mentioning it to John. Thankfully, things had quieted down after I submitted a change of address—to a post office box. If they wanted to harass me via mail, I was okay with that. As long as it didn't come with a side of anthrax.

"It came up at brunch. Must've been before you arrived."

"Right. My brother's big mouth strikes again."

John chuckled, and even through my car's speakers—or maybe because of the surround sound effect—the warm rumble rolled over me like a wave, raising goosebumps on my arms. I wondered what it'd sound like under my ear, which made me wonder if John had a hairy chest or if it was as smooth as his jaw always looked.

"Emily? Are you still there?"

I blinked, only then realizing he'd been talking while I'd been daydreaming. "What? Yeah, sorry. There's a . . . traffic . . . thing," I said with a cringe. Traffic thing? Come on, Em.

"I should probably let you go. Distracted driving is a bad idea."

"No, no, I'm sorry. I was distracted from the conversation, that's all. You're not distracting me." Never mind that it was thoughts of the hunky firefighter without a shirt on that were distracting me, not anything on the road. What in the world was wrong with me? First, the forearm gazing, and now this. John was a witch. I didn't date witches, no matter how sexy, brave, smart, artistic, helpful, and nice-smelling they were. Wow, that was a lot of complimentary adjectives. I might have been nursing a slight crush after all. "Fuck," I muttered, then clamped a hand over my mouth, hoping it hadn't been loud enough for the microphone to pick up.

"I was just saying that family is as much a blessing as it is a curse at times," he said.

"Amen to that." Though, mostly, mine had been a curse. "Do you have any siblings?"

"Three sisters. What about you? Other than Dan, of course."

We chatted through the rest of my drive, and even after I parked outside the Crow's Foot, I lingered in the car a few more minutes, enjoying the conversation as it shifted further and further from my current trials and tribulations. It was a pleasant distraction—an escape even. John had always been such a quiet presence in person, so I was pleasantly surprised at how easily the conversation flowed. There were no awkward pauses, no moments of hesitation or uncertainty. It was actually a little difficult to find a spot to wind down, though I knew I needed to so I could get back to the "real world." Because as pleasant a distraction as it had been, a distraction was exactly what the conversation was, and I couldn't afford to wallow in it forever.

"Well, I'm here, so I should probably go inside. Thanks for calling, John. It was nice to talk about something besides police business and the latest dumpster fire in my life."

"Hey, putting out fires is kind of my thing. But seriously, call me if you need a friendly ear. I can't promise to have all the answers, but I can listen. Sometimes it helps to just get it out."

"Thanks, I appreciate it. Take care."

I disconnected the call and fetched my phone from the dash mount, turned the car off, then slumped back in my seat with a sigh. Maybe effortless conversation was actually a bad sign. I'd had that with Matt, and look how that had turned out. Sure, he was still my bestie, but it could be argued that we were a little bit codependent. Or a whole lot codependent. I wasn't sure what a healthy relationship with a man looked like anymore, and that was all the more reason to keep my distance. But there was still a little part of me that wanted someone to look at me the way Russell looked at Suzi. Like she wasn't just the answer . . . she was the question.

Then again, I was a witch with no magic and more issues than *National Geographic*, living on my savings and the charity of my brother, being investigated by the Circle, and a budding civil rights warrior who had lately developed a nasty habit of landing on the business end of a gun.

God help the man who fell in love with me. He'd need all the help he could get.

12

The Crow's Foot was the closest thing to an Irish pub in Santa Fe. It occupied a corner unit of a small strip mall and wasn't burdened with an abundance of windows. The ones it did have were covered with colorful paper on the inside and bars outside. The result was a sort of jailhouse stained glass effect inside when the sun was at the right angle.

It was so much dimmer inside than outside that it always took a few seconds for my eyes to adjust. As the noisy music and conversation wrapped around me, I inhaled the scent of chalk dust, alcohol, and fried food. The place served the usual pub fare, which meant lots of greasy burgers and fries, but also fish and chips and the occasional shepherd's pie. Rumor had it they could also throw together a salad upon request, but I can't guarantee it wouldn't get a pass through the deep fryer before it hit the table.

Once my eyes adjusted, I found the ladies from the station gathered around the same pool table as the previous two weeks. Hands and drinks were raised as I approached, greeted by a chorus of "Emily!"

It wasn't that I was particularly popular, it was just their habit to greet everyone this way, like this was a place where everyone knows your name. I have to admit, it did make me feel welcome.

I dropped my purse on a nearby table and snagged the laminated menu from its metal stand. "Sorry I'm late. Mike says hi."

Most chuckled, but Jamie, a short young patrol officer with close-cropped red hair, harrumphed. "I'm still annoyed he didn't tell you about happy hour for months."

Rashida, the patrol officer who had finally tendered an invitation a couple of weeks ago, slung a friendly arm over Jamie's shoulders. "Don't be a sourpuss. She's here now, isn't she?"

I was tempted to ask about Marissa Gentry. It was a perfect opportunity. But I didn't see Lupe among those assembled, so I put it on the back burner. Maybe she'd turn up in a little while.

"It's no big deal. Anyone want to go in on a basket of potato skins with me?" Four enthusiastic hands went up. "Two orders it is. Anyone else need something while I'm at the bar?"

Two Manhattans, one IPA, one pear cider.

I repeated the drink order in my head on the way over to the bar, not wanting to forget anything. I was still the new girl in this little circle, and when exploring unfamiliar waters, it was usually best to try not to make waves. Granted, none of the girls had been anything but pleasant to me so far.

The bartender was the same one who'd been on duty for my last two visits to the Crow's Foot, and it turns out she was familiar enough with the regulars to match drink orders to tabs, so I didn't even have to pay for the round. She also loaned me a tray so I didn't have to make multiple trips back to the group. I made a mental note to tip as generously as my lean budget allowed when closing out my tab.

After drink distribution and tray return, I hovered on the edge of the group, listening in as they chatted about work and life and occasionally chiming in. The group of women—plus Jamie, who had recently come out as non-binary—was a warm bunch, and even though I didn't know most of them very well they made me feel more than welcome. The SFPD was a small department of fewer than 200 officers, but there was a disproportionately small number of women on the force, which wasn't unusual in law enforcement. Not all attended the weekly meetups at the Crow's Foot religiously, so I'd seen a few different faces each time I'd attended.

There was one person, though, who had been there every week: Rashida Abrams, the one who'd extended the invitation to me in the first place. She was a thirty-some-thing African American woman with laughing brown eyes and a boisterous personality—when out of uniform, anyway. At work, she was considerably more reserved, which I suppose one expects of police officers. As I got to know her better, I'd learned she'd moved to Santa Fe from Los Angeles a few years ago to get away from big city life. There was a dimness to her eyes when she spoke of it, and I got the feeling there was more to the story, but I hadn't wanted to press while we were still getting acquainted.

She did, however, have some hilarious stories about her time at the LAPD, and she was in the middle of telling one when Lupe Ortiz finally straggled in an hour or so after I got there.

"Lupe!" everyone greeted, interrupting the story.

The petite, older Latina flashed a tiny smile. "Sorry I'm

late." She had a drink in her hand, but it looked like a soda. I raised my ginger ale in salute, and she gave me a tight nod.

Maybe it's all the years I spent in nursing, but I can usually tell when people are hiding pain. Humans aren't as good at it as they'd like to think. Cats, on the other hand, by the time they show distress it's practically unbearable. Poor critters. But I digress.

Lupe was hiding pain, and while Rashida recapped enough of her story that Lupe could follow along with the rest, I studied her thoughtfully. She hadn't been limping. She held a glass in one steady hand and the other arm hung loosely at her side. The tension around her eyes could mean headache, but I suspected more when she declined Jamie's silent offer of a high stool to sit on. Her back, maybe?

The group broke out in laughter around me, jolting me from my musings. I laughed along, but I'd completely missed the rest of the story. After that, the group split up into teams for a round of pool, which Lupe politely declined, leaving us with an odd number.

"I'll sit this one out too," I said, lingering on my own tall stool.

"Are you sure?" Rashida asked. "I don't mind sitting out."

"Yup. Go get 'em, shark." I winked at her, and she laughed but turned to accept a cue from one of the other girls and walked over to one of the two closest pool tables.

Lupe drifted toward me and peeked into the baskets on the cocktail table. There was still one potato skin left in one of them, so I pushed the basket toward her. "Help yourself."

"Thanks," she said and did so.

I managed to restrain myself until she got at least a couple bites into the potato skin before asking, "Is your back bothering you?"

Lupe did that slow pan thing, turning her whole body

slightly toward me instead of turning her head. That's when I knew I was wrong.

"Ah. Your neck. I'm sorry, that's not fun. Is it a muscle strain? Nerve compression?"

She licked a little grease from her lips and smirked. "I thought I was the detective."

"Sorry, you know what they say, 'You can take the nurse out of the ER, but . . .'"

"I'm pretty sure no one says that."

I chuckled. "Probably not. Even if it's true. But seriously, have you seen a doctor?"

"Yeah. She thinks it's a pinched nerve. Prescribed a nice muscle relaxer, but it knocks me the hell out. I can only take it at night."

"There is such a thing as a day off, you know. I'm pretty sure the department has sick leave benefits." For full-timers, anyway. The subject of benefits made me think about my own—or lack thereof. It suddenly struck me that my health insurance would lapse at the end of the month when the hospital stopped paying its share. Shit. I was so preoccupied that I missed Lupe's reply entirely. "Sorry, what was that?"

"I said I'd rather save my sick time for something actually incapacitating. I can work through this." She paused for a moment, watching the others play over couple more bites of the potato skin, then asked, "You're Escobar's new consultant, right?"

We'd met, but I didn't hold it against her. Maybe she was just trying to make small talk. Not everyone is good at that, least of all me. "Yeah. Emily. I've been with the department a couple months, though. I think my new consultant smell is just about gone."

The joke fell flat, but Lupe nodded—or rather started to

nod but froze mid-motion. "How's he doing?" She popped the last of the potato skin in her mouth.

"Mike? Uh, fine I guess." I stirred my drink with my straw, ice cubes rattling against the sides of the glass. I was just about to take advantage of the golden opportunity to bring up my predecessor when a mix of cheers and groans sounded from the nearest table. Someone had sunk the eight ball, ending the game. Rather than start another, they stood around the table and chatted over their drinks while Rashida drifted over to us. It had been her partner who'd lost them the game, but she didn't seem to be taking it too hard.

"Either of you want to tag in?" Rashida asked.

"Nah, I'm not going to stay too much longer," Lupe replied. "I need to get home for dinner, but I wanted to make an appearance."

"Aw, that's sweet. We always like seeing you, girl." Rashida embraced the detective, who hugged her back stiffly, a look of such discomfort on her face that it would've been funny if I hadn't known it was at least partly due to pain.

Sensing my window to question Lupe was rapidly closing, I blurted out, "Did Mike's last consultant attend these happy hours?"

Both women turned toward me, brows lifted.

Heat rushed to my cheeks, and I hoped they weren't as red as they felt. "Just curious. Everyone keeps reminding me that I'm his new consultant. It makes me wonder about his last one. I don't know much about her other than that she died. Suddenly."

Features pinched with sadness, Rashida nodded slowly. "She was a regular, yeah. A real sweetheart. A bit on the shy side, but when she came out of her shell, she was fun to hang out with. Wicked sense of humor. Her death was a shock to us all. It was just so—so awful."

I glanced at Lupe whose lips were tightly sealed, eyes locked on the drink in her hand. "I'll bet. Sorry, I didn't mean to be a downer. Mike doesn't talk about her much. Sometimes I wonder if something was going on between them."

Lupe's brown eyes flicked up and met mine, but she remained silent.

"She definitely had it bad for him, but I don't know if anything came of it," Rashida said, then chuckled. "Escobar's such a stickler for the rules, he probably has the department's fraternization policy printed on his bedsheets."

"Hey now, that's my partner you're talking about." Still, I chuckled.

"Am I wrong?"

"I've never seen his sheets. How would I know?"

Rashida laughed and shoved my shoulder. "You're funny, Davenport."

"On that note, I need to head out." Lupe set her mostly empty glass on the nearby table. She hadn't even taken off her coat. But I couldn't blame her for wanting to get home to her meds, even if I suspected she was also looking to escape the conversation. I didn't intend to let her off the hook that easily.

"I'll walk you out," I said.

Lupe endured another hug from Rashida. The rest of the group were content to wave and call out their goodbyes, some expressing sadness that Lupe wasn't staying longer.

"Are you heading out too, Emily?" Jamie asked, hip propped on the edge of a pool table.

"Not yet. I'm going to walk Lupe out and get a fresh drink. I'll be back."

The cheers that news was met with did make me feel good, I'll admit. Maybe I'd play some pool when I got back and try to actually relax.

I stepped outside to find the sun setting behind the mountains to the west, painting the sky the color of orange sherbet with the occasional cotton candy-like pink cloud. A crisp breeze blew across the parking lot, making me wish I'd grabbed my coat on the way out.

"You didn't need to walk me out," Lupe said, not even pausing to admire the view on the way down the sidewalk.

"I know. What's the opposite of a police escort, anyway?"

"I don't think there's a word for it, because it's unnecessary," she said sourly.

"It seems like the Gentry case is a sore spot for you."

"What makes you say that?" Her tone was flat as she retrieved her keys from her coat pocket. She wasn't even trying to deny it, just deflect a bit.

"The way you clammed up and suddenly wanted to leave."

"I'm in pain, Davenport. I just want to go home, have dinner with my kid, and take a pain pill."

Referring to people by their last names is a default setting for some cops, but others revert to them when they're annoyed or trying to be formal. I wasn't sure which category Lupe fell into, but in the moment, she reminded me a little of Mike. "I'm sure that's true. But it's also true that you don't want to talk about the Gentry case. Why?"

She caught my arm and drew me to a halt, then turned toward me, meeting my eyes. "Let it go."

"With you, or in general?"

Her gaze was stern. "Yes. Just take my word for it. This

isn't a string you want to pull." She pointed her key fob at a green sedan and unlocked it with the press of a button. "Goodnight, Emily."

I watched her walk away and get in the car, then remained standing there as she backed out and drove off despite the goosebumps on my arms.

You know how someone telling you not to do something just makes you want to do it more? Yeah, it was a bit of that. Don't pull on the string, she'd said. What would unravel if I did?

13

"What happens if Alvin shows up?" Sitting on a bench at a bus stop under the midday sun, I did my best to look casual as the third bus pulled up to the curb in front of us, then drove off and left us behind. It didn't help that this was about as sketchy a part of town as you could find in Santa Fe. A phantom itch between my shoulder blades along with the urge to simply be anywhere else had been nagging at me since we sat down almost an hour ago.

Mike, on the other hand, appeared perfectly casual as he sprawled on the bench, legs spread and arms stretched out along the back to either side. "Alvin's not going to show up. He's dumb, but he's not that dumb."

"But what if he really is that dumb? Haven't you told me more than once not to underestimate the stupidity of criminals?" I hate to say that our entire plan hinged on Alvin not showing up for the drop, forcing his contact to report the incident to his superior, but . . . Our entire plan hinged on Alvin not showing up for the drop, forcing his contact to report the incident to his superior. Preferably in person.

"Then we'll arrest him again."

"But . . ."

"Relax, Em."

"Telling someone to relax is almost as bad as telling someone to calm down. It usually just pisses them off." I kept scanning the opposite side of the street while we talked. The drop was supposed to take place on the corner some twenty-five yards away. At least it was warm in the sun. Warm enough that I'd had to push my sunglasses up my sweaty nose a couple of times. Spring wasn't due for weeks yet, but a mid-February warm snap was normally welcome —if I was dressed for it. Which I wasn't.

Mike chuckled and poked my shoulder. "You're not mad, you're just impatient."

"I'm not impatient." I turned my head sharply and lowered my chin, glaring at him over the tops of my sunglasses. "I just like having contingency plans."

"*Madre de Dios*, you two argue like an old married couple." The earbud tucked in my left ear vibrated with the bass-y rumble of Xavier's voice. He was stationed in an unmarked car one block down, ready in case the perp got in a car or we were otherwise unable to follow on foot.

"Put a sock in it, Suarez," Mike replied without any particular vitriol.

"So much love. I knew you missed me."

I could practically hear my partner rolling his eyes. "Keep this channel clear, please. Our perp could show up at any time."

"Speaking of." I nudged Mike's foot with my own. A tall, heavily-tattooed lanky white guy in baggy clothes and a bulky jacket that was probably meant to make him look bigger and therefore more intimidating had begun loitering in the vicinity of the drop. He stood with his hands in his pockets, leaning against the side of the auto parts store on the corner. Sunglasses hid his eyes, but his head migrated left to right and back again as he kept an eye on his surroundings. He could've been missed as a customer of the auto parts store, but I'd watched him walk over and turn to prop up the wall without going inside. And, I dunno, something about him just said shady.

"Is that who I think it is?" Mike asked.

I squinted at the man from where we sat, glad my sunglasses hid my peering eyes. "Doesn't look familiar to me."

Meanwhile, Xavier cursed in my ear. "Ricky 'Lupo' Solomon? Yeah."

"He still running with Big G?"

"Last I knew," Xavier replied. "Christ, we shoulda known he'd be involved in this."

"Lupo? Big G? Why do I feel like I've just stepped into an episode of *The Wire*?" I asked.

Mike chuckled. "Big G's crew has been a pain in the ass around here for years. We're pretty sure he's got his fingers in all sorts of illegal pies—drugs, guns, gambling—but he's slippery as hell. His real name is Guillermo Ochoa, but I only know that because his son got into trouble a couple of years ago and let something slip while he was in custody."

"Kid shoulda gone to juvie," Xavier said. "Your partner's a softie, Davenport."

"He wasn't a bad kid, he just grew up in a bad environment and didn't have a lot of options. I gave him a second chance to make better choices, that's all."

"Once a punk, always a punk." I could practically hear Xavier rolling his eyes as he spoke. "Speaking of which, there's multiple warrants out for Solomon. Aggravated assault, trespassing, robbery . . . Maybe we should pinch him now."

I glanced at Mike, whose focus remained steady on the other side of the street. "He might lead us right to his boss's operation if we don't."

"I can flip him." Xavier's words oozed confidence.

"We stick to the plan," Mike said, finally breaking his thoughtful silence. "If we move prematurely, he might refuse to give us anything. Either way, he's going to end up in cuffs. We just need to be patient."

I couldn't make out Xavier's muttered reply, but that was probably for the best.

Time ticked by. Solomon lingered in place for a solid thirty minutes before pushing off the wall and starting back down the street in the direction he'd come from.

"He's on the move," I said. Probably unnecessarily, but it seemed like someone needed to say it.

Mike and I stood to walk up the sidewalk, keeping pace on the other side of the street. Ricky pulled out a cell phone and made a call, but of course we were too far away to hear what was said. After walking another block, he turned into a convenience store parking lot and got into a battered old sedan that had more primer gray on it than actual paint.

Lucky for us, he sat in his car for a couple of minutes before backing out, giving Xavier time to catch up to us with the car. We piled in and proceeded to follow the guy down the street.

"Watch your distance," Mike cautioned. "We don't want him to make us."

"I know what I'm doing," Xavier said, but shortly afterward the perp made a sudden left and accelerated down a side street.

Cursing, Xavier followed him, but the way Ricky rapidly picked up speed and made a series of aggressive turns, he knew someone was on his tail. I grabbed the "oh shit" bar over the window and held on as Xavier gave chase. Mike rolled down his window and slapped the magnetic emergency light to the roof, declaring the vehicle a police one but also serving as a warning to other drivers or pedestrians that might be in the way. He also called the situation in, which meant backup would soon be en route.

When Ricky pulled back onto St Francis Drive, he nearly side-swiped a landscaping truck but gained a little distance while Xavier braked to wait for an opening. It only took a few seconds for traffic to give way for a police vehicle, but they were seconds we didn't have. By the time we got around the corner, I'd lost track of Ricky's car entirely.

"Fuck! Where'd he go?" Xavier said as he practically rode the median, zipping down the left shoulder as quickly as he dared.

"There!" Mike pointed, and Xavier cursed again as he put on the brakes and executed a rapid U-turn right in front of a no U-turn sign.

Inertia threw me against the car door. Tires squealed, laying down rubber as the back of the car fishtailed. Horns honked. My heart raced. This was my first big police chase, and it was equal parts exciting and terrifying. Given the choice, I would've preferred to be in the driver's seat. At least then I would've felt like I had some sort of control over the outcome. As it was, I was just along for the ride.

"Jesus! Would you watch where you're going!" Mike hadn't reached for the bar over the window, but he did have a white-knuckled hand on the dashboard.

"Do you want to drive?" Xavier spat back.

"At this point, yes!"

I groaned. "Less arguing, more following!"

We careened around several more corners, chasing the barest glimpses of primer gray ahead. A black and white

SFPD cruiser with lights flashing and siren blaring soon fell in behind us. I hoped it was no one I knew. I'd never been so close to getting carsick in my life, and the fewer familiar faces there were to witness that, the better.

The suspect's car jetted through an intersection, blowing past a stop sign, and Xavier followed in hot pursuit, not so much as tapping the brake.

Mike shouted, "Look out!"

Movement in the corner of my eye drew my focus from the front just in time to see the grill of another vehicle bearing down on us.

Xavier swerved. I think I screamed. I really don't know. I don't remember the impact, just the jolt of panty-pissing fear before everything went black.

14

"She's coming to. Emily! Emily, can you hear me?"

I cracked my eyes open, squinting against the sudden brightness. Throbbing pain in my skull tagged along for the ride as I regained consciousness. The fuzzy oblong shape hovering over me slowly resolved into a familiar face.

I blinked a few times. "Michelle?"

"Hey, welcome back." She smiled down at me, the stethoscope around her neck swaying to clank quietly against the penlight clipped into the breast pocket of her uniform shirt. "Can you tell me what day it is?"

"Um." I blinked a few more times, taking in my surroundings. Wherever I was, we were moving. The metal ceiling, the storage units to either side, and the EMT's presence confirmed it even before I noticed the muffled wailing siren. Ambulance. Why was I in an ambulance? "Wednesday."

"And the month?" She drew her penlight and shone it in my eyes.

"February. What—" A sudden jolt as the ambulance

went over a bump of some sort, maybe a pothole, sent a bolt of agony shooting into my skull. I gasped and squeezed my eyes shut.

Michelle shot a glare in the direction of the front of the rig. "Careful, we've got a head injury back here!"

"Sorry," Andy's voice called from the front.

Michelle tucked her penlight away and held her finger up in front of me. It was right about then I realized she was doing everything one-handed. I tried to turn my head to see what her other hand was doing, but a neck brace prevented me from doing so. That plus another throb of pain was enough to keep me still.

"Follow my finger with your eyes. Don't move your head," she said.

I did my best. As my brain came more fully online, I told myself that the fact that I wasn't seeing double was a good sign. I'd obviously had some sort of head injury. "What happened?"

"You were in an accident, and you got a pretty good knock on the head. You've got a scalp lac, and it's bleeding like the dickens. Does anything else hurt?"

The pain in my skull was so intense I hadn't even been able to think about anything else. I took stock, wiggling fingers and toes. Everything seemed to be in working order, but I was strapped to the gurney for safety's sake, so it was hard to move much. "I don't think so.

"It probably will tomorrow." Her face twisted in sympathy. "Sorry."

I lay there staring at the ceiling for a few moments, half wishing for unconsciousness to return but half aware that remaining conscious would be better. Michelle asked me a few more standard head injury questions in an effort to get a read on how badly my brain was scrambled. Other than not being able to remember anything since breakfast, my memory seemed to be intact. She assured me that short-term memory loss was fairly common with head injuries, and I knew that, but it didn't make it any less unsettling.

"Was anyone else in the car?" I wondered aloud eventually.

"Yes, and they're both fine. Well, relatively. They were conscious when we left and didn't seem to have life-threatening injuries." She turned her head and called to the front, "Andy, can you get an update on the other two passengers?"

"Who are they?" I asked.

"I'm sorry," Michelle said. "I didn't catch their names. One of them was really worried about you though."

What had I done after breakfast that'd landed me in a car wreck with two other people? I strained my wounded brain, but it just made it throb more.

Michelle wrapped her fingers around mine and gave me a reassuring squeeze and a smile, perhaps reading the struggle on my face.

After a minute or so, Andy called back, "One is in transit, suspected broken leg. The other was cleared at the scene but is riding along to the ER."

I took that in, still distracted, but I was no closer to solving the dilemma when the ambulance slowed to a stop in front of the ER and the doors flew open. Michelle moved with me as the gurney wheeled toward the exit, rattling off information to the "pit crew" as I was unloaded.

"Twenty-eight-year-old female witch with head injury sustained in automobile collision. Unconscious when we arrived, but regained consciousness en route. Short-term memory loss, tested fine otherwise."

It was even brighter outside than it had been inside the rig, and I was too blinded at first to make out any faces of the ER personnel around me, but their voices were familiar and put me at ease. Or, at least as at ease as one can get in this sort of situation.

The sunlight was soon replaced by the fluorescent lights of the ER, and I was wheeled into a trauma room. As they unstrapped me from the backboard and prepared to transfer me to a hospital gurney, a familiar voice said, "Hey there, Emily. You know you're welcome to visit anytime, right?" Russell leaned over into my field of view and smiled, and I found myself smiling back, grateful he was currently on the day shift.

"You know me, always making a fuss," I replied.

Russ chuckled, then shifted to stabilize my head while the others lifted me from the backboard. The soft gurney pad beneath my back as they lowered me again was a relief. Plus, I could move my arms and legs enough to reassure myself that they still worked.

There wasn't much I could do but lie there while they did their jobs, and I was so grateful to be in their competent care that I didn't have the spare headspace to be anxious about being surrounded by former co-workers for the first time since I was fired.

The pressure on my head lifted momentarily, and my skin tingled as the wound on the right side of my head was exposed to air.

"That's a lot of blood for such a little split," Russell said. "Scalp wounds are the worst, aren't they Em?"

"Yeah," I mumbled distractedly.

"We're going to want to take some pictures to make sure there's no skull fracture or spinal issue," he said. "But I'll sew this up real quick for you. Can't have you bleeding all over the expensive equipment."

I chuckled at his joke, which was a bit darker than he

could usually get away with, but he didn't have to watch himself so much with me. I closed my eyes and lay there quietly while they bustled around me, too out of it to be embarrassed as Russell completed his examination and a pair of nurses replaced my clothes with a gown. Finding nothing immediately alarming, Russ stitched up my head while catching me up on the office gossip I'd missed out on, but most of it went in one ear and out the other.

By the time I was wheeled out from behind the trauma curtain, I was feeling pretty floaty thanks to pain meds, but I'd finally remembered what I'd done after breakfast. I filled up the tank in my car. That didn't explain how I'd ended up in a car with two others, but it was something. Wait. Had I wrecked my car?

I was mostly conscious for the X-rays, but I must've drifted off afterward because the next thing I knew I was in a hospital room, the afternoon sun slanting in through the mini blinds. My brain felt like it was too big for my skull. My pulse throbbed in my temple, and my tongue felt like sand-paper in my mouth.

I could move my head, which meant the neck brace was off. That boded well. The whiteboard on the wall opposite my bed was largely blank but did have my current nurse's name written in big block letters. The room was familiar in a generic way. It looked like a room at St. Vincent's. Other-wise, I had no idea where in the building I was. It was a private room, though, so someone there must've still liked me.

My eyes soon found Matt slumped in a chair beside the bed, his eyes glued to his tablet. He hadn't noticed I was awake yet, so I took the opportunity to observe him for a moment. His dark brown hair stuck up oddly from where he'd been running his fingers through it, as sure a sign as his bouncing knee that he was restless, worried, and possibly over-caffeinated. He had obviously rushed to the hospital from work because he still wore a polo shirt with the resort logo embroidered on it. Had he been surprised that he was still listed as my emergency contact? Maybe it was time for me to consider changing it. Okay, it was past time I changed it. But who else would I name? The list of possibilities was depressingly short.

"I hate to interrupt what is probably a good book, but what's a girl have to do to get some water around here?" I croaked.

Matt was on his feet in a flash, his tablet left forgotten in the chair. "Oh, thank God." He stepped closer and reached for my hand, cradling it in both of his. Relief shone in his hazel eyes. "How are you feeling?"

"Water?" I croaked again, and he hastily released my hand to pour a cup from the pitcher on the bedside table. I took it from him and sipped a bit through the bendy straw. The room-temperature liquid cascaded over my tongue like the sweetest ambrosia. I took another sip before passing the cup back to him. "Thanks. I feel like—" I laughed, but it was short-lived because it made my head throb uncomfortably.

"Shit?" he prompted, taking my hand again.

"I was going to say like I was hit by a truck, but that might be a little too on the nose."

He chuckled, stroking my fingers softly. "Is that what happened?"

It came to me in a flash. The chase. The big grill heading straight for me, then nothing. "Mike!" I bolted upright, which made the room spin a bit. Matt pushed me back down with a gentle but firm hand. "He's fine. A little banged up, but fine. He wanted to wait with you too, but I told him to go take care of cop business. That you wouldn't want any magic crimes to go unsolved while you were out of commission."

I furrowed my brow. "How long have I been out?"

"A few hours. But his pacing was getting on my nerves, so I figured he could use something to do. He said to tell you he'd stop by later, and that he and Xavier are fine."

"Michelle said one of them had a broken leg."

"Hmm. Well, there was nothing wrong with Mike's legs, so it must've been the other guy."

Something about the way he said that made me groan. "Please tell me you weren't checking out my very straight partner's legs."

"Oh sweetie, you know I'd never lie to you." He patted my hand.

There was a light knock on the door, and then it swung open and Russell strode in. "Ah, the patient is awake! How are you feeling, Em?"

I extracted my hand from Matt's and fumbled for the bed controls so I could sit up a little more. "Awake. Sore."

"Anywhere besides your head?" he asked, walking around to the far side of the bed.

"Just some general muscle soreness. No shooting pains or anything."

"That's good. Have you been out of bed yet?" He took out his penlight to check my pupillary reactions again.

"No, I just woke up a few minutes ago."

He checked my pulse and prodded my abdomen a little. It did hurt when he did that, and I winced, but he must not have felt anything alarming. "Your films looked good. No fractures, just that bump on the noggin. You have a mild concussion, so you might feel a little dizzy when you get out of bed. Don't do it without anyone in the room, okay?"

"I'll be here," Matt said from the other side of the bed.

Russell glanced at him and nodded. In that flicker of a moment before his attention returned to me, his entire demeanor changed. I got the suspicion that he didn't like Matt much, but I wasn't sure why. They couldn't have interacted more than a handful of times over the years. "I'd like to keep you overnight for observation."

"For a mild concussion? It was just a little fender bender."

"Any head injury bears watching, and with the memory loss—"

"Oh, I remember everything now."

His gaze grew shrewd. "Then you know full well it wasn't a little fender bender. You are extremely lucky, Emily. All three of you are."

"I can stay with her tonight if that will help," Matt said. "And I'll bring her right back if anything happens."

I looked hopefully from Matt to Russell, but the doctor appeared unmoved by my bestie's offer. "One night, Emily. Please."

I closed my eyes and sighed in frustration. I didn't like being weak or needing anyone to take care of me—ironic, I know—but I couldn't deny the throbbing of my seemingly cotton-stuffed head or the bone-deep fatigue that lingered even after a few hours of sleep. In my time as a nurse, I'd watched time after time as people checked themselves out of the hospital too early and ended up right back in the ER again.

"Okay, fine. One night. But I'm getting up now just to prove to you how ridiculous this is."

It turns out, it wasn't as ridiculous as I wanted to believe. My legs were rubbery, the room spun, and I wanted nothing quite so much as to crawl back under the covers even as I forced myself to shuffle to the bathroom and back with nothing but the IV stand to lean on and Matt standing aside practically clutching his non-existent pearls.

"I hope you're pleased with yourself," he muttered when I collapsed back in bed afterward, tucking the blanket around me.

I gave him the finger. As lovingly as possible.

Russell chuckled. "Good to see you haven't lost your sass. I'll leave you to rest."

"Hey Russ," I called out before he could make it out of the room. "How's Suzi doing?"

"Good. We have an appointment with that specialist next week. Thanks for making the call. You get some rest now, okay? Doctor's orders."

I was out cold before he finished closing the door.

15

Matt would've spent the night in my room watching me sleep if I hadn't put my foot down—at least as much as one can from a hospital bed—and threatened to have an orderly escort him out if it came to it.

Imagine my surprise when I woke in the middle of the night to find someone standing over me. I blinked in the darkness, unable to make out the features of the tall, darkened figure surrounded by a glowing nimbus of magical energy. I fumbled for the light switch built into the bed. When the light over the bed came on, it illuminated the features of a squinting Adrian Volkov. The aura around him vanished so quickly, I wasn't sure I'd actually seen it.

"What the hell are you doing here?" I demanded.

"Checking on you, of course," he said in his accented English. "Are you well?"

"Visiting hours ended hours ago. How did you even get in here? You know what? I don't want to know. Get out!"

I reached for the nurse call button, but he caught my wrist in a firm grip. "You don't want to do that."

We locked eyes, and I tugged my wrist from his grasp. "What do you want?"

"Must I want something?"

"Please, just . . . I can't even right now. Tell me what you want or go. I warned you what would happen if you didn't leave me alone."

He folded his hands behind his back in a sort of parade rest. "I have done as you wished."

"If that were true, you wouldn't be standing here."

"I do have a job to do, regardless of your wishes. But I have done my best to be more circumspect about it."

"Great. So you've still been following me around, just more discreetly?"

He inclined his head. "Something like that. I grew concerned when you didn't emerge from the hospital, so I decided to check on you."

"Which brings me back to how you got in here."

"The nurses were surprisingly cooperative when your brother came looking for you."

I frowned in confusion. "Dan was here?"

"Please, ma'am, just tell me if she's okay," he said, his accent melting away as if it'd never been. It reasserted itself when he spoke again. "I only sought information, but she practically insisted I come up to see you."

I stared at him in shock for a moment, then laughed. He gave me a puzzled look like he'd been expecting more outrage. I laughed harder. "Oh, man. Wow. Let me guess. A tiny illusion spell to alter the details on your ID?"

"Yes . . ." He looked distinctly uncomfortable, his features pinched, forehead so wrinkled a dark vertical line appeared between his brows.

I clutched my stomach, laughing so hard my face hurt. When the hysterical laughter abated, I lay there smirking up at him. "Well, I have good news and bad news for you. The good news is I won't be filing a restraining order."

"And the bad news?"

"Impersonating a police officer is a serious crime." Still, a quiet giggle bubbled to the surface at the thought of the big bad Deputy Archon being taken away in cuffs.

"Oh." His features smoothed. "Your brother is still in the academy. I doubt that qualifies."

"Maybe. Get lost and you won't have to test that theory."

Adrian emitted a heavy sigh and removed his sports jacket. As I'd expected, he wore a shoulder rig beneath it, but there was no weapon holstered there. It's harder to sneak a gun into a hospital than you'd think, witch or not. Illusion spells won't fool a metal detector. He draped it over the back of the chair by my bed, then settled into it. It was the first time he'd been anything but formal in my presence, which intrigued me, but it also wasn't him getting the hell out. Which only pissed me off. I reached for the nurse call button again, but a magical glow blossomed around him, and in the blink of an eye, he cast a spell that created a hardened shield of air around the buttons built into the side rail of the bed.

"Please, Ms. Davenport. Emily. Just talk to me."

Annoyance flared. "I don't have anything to say to you."

He shifted in his seat and pulled a smartphone from his back pocket, then fiddled with it in silence for a moment before leaning over and offering it to me. I took it with a frown. There was a picture on the screen of a mangled wreck of a car. The passenger side was completely caved in. I stared at it for a few seconds before I saw the little bubble light miraculously still attached to the roof. It was Xavier's car, the one we'd been chasing Ricky Solomon in before that idiot in the big pickup had failed to yield right of way.

It was nothing short of a miracle that the three of us had walked away. Especially me and Mike. But no. Miracles weren't required when magic was at hand. My eyes snapped from the phone to Adrian, who sat leaning forward in the chair, his forearms resting on his knees.

"How did you—What did you do?"

"Thickened the air inside the passenger compartment, giving you a bit of a cushion to blunt the impact."

I looked back down at the screen, taking that in. After thirty seconds or so, the screen automatically went dark. I set it aside. "We were in the middle of a chase. How were you even there?"

"Luck, actually. I had been following you, but I broke off when the chase started. Your path was a bit meandering. The collision was only a few blocks from where you started."

That was some crazy luck, but I believed him. That just left one question. "Why?"

"Despite what you might think, I don't wish you ill. And I like to think you'd do the same for me."

A mirthless laugh escaped me, and tears welled in my eyes as complex emotions stirred inside me. "Don't bet on it. But I wish I could." I swallowed and reached for the control panel again, forgetting that he'd shielded it. "I just want to sit up, can you . . ." The spell vanished, and I adjusted the bed so I wasn't reclined quite as far. "So, I guess I owe you now. Thanks."

"You're welcome," he said quietly.

An uncomfortable silence settled between us. I scratched around the edge of the tape holding the IV in place on the back of my hand. The adhesive was starting to itch.

"May I ask you a question?" he asked, breaking the silence.

"Sure. I suppose you've earned that much."

He studied me for a moment, and I felt the weight of his green eyes like a physical presence. Assessing. Judging. But his question surprised me. "What are you afraid of?"

"Snakes," I replied, though I knew full well that wasn't what he was asking.

"Be serious."

"I'm trying." I looked up at the ceiling. The shadowy tiles with their pinprick holes held no answers. But maybe I didn't have to tell him the whole truth to get him off my back. "I'm afraid of being thrown in a dark hole somewhere, I guess." That, at least, was the whole truth.

"Why would that happen?"

"I don't have magic, but . . ." Where to start? Heck, where to stop?

"I know, Emily."

My heart skipped a beat and my eyes slid to the door. Oh shit. He knew? Could I outrun him? Then I remembered I was still tethered to the IV stand. I swallowed and forced myself to look at him. "You do?"

He sat back in his chair and propped an ankle over a knee. "I've been following you for nearly a week now, and I've never once seen you cast a spell. Not even to save your own life. But I don't believe you're simply lying about being a witch to work with the police. That would be foolish at best. Especially given your family's reputation."

Oh. Was that it? I released a breath I hadn't realized I was holding and eased my sudden death grip on the top of my thin hospital blanket. "Right. Well, I may be a witch with no magic, but I am still a witch. I can see magical auras when witches are casting. I can see and identify spells and wards I'm familiar with and read residues. I can trigger charms that are keyed to witches. I am a witch in every way that matters except one. And it's an important one, but it's not the most important one." I still wasn't sure if I believed it wasn't the most important one, but I at least believed that I deserved to call myself a witch. Or, at least, that I couldn't call myself a mundie.

Adrian nodded, a thoughtful expression on his face. Nothing I'd said had shocked him. "That's not unusual. Nulls in general are uncommon, but magical affinity has been documented in them. Did your parents know?"

"Yes. I was tutored in magic theory and transcription, just not the actual spellcasting. But my mother made it clear in no uncertain terms that without the ability to cast spells I could not be a full member of the coven. She probably would've shipped me off to boarding school and forgotten about me entirely, but as much as she didn't appreciate having me around as a constant reminder of her failure, she didn't want word of my lack of talent to get out either. The Davenports have a certain reputation to uphold." I wrinkled my nose and shook my head. "I got out of there as soon as legally possible and cut all—okay, most of my family ties. I was content to avoid witches and live in obscurity, and it worked for ten years."

"What changed?"

A thin smile crept onto my lips. "A hapless human detective begged me to help him serve the witch community in Santa Fe. There are no witches in the SFPD. Well, except me. And Danny, if he manages not to drop out of the academy."

"I see." His eyes remained steady on me, his expression unreadable. "It seems dangerous for a witch without magic to investigate magic-related crimes."

I shrugged. "No more dangerous than it is for a human cop."

"Does he know? Your partner. About your . . . condition."

"My condition? Wow, thanks. Yes, he knows. I was upfront with him about it from the very beginning."

"And he still wanted you. I can see how that would be difficult for someone with your history to say no to."

I narrowed my eyes. "What's that supposed to mean?"

"Never mind." He waved a dismissive hand. "So, you registered with the state in order to work with the police, as you said before."

"Yup. And I guess word got back to my family somehow —I'm really not sure how—and my parents decided I was too big for my britches."

"So, here we are."

"Here we are." I rubbed my eyes, fatigue still lingering even if I was fully awake by then. "I don't want to give up my job. For one, it's the only one I have left. But beyond that, it's very fulfilling. I like helping people and getting threats to witches off the streets. Even when that means putting naughty witches using their magic inappropriately behind bars." My fingers went automatically to the St. Jude medal hanging from a silver chain around my neck. Matt had retrieved it from the sack with my personal effects for me before he'd gone home for the night. The metal was warm from contact with my skin, and rubbing it soothed me.

"Have you considered changing your name?"

"Pardon?"

"To appease your family. Much of the source of the conflict here is the Davenport name, and your parents' desire—however cruel—to not have it associated with your 'lack of talent.' You wouldn't be the first witch to do that to keep their family ties on the down-low."

I appreciated his use of air quotes, even as I bristled at the suggestion. "That feels an awful lot like letting them win. I'm tired of being the family's dirty little secret. I just want to live my life in peace. Would it help my case with the Circle if I joined a local coven?"

"Yes. It was a simple matter to confirm that you did not list a coven on your registration, but if another coven were listed, that would be a concrete statement that you do not claim to be part of the Davenport coven or, therefore, the Circle."

Maybe it really was that simple. Hope blossomed in my chest. "So, I do that and you go back to Utah and tell the Archon it's dealt with? I don't have to show up for some bullshit witch test I probably wouldn't pass?"

"Pretty much." He uncrossed his legs and stood, reaching for his coat. "But there's just one small problem."

"You really know how to burst a girl's bubble. Has anyone ever told you that?"

He cracked a small smile. "Once or twice."

"Okay, I'll bite. What's the problem?"

He put on his jacket and buttoned the top button, the smile fading from his thin lips. "I don't believe you."

"Are you kidding? I just bared my soul in here. Test me if you want. I'll be able to see it as soon as you call on your magic."

"Oh, I believe you about that part. But there's still something you're not telling me."

He stepped closer to the bed and laid a hand on the railing. The urge to recoil was strong, but I fought it and met his eyes evenly, glad I wasn't hooked up to a heart monitor so he couldn't hear how mine was hammering. "Oh?"

"Mm-hm. My intuition rarely leads me astray." He removed a business card from an inner jacket pocket and leaned over to place it on the rolling table beside the bed. "My number. Call me when you're ready to talk again." With that, he turned and headed for the door. "Oh, and Emily? Make it soon. You have four days left."

I sagged against the mattress when the door closed behind him, fighting back tears. I told myself they wouldn't do me any good, just make my headache—worse? That was when I realized I didn't have a headache. My hand flew to the bandage on my head, and I winced instinctively, but there was no corresponding twinge of pain when I touched it. I was extremely tired but clear-headed, nothing like the foggy double-stuffed skull feeling I'd had in my conscious moments ever since the crash. I'd been so distracted by Adrian's visit that I hadn't noticed.

The memory of him standing over my bed with a magical aura around him flashed through my mind. That hadn't been my imagination, had it?

There was no other explanation. He'd healed me.

Shit. Now I *really* owed him.

16

The next morning, my nurse was unsurprised to find me perched on the edge of my bed in street clothes, demanding to be discharged when he dropped by for the morning check-in. He was surprised, however, to find me completely recovered from my injuries. Rather than go into the whole story about my late-night visitor, I explained simply that a witch friend with a knack for healing had paid me a visit.

I had to cool my heels for a while, of course, until a doctor came by to check me out and sign the proper form to release me. This time it was someone I only knew in passing, since we weren't in the ER anymore. I considered that a blessing. It meant I was spared some of the explanation and small talk. I was a free woman by 9 a.m. and called Mike on the way home to shower and change. I was still a little tired —magic healing takes a lot out of you—but it wasn't the bone-numbing fatigue of the day before, so I considered that a win.

Mike's skepticism was clear when I told him I'd drop by the department in a little while, but he didn't fight me too hard on it. Maybe he wanted to lay eyes on me for himself, since the last time he'd seen me I was in a hospital bed.

I rolled into the station around ten-thirty and found Mike at his desk. He had a couple of butterfly bandages on his forehead, but that was the only obvious injury I saw as I set a to-go cup of coffee in front of him. "Morning."

He looked at the cup, then up at me. "Thanks. Concussion looks good on you. If I didn't know any better—"

"I'm fine. No concussion, not so much as a hangnail. How's Xavier? I heard he broke his leg?"

His brows went up, but he didn't challenge me. "Yeah, broken tibia. He's going to be out of commission for a while, but they gave him some happy pills."

"A clean break, I hope?"

"Yeah, he didn't need surgery or anything. They fixed him up in the ER and released him once the cast was on."

"I guess that means he's off the case." I tried not to sound excited about that, but given that Mike eyeballed me a bit, I may not have been one hundred percent successful.

"Unless it drags on a few more weeks. But I don't expect it to."

I dropped into my chair off to the side of his desk and sipped my coffee. "Did you find Ricky Solomon yet?"

"Yeah. He actually ran out of gas a few miles from the site of the collision. Can you believe that? A couple of uniforms found the car abandoned on the side of the road, and him walking on the shoulder half a mile away."

"Wow. Did you interrogate him yet?"

His smile told me all I needed to know before he opened his mouth. "Yup. He rolled over in record time. I've got the location of their distribution hub."

"We need to move on that fast. Someone's going to raise a red flag when Ricky doesn't check in, right?"

"Yeah, but we did get him to call his boss and tell him about his car trouble, so that bought us enough time to do some recon." He turned his monitor a little so I could see it better and brought up a web browser to show me pictures of the building and a map of the area. It was a strip mall containing a nail salon, a coffee shop, and a carniceria—a Mexican meat market—among other things.

"That's not far from the drop location. Do we know which unit?"

"Yup. The one on the end. Google Maps says it's a payday loan place, but when I drove by there was a For Lease sign in the window. The windows around it were blackened, so I couldn't see inside."

"I don't imagine they want any passersby watching them count money and weigh drugs. So, when's the raid?"

"Tonight. We want to try and round up as many of the people involved in the operation as we can, and the roaches all come out after dark."

"Sounds good. I wouldn't mind a nap this afternoon." Just mentioning it made me yawn.

"How are you, really? Should I be trying to make you take a couple days off?" He turned his chair more fully toward me and leaned back, folding his arms across his chest.

"I'm fine." I held up three fingers in a scout's pledge, hoping he wouldn't press the issue. I really didn't want to get into the subject of Adrian Volkov or the Circle with him. "Scout's honor."

"Matt said you had a concussion."

"It wasn't as bad as they thought."

"You had a head wound at the scene. I used my shirt as a compress until the ambulance arrived."

Oh god. No one had told me that. "Hey, do you want me

to warm that up for you? It was a bit of a drive from the coffee shop."

"Emily . . ."

"A witch healed me, okay? Can we just leave it at that?"

He studied me for several long seconds. "You're not kidding, are you?"

"Of course not. Jeez." I stood and reached for his coffee, but he unfolded his arms and picked it up.

"If you knew someone who could do that, why didn't you have them heal you when you messed up your shoulder on the Reed case?"

"He's a more recent acquaintance."

His brows went up, but he nodded. "Say no more."

I wanted to put my face in my hands and protest that he wasn't that kind of acquaintance. But why bother? He could think what he wanted. He was my partner, not my mom. Still, my cheeks heated. "Great. Is there anything I can help with today, or should I just come back for the raid?"

He let his chair return to an upright position and leaned over to set the coffee down on the edge of the desk nearest me. "Yeah, heat that up for me."

"Sure thing, boss," I said tartly and snatched it up, turning away before I could get myself in any more trouble.

The walk to the break room was good for me. It gave me a chance to calm down, and if I stared at the microwave in annoyance while watching the paper cup inside rotate, well, it wasn't hurting anyone. Except myself, if those old wives' tales about microwaves had any truth to them at all.

"Emily, hey!"

I turned at the sound of Rashida's voice and offered her a smile but she didn't stop there and enfolded me in a warm, if gentle, hug. "Hey yourself."

"I'm so glad to see you." She stepped back and held me

at arm's length, looking me over. "I heard about the wreck. Crazy, huh? You feeling okay?"

"Yeah, um, head wounds always bleed a lot, but it was no big deal."

"I'm so glad to hear that. Rodriguez showed me some pictures from the scene. I don't know how the three of you walked away, but thank God you did."

Yes, thank God . . . and Adrian Volkov. Dammit, I really needed to figure out what to do about him. The microwave beeped behind me, and I jerked a thumb over my shoulder. "That's me."

Rashida's hands fell away from my arms. "Sure, sure. Actually, do you have a minute? There's something I wanted to talk to you about."

"Uh, sure." I fetched the two cups from the microwave and put the lids on them. Fortunately, the milk in mine made it easy to identify when compared to Mike's plain black coffee.

She wandered closer to lean against the counter and lowered her voice. "It's about Marissa."

"Oh?" That certainly got my attention. I turned toward her with cups in hand.

"Yeah. Before she—um, passed—she was working on something. Off the books."

"I'm all ears."

"I don't know much. She was close-lipped. But—" She glanced toward the door and leaned a little closer, lowering her voice even more. "I think it had something to do with narcotics."

"Hmm. I wonder if it had something to do with this case we've been working on. Her death was only a few weeks before the first OD popped up on my radar."

Rashida bit her lower lip. "No, I mean—"

A pair of off-duty uniforms wandered into the break room and headed for the coffee pot. I waited for them to leave so we could finish our conversation, but Rashida glanced at her watch and winced. "I've gotta go. We can continue this later, Em."

She left me standing there with thoughts swirling through my head. What had she been about to tell me? She'd said Marissa had been investigating something off the books about drugs. No, narcotics.

Wait, not narcotics. Capital N. Narcotics. The department.

Lupe's words of caution came back to me, advising me not to tug on stray threads. Was that what had happened to Marissa? Had she discovered something dicey was going on in Narcotics?

And if so, had she really killed herself? Or was she silenced?

17

I spent the rest of the day filing reports and going over the new information Mike had obtained from Ricky Solomon. It seemed like the fairy dust operation was fairly compartmentalized, which Mike assured me was normal. The distribution hub we were set to raid that night wasn't probably the only one, but hopefully, we'd walk away with a considerable amount of the drug and a few more of the criminals involved in the enterprise, any of whom might have key information that could lead us to their manufacturing operation.

But even as I turned my thoughts toward our open case, thoughts about Marissa's off-the-books investigation percolated in the back of my head. I almost brought it up with Mike several times, but there had been nothing about it in his handwritten notes. Clearly, she hadn't told him about it. But why?

Mike had been in Narcotics before transferring to the newly minted Magic Crimes department. Was he involved somehow? That seemed impossible. Mike was as straight a shooter as they came. But the thought nagged at me all afternoon until I had to get out of there before the questions came flying out of my mouth. Once that happened, I'd have to admit to invading his privacy and looking into Marissa's death behind his back, and . . . yeah. The guilt from all of that was starting to get to me. Something had to give eventually.

I headed home for some leftover Thai and a nap, then reported to the station an hour and a half before go-time for the pre-raid briefing and gearing up. I put on my vest with its bright white reflective lettering and double-checked to make sure my blindfold was in my pocket and my charms were in place and touching skin. Fortunately, things moved quickly enough from there that I wasn't left alone with Mike or my thoughts long enough to get myself in trouble.

We sat across from each other in the back of the SWAT van on the way to the target location, swaying with the motion of the vehicle as it maneuvered down the quiet streets. Why hadn't she told him? Why? He caught me staring at him and arched a brow. I forced a smile and a thumbs-up before looking away and telling myself to get my head in the game. I couldn't afford to be distracted. Everyone was depending on me to be on the lookout for magic wards, traps, and of course witches themselves among the bad guys.

By the time we spilled out of the van behind the building, focused breathing had given me some clarity, and I was ready for the task at hand. Or at least as ready as I was going to get for my first real live police raid. This time the guns were real, and there was more at stake than an inter-department rivalry. Nervous energy shot through my limbs as I formed up at the back of the line, shifting my weight between my feet and shaking out my hands.

A hand clamped down on my shoulder and I met Mike's gaze. "Deep breaths, Davenport. Remember your training."

I nodded and he squeezed my shoulder before walking up the line to take his place more toward the middle. Our plan was a two-pronged strike, with one group going in the front while ours went in the back. There was little comm chatter as the teams assembled, and the countdown began once the team leaders confirmed both were in position and ready. I shifted my weight between my feet, breathing in the crisp night air with its faint hint of woodsmoke and fidgeting with my charms for lack of anything better to do with my hands.

The order to breach sounded over the comm. Even prepared for it, the sound of the battering ram hitting the door was loud in the relative stillness of the night, followed a few seconds later by the expected booms of a flashbang grenade. Ahead of me, the line surged forward. It felt weird being the only one without a gun, but I wasn't completely unprepared. I had my wits and my charms, not to mention a whole SWAT team to look out for me, and if everything went according to plan ...

Let me stop right there, because nothing went according to plan.

The first shout of "Santa Fe Police!" was met with gunfire, so I activated my shield charm before I even stepped into the building, sticking behind the broad back of the SWAT guy in front of me as I'd been instructed. Inside, a haze of smoke drifted through the darkened room, which was lit only by the neon exit sign over the back door, muzzle flashes, and the barrel-mounted flashlights on the SWAT team weapons.

A bullet pinged off my shield, and I spun in time to see a figure dart behind a shelving unit. Before I could even think about finding somewhere to take cover, the big guy in front of me staggered backward and knocked me into the wall. The air rushed out of my lungs as he pinned me to the wall for a moment, then dropped to his knees and fell forward in a faceplant. I knelt beside him and struggled to roll him over. A bullet had taken him right under the chinstrap and lodged in his neck. I covered it with my hand instinctively, applying pressure, but I had the sinking feeling that there wasn't a damn thing I could do to keep him from bleeding out before help arrived. He looked up at me, eyes wide as he choked on his own blood.

Two more bullets pinged off my shield. I threw myself instinctively over the wounded officer, plastering myself to him. I could feel the shield shudder around me each time it deflected a round, releasing a pulse of magic. I wasn't sure how many bullets it could take before dissipating. As Tracy had warned, it wasn't intended for a shooting gallery.

Firm hands grabbed the back of my vest and yanked me to my feet. I struggled at first, landing a few ineffective blows before my panicked eyes found Mike's grim face. He didn't say a word, just shoved me out the back door and slammed it shut, leaving me dazed outside with blood on my shaking hands and my heart beating against my ribs like a jackhammer. I was so stunned that I couldn't do anything but stand there with my ears ringing as the now-muffled gunfire continued inside the building. It didn't take long to taper off after that, and the "All clear" chatter in my earpiece told me that the good guys had won. But at what cost?

I lunged for the door and yanked it open, leaving smears of blood on the handle. It was still dark inside, but the lights flickered on a few seconds later, illuminating a grim scene. Three of the eight SWAT team members that had gone in the back with us were down, and from what I could tell from the comm chatter, the front room wasn't any better off. The place was a mess, with overturned boxes and spilled packing peanuts everywhere, many of them bloody. The still-standing police were assessing the wounded from both sides, kicking guns out of the reach of still-living perps and deploying zip ties.

I'd heard Mike's voice on the comm, so I knew he was still up, but I didn't see him in the room.

"Mike!" I called, forgetting that I didn't need to yell thanks to the throat mic.

"Up front," he replied in my ear.

I picked my way across the room, stopping along the way to triage the injured I came across. The urgency to lay eyes on my partner was a constant buzz in the back of my mind, but my priorities were an ever-shifting bog. I couldn't turn off years of training, even if all I had to work with was the glorified first aid kit from the SWAT van. Adding a trauma kit to my standard raid loadout went on my mental to-do list.

When I got there, the front room looked much the same as the back, except with fewer boxes and packing peanuts and more money. Yes, money was scattered everywhere like it'd started raining from the ceiling during the fight. Mike stood in the center of the room beside a long folding table littered with scales, baggies, and a big plastic bin of a suspiciously glowing white substance. The fact that it was glowing distracted me at least briefly from my relief to see my partner standing and whole.

I approached the table slowly, like its contents might lunge at me. "Holy shit."

"Yeah," he said. "A lot more than I expected, too."

I drew closer and leaned over to peer into the container, but covered my nose and mouth with my hand, not wanting to accidentally inhale any of it. The grains of fine white powder had an iridescent sheen, and each glowed with a faint shimmer of gold. "I've never seen anything like it before."

"No?" he said. "Looks like cocaine to me."

"That's because you're not a witch. It's like it's infused with magic. Every grain."

"Hmm. I guess that means whoever's cooking it is a witch."

"They'd have to be. But there weren't any witches here. Or, at least not in the back." I straightened and looked around, but none of the survivors bore any trace of magic as far as I could tell. That didn't mean none of the fallen were witches, of course. I couldn't detect dead witches the same as I could living ones.

Mike found a discarded lid on the floor under the table and snapped it on the bin of magic fairy dust, or whatever the hell it was, blocking me from examining it further. "Why don't you see what you can do for the wounded? EMS is on the way."

I nodded and went back to work, finding the routine fairly calming, but my newfound knowledge of fairy dust lingered in my mind. I don't know what I had expected of it, but I hadn't expected it to be magical in nature. Sure, it was strange that it only affected witches, but I'd figured modern chemistry would have an answer for that somehow.

The ride back to the station was somber. We were all keenly aware of the empty seats in the back of the van.

"Jesus," someone muttered, raking his fingers through his short dark hair. "Who's going to tell Foster's wife?"

"The captain will take care of it," the woman across from him replied. "I'm going to get cleaned up and head to the hospital after debrief. Wait for news on Winters and Royce."

"Me too," another said.

"That wasn't normal, was it?" I asked.

"No," the woman said. "That was a goddamn ambush."

I glanced at Mike who sat in silence, this time beside me, staring straight ahead with the tub full of fairy dust in his lap. I had more questions, but I didn't think he had any more answers than the rest of us did. And a lot of them started and ended with the contents of that tub.

18

There was a lot of yelling when we got back to the station. The only time I'd ever been called into the captain's office before was to be praised after apprehending a witch who'd killed a personal friend of the mayor. He'd always seemed like a level-headed fellow. Fatherly, even. I had no idea a man's face could turn that red, and I had worked my actual father up into quite a few rages in my rebellious teenage years.

The captain wanted answers, and we didn't have any. We'd had no indication that they were expecting us, nor any idea how. There were only two things I could think of. The first was that maybe Ricky Solomon had tipped them off with some sort of code word during his check-in call, but when I suggested it, the captain told me I'd watched too much *Law & Order*. The joke was on him since I'd never seen an episode in my life, but I thought it unwise to point it out while that vein was visibly throbbing in his forehead.

The other thing I could think of—that there was a leak in the department somewhere—I hesitated to voice until Mike and I were alone. But after we were ejected from the captain's office—and I could not have sprung from that chair faster if it had been spring-loaded—we were immediately pulled into an after-action meeting, and about midway through that, he stepped out to take a call and never came back.

When that meeting let out, I stood and turned around, surprised to see Xavier leaning against the wall at the back of the room, crutches propped against the wall beside him and muscular arms folded across his broad chest. Most of the officers filed past him without comment, though a couple clapped him on the shoulder and said a few words in passing. As I drew nearer, he met my eyes and lifted his chin in silent greeting. I nodded back, altering my course to approach him.

"Shouldn't you be on medical leave or something?" I motioned at the cast that covered his left leg and foot below the knee.

"When I heard what happened, I couldn't just sit in that damn recliner." He squinted at me. "You look better than the last time I saw you."

"Yeah. I'm good. Mike was here"—I glanced at my phone, finding no new messages—"but he had to go. Not sure what's up with that."

"Must've been important."

"Yeah." I sent Mike a quick text message, and stared at the "delivered" status for a few seconds, but it didn't flip to "read." What the heck was going on? "Hey, are you going to be hanging around for a bit?"

He reached for his crutches and straightened to tuck them under his arms. "As long as I can get away with it, yeah. If my LT catches up to me, I'll be sent back to my recliner."

I glanced over my shoulder to where Lieutenant

Roberts, the head of the Criminal Investigations arm of the SFPD, stood conferring with his counterpart from the Patrol division and a few sergeants at the front of the briefing room. "Isn't this a dangerous place to linger if you're worried about that?"

"I'll be gone before he makes it back here."

"Fair enough. I've got to make a few calls, but I may have a favor to call in if Mike doesn't turn up."

"Sure. Text me and I'll hobble wherever you need me. In the meantime, can you hold this door open for me?"

After aiding and abetting Xavier on his clandestine trek to the Narcotics corner of the squad room, I headed for Mike's desk. He wasn't there. I hadn't expected him to be but felt a faint sting of disappointment nonetheless. Dropping into his chair, I leaned back and stared up at the ceiling, pondering my next move. Until Mike resurfaced, I had to keep my concerns about a leak in the department under wraps, and I should probably be careful with whom I shared any new information with. Not that I generally chatted about our cases with anyone but Mike, but considering anyone with access could look up our case files, the idea of an inside man in the SFPD chilled me.

Rather than dwell on that lovely thought too long, I turned my attention toward the investigation itself. The raid was technically a win, as we'd gotten a significant quantity of fairy dust off the streets and arrested a few of the people involved in its distribution. I wasn't about to try and interrogate anyone without Mike, but I could see what I could figure out about the mysterious magical drug itself. And for that, I was going to need help. Normally, I'd bring Dan in on something like this. He may've been a pain in my ass, but he'd proven to be a valuable source of information in the past. With him closeted away at the academy, that wasn't an option this time.

I briefly considered Kara Seaver, the State Police's new witch, but she'd had such a chip on her shoulder that the idea of giving her a call didn't sit right. Also, I wasn't sure quite what the protocol was for requesting State Police help with our investigation. Did that have to go through some sort of official channel? What were the ramifications?

So, if not Dan, and if not Seaver, who did that leave? Tracy? But she didn't have the same level of magic education Dan did. Or maybe that was just my Davenport privilege rearing its ugly head. After all, she'd figured out the trigger for my shield bracelet after Dan couldn't. In the end, I decided I didn't know her training and experience well enough to bring her into something like this. John? He was one of the strongest witches I'd ever met, but brute magic force wasn't what I needed. Kassidy? Her archive might contain relevant information, but there was no way I could convince her to come to the police station and no way I could get a sample of the drug out of evidence to take to her. What I really needed was someone with rigorous magic training, a wealth of magic theory knowledge, and access to an arcane library.

What I needed was a Circle witch. I smacked my palm to my forehead and groaned.

I needed Adrian Volkov.

Even with the answer staring me in the face, I hesitated. What would the price of his assistance be? I didn't have to think too hard about that. He'd want to know the rest of my story, or he'd want me to comply with one of his original demands. How far was I willing to go? I didn't know the guy well enough to trust him, but he may have saved my life—and Mike's—with his little magic trick the day before. And any witch who could cast a spell like that in a fraction of a second at the drop of a hat ... That was beyond impressive.

Unfortunately, I had no idea where the card with his phone number on it had ended up. It was probably at home on the dining table with the pile of discharge paperwork from the hospital. I might've tucked it in my purse, but that was currently locked in Mike's desk. Along with my car keys.

But did I really need to call him? He was still following me around town; he was just being more discreet about it. I made my way out of the police station and stood in the dark outside, peering around the mostly empty but well-lit parking lot. Volkov's SUV was nowhere to be found, but he couldn't be far.

I cupped my hands around my mouth and did my best Rocky impression. "ADRIANNN!" Then I waved my arms a bit for good measure.

A few seconds later, my phone rang. It was an unknown number. I usually don't bother answering those, but considering the timing, I didn't hesitate to tap the green button and put the phone to my ear.

"I know you're out there," I said, foregoing any pleasantries. "Do you want to see something really cool?" I'd learned over the last few months to avoid words like 'help' or 'favor' with Dan. Hopefully, that'd serve me well with Adrian too.

"Good evening to you too, Ms. Davenport."

"Oh, come on, man. I thought we were past the formalities."

A pause followed, then, "What can I do for you, Emily?"

"That's the spirit. But really, I've got something in here you need to see. It's nuts." I jerked a thumb over my shoulder for emphasis.

"Does it involve your witch status?"

"Not really. But if you come take a look, I'll call it a night afterward, and you can go back to your hotel for your beauty rest."

"It's after midnight. You can't possibly have that much to do that can't wait until morning."

"After that shitshow of a raid? I'm up to my eyeballs in paperwork." That wasn't entirely true. Mike was responsible for most of that. But he wasn't here, so maybe I'd end up having to do it myself after all.

He breathed a sigh. "Fine."

At the farthest edge of the parking lot, a lamp I hadn't realized was off flickered on, illuminating the black SUV parked beneath it. The driver's door opened and Adrian stepped out. He closed the door and the SUV's lights flickered on briefly as it locked. I waited, rubbing my bare arms against the chill of the night while he crossed the parking lot at an unhurried pace. He looked as fresh as I'd ever seen him, his hair slicked back and eyes alert.

"Do you ever sleep?" I couldn't help but ask.

"Occasionally. What is it you want me to see so badly?"

I reached out and flicked his jacket open, checking his shoulder holster since he wouldn't be allowed to bring a gun into the station, but I needn't have worried. It was empty once again. "Do you actually have a gun for that thing?"

He arched a brow and said nothing.

"Right. Stupid question. Come on."

I hauled open the door and got him signed in at the front desk, then led him down the hall to the squad room. I found Xavier parked right where I'd left him, sitting at his desk with his cast propped up on a chair from one of the conference rooms. He looked up from the computer screen on his desk, eyes flicking from me to Adrian and back, a clear question lurking in them.

"Adrian, Xavier. Xavier, Adrian."

Adrian leaned over the desk to offer a handshake, which Xavier accepted. "Nice to meet you, whoever you are. Forgive me if I don't get up. What's up, Emily?"

"Mike's still AWOL. Can you sign out some evidence for me?"

He hesitated a moment, glancing between me and Adrian again. "Why?"

"I want to show it to Adrian."

Frowning, Xavier scratched his stubbly jaw, then removed his foot from the chair beside his desk and pulled himself to stand. "Okay, but this had better not be about getting into his pants."

"I assure you, detective, my relationship with Ms.— Emily—is strictly professional," Adrian deadpanned.

Xavier's hand paused, hovering over his crutches as he gave Adrian a long look.

"I'm bringing him in to consult on the fairy dust case," I said.

"A consultant for the consultant?" Xavier smirked, grabbing his crutches and tucking them under his arms. "Does Esco know about this?"

"Not yet, but it'll be fine. We've brought in subject matter experts before." I ignored the searching look Adrian gave me. Maybe I should've told him a little more about what I wanted him to see and why. Oh well, hindsight and all that.

Xavier hobbled around the desk. "Okie dokie. But it can't leave the evidence room. Or my line of sight."

I bit back the first response that came to mind. I knew full well how chain of custody worked, and there was no way I'd risk our case by screwing that up. I forced a smile, reminding myself you catch more flies with honey. "You're the boss."

I took the lead once more, making sure the coast was clear for Xavier to move through the squad room and down the hall to the elevator without getting busted. I felt a bit like a sitting duck waiting for the elevator doors to open. There was no telling who might be inside, but it couldn't be helped. Evidence was on the second floor and Xavier was in no condition to navigate stairs.

We made it upstairs without incident and soon stood at the counter. Soft snores rose from the officer behind the counter, a stocky older guy who was tipped so far back in his chair I half expected it to dump him on his back at any moment. So much for justice never sleeping.

Xavier rang the bell on the counter a few times in rapid succession, startling the officer awake. He jerked upright, blinking at us as his brain came back online. "Case number?" The words tumbled from his lips by rote.

Fortunately, we'd been working on this one long enough that I knew it off the top of my head. The officer typed it into his computer and clicked a few times. "You need all of it?"

I thought about the giant tub full of the drug Mike had turned in when we got back from the raid and grimaced. "No, just the first one."

He nodded and typed some more, then had Xavier sign on a tablet before disappearing into the back. When he returned a few minutes later, he slapped the evidence bag on the counter. Inside was the plastic bag we'd gotten from Alvin, which contained a dozen or so other tiny bags of white powder. I hadn't seen it before with my own eyes, hadn't even realized I'd needed to. How could I have known or even suspected it could have magical properties?

And yet I quickly realized . . . it didn't.

I picked up the bag and looked more closely, but the contents just looked like ordinary white powder. No glow of magic, no iridescent sheen. I could've blamed the lack of color on the bland fluorescent lighting, but the absence of magic glow was definitely odd.

"Has anyone checked this out since it came in?" I asked the clerk.

He consulted the computer. "A sample was taken for lab analysis by Detective Suarez."

"Hmm. On second thought, can we see the second batch?" I asked.

The stocky officer sighed and went back to his computer, repeating the process for the other piece of evidence logged under the case.

"Something wrong?" Xavier asked, taking the bag from me and inspecting it while Adrian observed the whole thing quietly from a few feet away.

"This doesn't look like the same stuff we confiscated after the raid," I said.

"Could be cocaine. Maybe Alvin was dealing more than just fairy dust," Xavier said, placing the bag on the counter. "Or maybe he was carrying a decoy. I've seen it before."

"Maybe," I said. Either explanation could be true. But why would he have been carrying a decoy? The question was poised on the tip of my tongue, but I held it back. Those thoughts about a leak in the department resurfaced.

Had someone tipped Alvin off that we were looking for him? But if so, why would he have been at the park at all? No, he'd been freaked out when he saw Mike and Xavier. He'd tried to run, even pulled a gun on them. Those weren't the actions of a kid who knew what was coming and had fake drugs in his pocket. Unless whoever had given him the package had known? But that assumed that a drop had occurred between when we started looking for Alvin and when we actually found him. And if Alvin didn't know about it, he might've sold some of it.

Xavier nudged me with an elbow, jostling me from my thoughts. "Careful over there. I think I smell smoke."

"Hmm?" I blinked a few times before focusing on him and offering a tight-lipped smile. "You're not as funny as you think you are."

"Nah. I'm funnier." He grinned, but there was something in his eyes that made my stomach tighten.

What if the leak was standing right in front of me?

I dismissed the thought as soon as it surfaced, but it fought to re-emerge while we waited for the officer to bring out the rest of the evidence. This time, the package was too big to fit through the slot on the counter. A door opened into the reception and the night clerk brought the big tub out and set it on a table to our left.

We gathered around the table. The tub was opaque, so I couldn't see its contents. I eyed the tape sealing the tub shut. "Anyone have a knife?"

Xavier passed me his pocketknife, and I sliced carefully along the edge of the rim. Once the seal was broken, I opened the tub carefully, not wanting to send up a cloud of the stuff. As soon as I cracked the lid, a golden magical glow spilled out of it. I glanced at Adrian, who was suddenly gazing intently at the tub. He saw it too.

I took the lid off fully and set it aside, revealing the shimmering powdery contents. Adrian stepped closer and leaned over for a closer look. I put a hand on his shoulder. "Careful. Don't inhale any. We still don't entirely know what this stuff does or what a safe dose is. If there is one." He shot me a withering glance, and I removed my hand. Was womansplaining a thing?

Xavier opened the original evidence bag and took Alvin's

baggie full of baggies out, holding it up and looking from it to the tub's contents and back again. "Looks the same to me."

I glanced between the two samples, but the first one definitely didn't have the same magical glow as the second. "Let me see."

He handed me the bag and I opened it, then took one of the smaller bags out from inside and opened that too. Maybe the plastic was interfering with my perception somehow? But no, when I squeezed the edges of the plastic zipper enclosure to hold it open and peered inside, the contents were flat white powder—no magical glow, and no iridescent colors. I sealed the small bag back up again and dropped it in the larger one.

"Satisfied?" Xavier asked.

I wasn't, but my gut told me to keep that to myself. I nodded absently and turned my attention back to Adrian and the "good" sample. Adrian had produced a pair of small round spectacles with green-tinted lenses from somewhere. They were now perched low on his nose.

"May I?" Adrian motioned at the pocketknife, so I handed it to him and he scooped a little of the powder onto the blade, bringing it closer to peer at it. "Interesting."

"What do you make of it?" I asked.

"It's clearly magic-infused. The grains are tiny, so if there are any sigils engraved, they'd be at the microscopic level. Impractical at best. What did you say this did again?"

"I didn't. But it makes witches stronger, faster. Too much can be fatal." I glanced at Xavier. "Has the lab analysis come back yet for the first sample?"

"Let me check." He tossed the baggie on the table and took out his phone. After a few seconds of tapping and scrolling, he shook his head and tucked his phone away again. "Not yet."

Odd. It'd been several days since we arrested Alvin. Before I could ask any other questions, the hairs on the back of my neck stood up and a magical glow appeared around Adrian. I grabbed his arm, my first instinct to drain his magic away to keep him from tampering with the evidence. I managed to stop myself, thank god. "What are you doing?"

"Do you want me to fully assess this or not?"

"Okay, but don't alter it in any way."

He shot me an affronted look. "I will not."

I released his arm but kept careful watch as he stood there gazing intently at the sample, wreathed in a magical glow. He didn't cast a single spell, but tiny sigils etched into the arms of his glasses began to glow. They were so small that I hadn't noticed them until they lit up like red-hot metal. After a few minutes, the glow around Adrian winked out and he dumped the sample off the knife blade and back into the storage bin, tapping the blade against the rim a few times to get rid of any lingering grains.

"Well?" I asked.

He closed the pocketknife and handed it back to Xavier, then removed his glasses and began to polish them with a cloth from his pocket. "It has a crystalline structure, so I suspect a spell was cast on a larger crystal which was then ground or crushed into a powder. Though I'm unsure how the spell survived the crushing process."

"You can tell that just from looking at it?" Xavier asked.

"With the aid of a little magic, yes." He wrapped the cloth around the glasses and tucked them away again.

I wondered what those glasses did, what they were spelled to allow him to see, but there would be a time and a place for that discussion. Possibly never and nowhere.

"You said a spell was cast on it before it was ground or crushed. Are you familiar with spells that make a person—or, specifically, a witch—faster or stronger?"

"No. A levitation spell could be cast on an object while someone pretends to lift it. But directly affecting physical strength, speed, or endurance? Pure fantasy. It's more likely that the magic is reinforcing existing chemical bonds, making them stronger, enhancing the effect of the drug."

"So, maybe some kind of steroid?" Xavier said.

"Steroids aren't like Popeye with a can of spinach." I eyed Xavier's big arms and chest. He obviously worked out, and he was a Narcotics detective, so I was surprised he didn't know this. "Some steroids will help you build muscle faster, others will reduce recovery time so you can work out more, but you still have to work out and train."

"Right, right," he said, waving me off. "Hmm. I've seen some guys do some pretty extraordinary things on speed . . ."

"Amphetamine doesn't actually make people stronger, it just inhibits their pain receptors so they don't know what their limits are."

Xavier eyed me. "You sure you don't want to join Narcotics?"

"Maybe if we had a Magic Narcotics department," I said, then thought better of the implications of it and shuddered. "I hope we never need a Magic Narcotics department."

We got the evidence sealed back up and checked back in, then I smuggled Xavier back to the squad room before walking Adrian out.

"Thanks for that," I said, lingering outside the front doors in a pool of light from one of the exterior floodlights. "I owe you one."

"You're welcome. I'd be interested to learn what that

substance really is when you figure it out." He tucked his hands in his slacks pockets. "But I'd settle for your cooperation so I can go home."

My back stiffened. Hell, my everything stiffened. "I cooperated."

Adrian inclined his head, and one dark brow inched upward. "Did you?"

He waited for an answer, but I kept my lips firmly pressed together. I had cooperated. I'd told him everything he needed to know. It wasn't my fault that he wasn't satisfied with that.

After a few tense seconds, he nodded. "Alright, then. Goodnight, Ms. Davenport."

"Emily," I muttered in his wake, then turned on my heel and stalked back inside. How on earth was I going to get him off my back without giving everything away?

19

Mike was still nowhere to be found when I got back to his desk, so I sent him a text message and dropped into his chair. It was well after midnight, and I really wanted to go home for some quality pillow time, but my purse was still locked up in Mike's desk and my phone wouldn't get me into my car or my apartment. I never thought I'd regret shipping Dan off to the police academy quite so soon.

I considered calling Matt. He had a key to my place, and wild horses couldn't have kept him from coming to pick me up if called, even in the middle of the night. But it was a weeknight and he had to be up early for work. I couldn't bring myself to roll him out of bed. With my luck, Mike would reappear while Matt was on his way, rendering the whole exercise moot.

With nothing better to do but wait, my thoughts turned to the case. Or, more specifically, the case's evidence. The two samples didn't match. There was no disputing that. The question was, why? Alvin carrying a decoy made little sense. But did that mean the evidence was swapped with a decoy before it was entered into evidence or after? The evidence clerk had said that Xavier was the only one to check it out, when he'd collected the sample for the lab, and only two people would've had access to it before it was checked in: Mike and Xavier.

Was Xavier dirty?

I could only let myself think it now that he wasn't in the room. What evidence did I have that suggested it, besides the bagged evidence that wasn't what it was supposed to be with his signature on it? My own petty jealousy aside, he'd been nothing but helpful since signing on to help with the case. Mike trusted him. They were friends. Former partners, even. But that just meant I couldn't say anything to Mike until I had solid proof.

Wait, wait, wait.

Was that why Marissa Gentry hadn't told Mike about her off-the-books Narcotics investigation? Because it involved his old partner?

"Hey, Davenport."

I nearly jumped out of my skin at the sound of Xavier's voice. I'd been so preoccupied with my thoughts that I hadn't heard him approach. I put a hand over my pounding heart and hoped he'd brush off my anxious laugh as a side-effect of being startled. "Sorry, I was off in my own world. What's up?"

"Mike's going to be a while yet." He shifted on his crutches, glancing over the top of the cubicle wall briefly. "There was a break-in at his house. He asked me to take you home."

I reached for my phone on instinct, checking for missed calls and messages. There were none, which only ratcheted my suspicion higher. Why would Mike reach out to Xavier but ignore my messages? My heart's pace quickened further, but before I could figure out how to answer, my phone rang. It was Mike.

"Speak of the devil . . ." I tapped the screen and answered. "Hey, is everything okay?"

"Yeah. Well, sort of. Still trying to figure that out. There was a break-in at my house, so I've been a bit preoccupied. Sorry I didn't respond sooner." He sounded stressed, but that was understandable.

"Wow, that sucks. I'm sorry, man. Don't worry about it," I said, very conscious of Xavier hovering nearby, overhearing every word I said.

"I just remembered your stuff was locked up in my desk. I'm so sorry to leave you stranded there. I asked Xavier to give you a lift."

I met Xavier's eyes across the desk. At least that part of his story checked out. Still, I wasn't terribly enthusiastic about the notion. "It's not a big deal, really. I can wait."

"He doesn't mind," Mike said.

"I don't mind," Xavier said at the same time.

I forced a chuckle. "In case you forgot, the last time I was in a car with him, I ended up in the hospital."

Xavier smirked. "No high-speed chases this time. Cross my heart."

I can't say the idea of going anywhere with Xavier at that point sounded like a good idea, but how much trouble could a guy with a broken leg be?

"It's up to you," Mike said. "But it's late, and I'd feel better if he did it. I could be here for hours yet."

I scrambled for a good excuse that wouldn't tip Xavier off that I was on to him—if I even was—but came up short. "Okay. I'll call you when I get home."

He hadn't asked, and it was weird for me to volunteer, but Xavier didn't have to know that. All he had to know was that Mike would be expecting a call from me, and if he didn't get it, the cavalry wouldn't be far behind.

I ended the call and stood, tucking my phone in my pocket and swallowing as much lingering apprehension as I could. "Lead the way."

Any hopes I might've had about Xavier being parked in front where Adrian might see me leave were swiftly dashed as he led me toward the back exit. The employee parking lot sported fewer cars at night than during the day, and his fancy sports car was nowhere to be seen.

"Where's your car?" I asked, unease building in my stomach.

"Home. It's a stick, so . . ."

I glanced at his casted left foot. "Yeah, I guess it's hard to work a clutch right now."

He stopped near a white minivan and fished keys out of his pocket. "This is my wife's ride." He clicked the button to unlock the doors and the hazard lights flashed briefly. "Gas mileage isn't great, but it's got great safety ratings."

"Good to know. You need any help getting in?"

"Nah. Believe it or not, this isn't my first time on crutches." He disappeared from sight, heading for the driver's door, and I took the opportunity to snap a quick picture of the license plate. What I didn't count on was the flash. I froze for a split second, then scurried around to the passenger's side, sending the picture with a brief message to Matt along the way. It wouldn't be the first time he'd gotten a "if you don't hear from me in an hour, call the cops" message from me, and probably not the last. Hopefully, he was still awake.

As I climbed into the passenger's seat, a crucial piece of information surfaced in my brain. "Shit, I just realized . . . I can't get into my apartment without my keys either. I guess this is a no-go."

I reached for the door handle, but all the locks in the van suddenly engaged with a telltale surround-sound click. When I looked over at Xavier again, there was a gun in his hand, pointed at me. My stomach sank.

"Put your seatbelt on," he said, his dark eyes cold. "We're going for a ride."

My fingers twitched to reach for the buckle automatically, survival instinct telling my lizard brain to do what the man with the gun told me to do. But my logic center kicked in a moment later, though my mouth was suddenly so dry I had to peel my tongue off the roof of it. "You're not going to shoot me."

He kept the gun steady on me. "You sure about that?" In a movie, this is the part where the bad guy cocks the gun, but real bad guys do it ahead of time. I had no doubt he had a bullet ready to go in the chamber, I just didn't think he would use it. Not right then, anyway.

"Here? In the van your wife drives your kids around in? In the SFPD parking lot?"

He smirked. "Try me."

"It'll be awfully hard to make it look like a suicide that way." As soon as the words left my big dumb mouth, I knew I'd tipped my hand too soon.

He lunged for me and I cringed away, fumbling with the door lock but ending up pinned between him and the door, the barrel of the gun pressed painfully into my side. "Now you listen to me, you mouthy little bitch," he said, getting right in my face. His breath smelled like onions and betrayal. "You have no idea what kind of shitstorm you're stirring up."

I sat there for a moment, heart racing, trying to figure

out what to do. I couldn't leave the parking lot with him now. If I did, I was as good as dead. I didn't think he'd actually shoot me here, but I wouldn't like the consequences of being wrong. Then I remembered I was still wearing my raid charms. I brushed a fingertip across the coin on the inside of my wrist with a subtle movement, taking some comfort in the tingling golden sheen that covered my body, though I wasn't sure if it had enough juice left to stop a bullet at such close range. Still, it gave me enough courage to challenge him as my fingers inched toward the lock again. "I know you're a dirty cop who turned in fake evidence, and it's probably not the first time. Is that what Marissa figured out? Is that why she had to go?"

"Shut up!" he screamed, his free hand finding my throat, fingers clamping down. "You don't know what the fuck you're talking about. The people I work for won't stop at killing me if I get burned. Hell, they won't even start with killing me. They'll go after my family. My fucking kids!" Heavy breaths sawed in and out of his lungs as he struggled to compose himself. Some of the wildness left his eyes, but the stone-cold stare that replaced it was even more terrifying. "You know, I thought maybe we could talk this out. That you'd listen to reason, unlike your holier-than-thou predecessor. But now I see you're just another ornery slut with a martyr complex. At least this time Esco had the sense to keep his dick in his pants."

My heart ached for Mike at the confirmation of my suspicions, but this was neither the time nor the place. Also, my air supply was rapidly dwindling the way Xavier's thick fingers squeezed my windpipe. Dan's shield spell hadn't been designed to repel this kind of attack. It had to be able to bend and flex with my movements, so its magic must've only repelled things coming at me with considerable force. I opened my mouth to reply, but the words died on my tongue. I couldn't choke them out.

"Where's that smart reply now, eh?"

His fingers dug more tightly into my throat. My lungs burned for lack of air. Spots danced before my eyes, the sight of Xavier's flushed face blurring as tears welled. The urge to fight back, to punch or slap or claw or kick, warred with the knowledge that he had a gun jammed into my side. A twitch of his finger could set it off, and I didn't trust the dwindling shield enough to test it. After what felt like an eternity, the tips of my fingers finally brushed the door lock and I pushed it frantically. The door unlocked and I grabbed for the handle, yanking it before he could stop me.

The gun went off with a deafening bang as the door flew open. I was ejected from the van by the blowback from the bullet shattering the shield spell—and possibly a rib or two. What little air I had left in me flew out when I hit the pavement, and I cracked my head but good for the second time in as many days. Fortunately, air rushed right back into my lungs just as fast, but I spent several precious seconds lying there in a daze while Xavier scrambled to lean out and look down at me. His eyes were full of weary resignation as he pointed his gun at me again.

Ignoring the pain in my side, I rolled farther into the empty space next to the van, and the next shot pinged off the pavement instead of striking me. I scrambled to my feet and clutched my side as I ran for the back of the van, unable to think past getting out of his line of sight. Once I got there, I knew I had the edge only on account of his limited mobility. I took my phone out and quickly dialed 911. Before dispatch could answer, the van's lift gate clicked and began to rise with a motorized whir behind me. Shit.

I scuttled around to the driver's side of the van, ducking

to stay below window level, then ran for the next car down, some six or seven empty parking spaces away. No gunfire followed me as I threw myself around it to the far side to crouch beside the wheel well, pulse pounding in my aching head.

Pressing the phone to my ear once more, I heard nothing on the other end. "Hello?"

"911, what's your emergency?"

Behind me, an engine roared to life. "Someone's trying to kill me in the parking lot behind the police department!"

That got the dispatcher's attention, but before I could answer further questions, Xavier's van went flying past me toward the exit. I slumped against the wheel beside me and filled in the dispatcher on the need-to-know details. Maybe twenty seconds after the van peeled out into the street, the station's back door flew open and numerous officers in uniform spilled out into the parking lot.

It was over and I'd survived. Now I just had to figure out how to break the news to Mike that his old friend was on the take, had sabotaged our investigation, and had killed the woman he loved when she got too close to the truth.

20

I n the end, I was very, very lucky. I ended up with a heck of a tender bruise from the shield-breaking, point-blank gunshot and a few scrapes from rolling around on the ground, but that was the worst of it. Even the konk on the head didn't concuss me, and the EMTs were able to clear me at the scene so I didn't end up in the ER again. I had to give a statement about what had transpired between me and Xavier in the parking lot, and a warrant was issued for his arrest, but he wasn't home when they went looking for him. I was sure to mention what he'd said about his family being in danger, so they parked a unit outside his house both to keep an eye on them and keep watch in case Xavier returned.

I texted Matt early on to let him know all was well after my mysterious license plate text, but I waited as long as I could to call Mike. Call me a coward, I suppose. I was kind of hoping to leave a message and avoid going into it until morning, but naturally this time he answered. I didn't want to drop the bomb over the phone, so I just told him there'd been a major development in the case and that he was needed at the station ASAP. Twenty minutes later, I delivered the bad news in a conference room over two awful cups of stale coffee, one of which ended up splattered all over the wall. Honestly, it was probably better off there than in anyone's stomach.

Mike leaned over the table, pressing his palms to its cool surface, his eyes closed and his face awash in fury and pain. I wanted to help him, to comfort him, but I didn't know how. So I did the best thing I could think of—nudged the remaining cup of coffee toward him in case he wanted another go and found somewhere else to look while he composed himself.

"I'm sorry," I said after a long pause. "For invading your privacy and digging around about Marissa behind your back."

He didn't answer for a long moment, but he did turn and retrieve the chair from where it'd rolled when he'd stood abruptly. Once he was settled again, he rubbed a hand down his face. "It's partly my fault. If I'd been more open about it, you wouldn't have felt like you needed to hide it."

"That's kind of you to say, but . . ."

He met my eyes, and though the sorrow in his gaze about broke my heart, his words swiftly mended it. "I forgive you, Emily. Let's leave it at that, okay?" Maybe Xavier's much deeper betrayal made mine easier to handle.

I swallowed the lump in my throat and nodded. "Okay. Do you want to, um, talk about Xavier?"

"No," he said quickly. "Not right now. It's so hard to believe he could . . ." His eyes grew distant, and though I waited for him to finish the thought, he didn't.

A subject change seemed prudent. "Is everything okay at your house?"

"Relatively. The place was trashed, but I don't think

anything was stolen. At least nothing was set on fire," he said like this wasn't the first time something like this had happened.

I whistled low. "Yikes. Any idea who did it?"

"Not yet, but I've got a few ideas. Nothing more to be done until CSI finishes up. I'm probably better off out of their way anyway."

"Do you want to stay at my place tonight? My couch is apparently comfortable. It took months to pry Dan off it."

He studied his hands for a moment. "Yeah, actually that sounds like a good idea. I was going to suggest you staying with me or parking a uniform outside your place, since— since he is still out there. But my place is a wreck, so . . . yeah."

After finally retrieving my purse from Mike's desk, we left the station and headed for my place. He followed me rather than leave his car at the station, and when we got there, he climbed out and stood watching the street for a moment with a frown.

"What's up?" I called from the sidewalk.

"Someone followed us here, but when we pulled into the parking lot, they kept going. I should call it in. I got most of the plate."

Adrian. I grimaced. "It's probably nothing. It's been a long night—I don't blame you for being a little on edge."

He shut his door and approached me, frowning. "Someone tried to kill you tonight. Now someone's following you, and I'm a little on edge?"

"It's not, uh, related. I'm sure. Come on, let's go up."

He got that relentless investigator look in his eyes, but he didn't follow up on it. I thought maybe I was off the hook. I should've known better. Once we were safely in my apartment, our coats shed and hung up, he turned to me and cocked his head. "What's going on?"

"I'm not sure what you mean." I was completely sure what he meant, and he knew it. What's more, he knew I knew he knew.

His narrowed eyes confirmed it. "We're partners, Emily. You know what that means?"

"Yes, of course. I—"

"It means we need to be able to trust each other. Completely and without reservation."

"I do trust you." No sooner were the words out of my mouth did I realize that me trusting him wasn't the issue. He needed to trust me too, and I couldn't build trust by keeping things from him. Not now, when the memory of his former partners' secrets was so fresh in his mind. I looked away from him and sighed, sinking onto one end of the sofa. A wave of fatigue washed over me, as if now that I was home and my extremely long day was near an end, my mind and body were eager for the blissful reprieve of sleep. But I couldn't acquiesce. Not yet. "Do you know what the Circle is?"

He lowered himself onto the other end of the couch, angled slightly toward me, and draped an arm along the back. "Yes."

"Great."

That saved me at least some explanation, though I was more surprised than I should've been that he knew of the Circle. After all, he was a Magic Crimes detective. He probably knew—or should have known—more about the magical world than the average human. I explained my situation to him while he listened quietly, frowning but not interrupting as he rubbed my cat's head and ears.

Barrington had appeared in his lap within seconds, begging for his attention while ignoring me completely—as usual.

Eventually, the story got back to tonight's tail. "So if whoever was following us was driving a black SUV, it was probably the Circle's rep. I know he was still at the station as of a couple hours ago because I brought him in to consult on the fairy dust case."

His frown deepened. "Without talking to me about it?"

"If you want to be in the loop, you should consider answering your phone."

"Fair enough. Was he at least helpful?"

"Yeah, actually. He was able to tell that it has a crystalline structure, and he thinks the crystal was infused with magic before it was crushed to a powder. But it wasn't done like a normal charm, because crushing would destroy the spell."

"The lab analysis told us half of that."

"Lab analysis? But Xavier told me—oh." He'd been lying. He was good at that, apparently. "Right. Okay. So what did the lab analysis tell us?"

"Let's focus on one thing at a time. What are you going to do about the Circle?"

I rubbed a hand down my face and sighed. "I'm not sure. I told Adrian most of the story, but I didn't tell him about being a Conduit, and somehow he knows I'm holding something back. He's like a human lie detector. Or, in this case, an omission detector."

"To be fair, you're not a very good liar."

"Thanks for reminding me." My tone was a little snappish, and I immediately regretted it. "Sorry. I'm tired. Maybe we can finish this conversation in the morning."

"Marissa was a Sandoval."

I nearly got whiplash from the sudden change of conversational direction. "What?"

"Of the Sandoval Coven. You're familiar with it, I assume."

I was. The Sandoval Coven was as old as—if not older than—the Davenport Coven, and was also a Circle coven. "Yeah, but I thought . . ."

"Gentry was her mother's maiden name. She took it after she left the coven to avoid any issues with the Circle."

"You think I should change my name?" He wasn't the first one to suggest it, and I began to wonder if dismissing it out of hand was childish.

He shrugged. "Just saying it's an option. But either way, I'm not going to let some Circle witch cart you off to Utah against your will. This is still America, and witches have rights the same as everyone else."

"But for how long?"

That gave him pause. He even stopped petting Barrington, who after a split second of inattention butted his head against Mike's hand to get it going again. "What do you mean?"

"Witches are under attack in this country, Mike. Our rights are challenged every day. I've been attacked, verbally and physically, since registering with the state. I was fired from the hospital over it. Who's going to raise a fuss if one pesky little nobody witch disappears?"

"I will, Emily." He was so sure, so steady, that I almost believed it would make a difference.

"Thanks. But I'm not sure it's enough. No matter what I do, I'm screwed."

The cat vacated Mike's lap as he scooted closer to me and reached for my hand. I let him claim it, and he threaded our fingers together. It was a little weird, holding his hand, but strangely comforting as well.

"We're a team, Em. Whether you're a Davenport or not."

"I don't have to change my name to get out of this mess. All I really need to do is join a coven and convince Adrian he's got the full story—without actually telling him the full story. But I don't know how to do that. And if the Circle finds out I'm a Conduit—" My throat closed suddenly and a sob threatened to break free. Terror gripped me for a moment, the fear of the unknown rising like the darkness at the edges of a guttering fire. All the stories I'd been told all my life with the Circle as the boogeyman came racing back. Maybe it was unrealistic to think they could hold that kind of power over witches' lives in the modern era, but people— normal people—disappeared without a trace every day.

I wasn't fully aware of Mike's arm curling around me until my face was pressed against his neck and I clung to him like a piece of driftwood in raging floodwaters. Hot tears spilled down my cheeks, and for once I just let them flow. I'm not sure how long we sat there like that, my tears dampening the collar of his shirt while his warm hand rubbed my back, but eventually, the flood ran its course, and I was just another piece of debris cast upon the muddy shore, waterlogged but whole. Safe.

I pulled away and wiped at my cheeks. "Sorry. It's been a long day."

"I know you think the Circle is somehow above the law, but I promise you it's not. The only power they have over you is what you give them."

I sniffled, wanting a tissue but too tired to get up and get one. "I threatened to file a restraining order when he first showed up. Maybe I should make good on that. But he hasn't been a total dick since then. He's the one who healed me after the wreck, and he doesn't seem eager to truss me up with magic and throw me in the back of his SUV. He seems like he'd rather be able to report back that the situation has been dealt with, but I get the sense he'd be forced to take action if I fail to meet the deadline."

"How much time do you have left?"

"Three days." It was so absurd I couldn't help a snort of laughter. "Three days to find a coven and convince him that there's nothing special about me at all, but I deserve to call myself a witch."

"What did you say the guy's name was?" He took out his phone.

"Volkov. Adrian Volkov. Why?"

He tapped at the screen a bit. "Have you put out any feelers for a coven yet?"

"When would I have had time to do that?"

"See what you can do about that tomorrow. I'm going to see what I can dig up on this Volkov guy. The best defense is a good offense, after all."

I lingered there for another minute or two, watching him tap away at his phone, then reached out and plucked it from his hand.

"Tomorrow," I said. "Tonight, we both need some sleep." I hauled myself from the couch with a groan and dropped his phone face down on the coffee table. "Let me just grab you some bedding and a pillow."

"Thanks for letting me crash here."

"I'm glad to have you. Truth be told, the nest has been a little empty without Dan." I gave him a stern look. "But if you tell him that, I'll deny it to my dying day."

21

"Emily, wake up."

I groaned and tried to roll away from the hand shaking my shoulder, but the pillow was yanked from beneath my head, giving me enough of a jolt to drag my eyes open and blink blearily up at my meaniehead partner. His jaw was shadowed with at least one day's beard growth and his clothes were rumpled from being slept in, but his eyes were alert.

"What time is it?" I croaked.

"Ten past eight. We need to get a move on."

Even by my half-asleep math, that meant I'd been asleep less than six hours. "Huh?"

"They picked up Suarez."

Four simple words, but they were more than enough to jumpstart my brain. "I need a shower. And coffee."

"Go ahead and tackle the first, and I'll get the second going." He turned on his heel and marched out of my bedroom.

"Make yourself at home," I muttered in his wake,

allowing myself a few moments of blinking up at the ceiling before I rolled over and hauled myself out of bed, stiff and aching in several places from my tumble out of the minivan and graceless rolling across the pavement.

I took stock in the bathroom while the water heated. I had a small knot on my head and a scraped palm, neither of which was too bad. The big purple bruise spreading from a point just under my ribs on my left side looked worse than it felt—as long as I didn't touch it or attempt a side bend. I was lucky the blast hadn't cracked a rib. Hell, I was lucky to have escaped at all. If Xavier hadn't been hampered by a broken leg . . .

I shook the thought off and threw myself in the shower, letting the hot water ease the stiffness from my limbs and soothe my aches. By the time I emerged from the bathroom, the smell of fresh-brewed coffee awaited to draw me into the kitchen like a siren's song. Mike stood at the stove, yesterday's shirtsleeves rolled up, stirring eggs in a pan while Barrington crunched kibble in the corner.

Mike glanced at me as I wandered in. "That was fast."

"Have I ever struck you as the kind of girl who takes two hours to put on her face?"

He didn't answer, and I chose not to dwell on it. Instead, I made a beeline for the cupboard housing my mismatched mugs.

"Might want to grab a travel mug," Mike said, glancing over his shoulder.

"Am I eating in the car too?"

"No one likes a smartass, Em."

"You keep saying that, but admit it. You like me." I batted my lashes at him. "Thanks for making breakfast. And feeding my cat. I'm a pretty shitty hostess, making you sleep on the couch and cook."

"I've slept on worse. You were right—it is pretty comfy."

"Maybe I should swap it out for something less inviting before Dan gets back."

He chuckled. "Maybe."

Once I poured and doctored my coffee, I leaned against the counter and watched Mike continue to stir a jumbled mix of egg whites and yolks. I was no chef, but even I knew how to scramble an egg properly. "Why didn't you beat the eggs before putting them in the pan?"

"Would you rather do this?" he said, giving me a bit of side-eye.

"Yum. Bachelor eggs are the best."

He snorted, transferring the culinary crime scene to a couple of plates already adorned with buttered toast before offering me one. I took it, fetched us both forks, and we leaned against opposite sides of the galley kitchen to eat as if taking a few steps to the table would be a waste of precious time.

"You said last night that the fairy dust lab analysis was in. Can I see it?"

"Sure, but I can sum it up. Talcum powder."

"Seriously?" I frowned, then snapped my fingers. "That must be the first sample, the one we got from Alvin. What about the second one?"

"I haven't had a chance to request the lab analysis yet. I thought it was the same as the first, so it wasn't a high priority."

I sighed, watching Barrington rub against Mike's ankles. "And I didn't notice the discrepancy until last night. I wish I'd been paying more attention when Alvin was searched. We may never know if he was carrying a decoy or if Xavier swapped it out."

"Don't beat yourself up. You were a little shaken up after

the shooting, and you had no reason to suspect the drug itself would be magical."

"Be that as it may, it still set us back three freaking days. We're going to want to get that second batch checked out ASAP. In fact, I don't suppose you'd be willing to check a sample out for me? I don't need much, maybe a tablespoon."

"Why?" He eyed me. "You're not thinking of trying it out, are you?"

"What? Hell no." Though, now that he mentioned it, I wondered if it would have any effect on me. "I was just thinking that Adrian's input was helpful, but the person I really want to get it in front of . . . They're a bit of a recluse. There's no way I can get them to come to the police station."

"I can check it out, but I can't let it out of my sight. It's evidence."

I grimaced, knowing there was no way I could take Mike with me to visit Kassidy. "My contact is also a bit shy. I guess sneaking a little out is a no-go?"

"I'm not even going to dignify that with a response."

I speared the last bit of egg from my plate and popped it in my mouth, following it with the last of my toast. "Too bad we don't know what, if anything, Xavier did with that first batch."

"It's still evidence."

"Yeah, yeah, I know. But no one would know if we checked it in with a tiny bit missing."

"We'd know. That's . . . unethical at best, and could get both of us fired if anyone found out."

"Don't you want to know what this shit really is?"

"Honestly? I'd settle for getting it off the streets and whoever's responsible for cooking it behind bars."

"There's more to this than the average street drug. There

has to be. Think about it, Mike. What are criminal drug rings after? Money. Why would anyone sink time and resources into a drug that only works on witches? That's a niche market, especially when meth, pot, cocaine—all the normal shit—affects witches and humans equally."

"How does knowing what it is get us closer to knowing why it was created?"

"It's a piece of the puzzle. The more pieces we have, the clearer the picture will be."

He grunted, seeming unconvinced as he crossed the kitchen to rinse his plate. I pitched in with cleanup, and then we headed out with travel mugs in hand, arriving at the station less than an hour after I rolled out of bed. Before we got down to business, Mike had an admin assign me a locker where I could stash my stuff in the future so I'd never end up stranded and waiting for him again.

With that taken care of, we went looking for Xavier. Mike may have ix-nayed my idea about what we could do with the missing evidence, but we still had plenty of questions for him. We tracked him down in interrogation, where Internal Affairs was already having a go at him. I inclined my head toward the observation room door, but Mike shook his head and leaned against the wall opposite the interrogation room door a few feet away.

"Why not?" I leaned against the wall beside him and folded my arms across my chest.

"IA plays by a different rulebook. No one's allowed in observation without approval."

Fifteen minutes later, the door opened and a man and a woman came out of the room. I caught a glimpse of Xavier through the open doorway before it closed, slumped in a chair with his hands cuffed in his lap and his crutches leaning against the table beside him. He must've been cooperative enough if they'd let him hobble here from holding on his crutches, because he wouldn't have been able to do that while cuffed.

I hadn't had the occasion to meet many people from IA since signing on with the SFPD. They tended to keep themselves apart from the rest of the force for obvious reasons. Mike knew them both, however, and introduced the man as Detective Baldwin and the woman as Detective Hannover. Both recognized my name upon introduction and gave me assessing looks.

"I read your statement about the shooting, Ms. Davenport. Do you have a few minutes to chat?"

"Um, sure. Is it okay if Mike sits in?"

The two detectives hesitated, glancing at each other.

"It's okay," Mike said. "Actually, I'd like to talk to Suarez. Alone."

The detectives exchanged another glance, and Hannover fidgeted with the file folder in her hands. "I'm not sure that's wise."

"You can watch from observation, but I need the room to myself."

"The conversation will be recorded," Baldwin said.

Undeterred, Mike pushed off the wall and headed for the interrogation room door. "Understood."

I would've liked to have been a fly on the wall for that one myself, but it wasn't in the cards. In the end, Mike disappeared into the interrogation room and Baldwin into observation, leaving me and Hannover in the hallway.

"I see you have a cup of coffee, but I could use one," she said. "Walk with me? I'd like to ask you a few questions about what happened last night."

After exchanging enough small talk to set my teeth on edge and fetching her coffee, we found a conference room and I ended up telling the whole story all over again. I held nothing back, explaining all of my suspicions about him leaking information about the case, tampering with evidence, and his involvement in Marissa Gentry's death. I even mentioned Detective Ortiz's cryptic warning, at which point I learned that Xavier hadn't been flying as far under the radar as he'd thought. IA had been quietly looking into suspicious activities in Narcotics based on a tip from Ortiz a few months back. It comforted me to learn that Lupe hadn't been in on the scheme too, and I supposed I understood a bit better why she'd urged me not to pull at strings. I could've blown IA's investigation.

Then Hannover asked the question that'd been rattling around in my head since last night. "If you suspected he was dirty, that he'd killed at least once to protect his secret, why did you get in the car with him?"

I fidgeted with my travel mug, thumbing the button that held the spill-safe seal closed. "I wasn't sure I was right. I didn't want to be right, you know? For Mike's sake, if not my own."

"Sometimes you have to trust your instincts, especially when your safety is concerned."

"I'll try to remember that. Is he talking?"

"Suarez? Nope. Whoever he's working for has him scared shitless."

I tried to imagine the big detective scared of anything and came up empty. But I suppose if there's anything a person ought to be scared about, it's a threat to people they love. "I would be too. Do you know if there's still a unit keeping an eye on his family?"

"As far as I know." She scribbled something on her notepad. "I'll follow up and check."

"Thanks. Are we done here?"

She nodded and passed me a card. "If you think of anything else, give me a call or shoot me an email."

I took the card and nodded, then checked my phone as I stood. My interview had taken less than twenty minutes. Mike's took even less. He was waiting for me outside the conference room when I stepped out. I searched his face for some indication of how the conversation had gone, but it was an emotionless mask.

"Detective," Hannover said, nodding to him in passing.

He nodded back, watching her as she headed off down the hall.

"How did it go?" I asked. Mike didn't answer right away, his eyes still on Hannover as she strode away. I poked him. "Quit checking out her ass."

His eyes snapped to me, but there was more confusion than guilt in his expression as he shook his head. "I have to take a leak. Can you hold onto this for me?" He pushed an evidence bag into my hand, and I blinked as I caught the magical glow emanating from it. Or, rather, from the crystalline white powder within the small baggies within the larger baggie within the unsealed evidence bag in my hand.

"Is this . . .?"

"Yeah."

"Where did you—"

"I'll be right back." His eyes met mine, and there was meaning in the glance I didn't understand until he turned and walked away, leaving me standing there with the missing evidence in hand. He was providing me an opportunity to take a sample and giving himself plausible deniability.

I ducked back into the conference room and shut the door, then leaned against it. The evidence bag crinkled noisily as I opened the plastic bag inside it and took out one of the smaller bags, which couldn't have contained more than a teaspoon of the drug. What would Kassidy make of it? Would she be able to shed any more light on it than Adrian had?

Even though this had been my idea to start with, now that the moment had arrived, I was struck with a sudden crisis of conscience. If I did this, if I kept a sample, that made me just as guilty as Xavier was when it came to tampering with evidence.

Okay, maybe not just as guilty. He'd turned in fake evidence. All I was doing was taking a tiny sample. Compared to what we already had in the tub, it was nothing. But my conscience still tugged at me, and I put the tiny baggie back in the larger one only to take it back out a few seconds later. I'd find a way to put it back. That was a compromise worth making to get to the bottom of this case and save witch lives. Mike seemed to think so, even if he didn't want any active part in it.

I sealed the evidence bag shut and stepped back out into the hallway, the tiny baggie practically burning a hole in my pocket. I passed the bag back to Mike when he got back. He accepted it without comment, his mask still in place.

"I've got an errand to run," I said.

"I'll get this logged in, and I'll call if there are any new developments." He turned to go, but I caught his sleeve. He turned back and I met his eyes.

"You can count on me."

That mask cracked, giving me a fleeting glimpse of the wounded man beneath it, and it was all I could do not to wrap him up in a hug. He nodded slightly and turned again to go, but I caught his murmured, "I hope so," as he strode off.

I hoped Xavier Suarez rotted in prison for the rest of his life—and vowed to do anything in my power to make sure it happened.

22

The last time I'd paid Kassidy a visit, she'd told me I didn't have to go through John to get to her. However, I didn't exactly have anywhere else besides John's place to park. I probably should've called ahead, but I hoped he would be at work and I could be there and gone without him even noticing.

That hope was on thin ice when I arrived at his place to find his truck in the driveway, and it plunged through the ice and into the icy depths below when I opened my door to the sound of his dog's deep booming bark. I had yet to lay eyes on the critter, but it sounded like a big hound dog of some sort. I imagined long droopy ears and jowls you could lose a hand in trying to rub its chin.

I had a split second to decide if I wanted to tear off down the road before he could be roused to investigate, or try and be friendly—not that being friendly with the handsome witch was difficult. My problem was with how friendly I wanted to be with him, despite my logic center screaming about what a bad idea it was. That same logic center that now told me there was a fine line between not being friendly and being outright rude, and taking off without a word was on the other side of that line.

Breathing a resigned sigh, I shut my door and approached the gate in the tall weathered blue privacy fence. The dog on the other side had gone quiet, but when I got within a few feet of the gate, it rattled in its housing as if something heavy leaned on it from the other side, and a few more of those booming barks sounded. Yeah, there was no way I was opening that gate if the giant on the other side could reach it.

I took out my phone instead, but before I could fire off a text message, a whistle silenced the bark and the gate swayed back in place.

"John?" I called. I'm not sure why it was a question. Who else would it be?

"Come on in, I've got him."

I unlatched the gate and pulled it open to peek inside. A wide yard circled the adobe house on the other side, featuring a few scraggly trees and little else in the way of landscaping. A well-worn path ran from the gate to the front porch, where John stood holding the collar of a dog nearly half as tall as he was. I didn't know much about dogs, but I wasn't wrong about the jowls. The dog had a black muzzle and floppy black ears, but the rest of his short hair was light brown, like beach sand. He pulled against the grip on his collar, his eyes fixed on me, but his tail wagged hard enough to shake his massive rump.

"Sorry to drop by unannounced," I said, lingering at the gate. "Do you mind if I park here while I go see Kassidy?"

John glanced down at the dog and said something I couldn't make out from afar. The dog sat, but his tail still thumped the porch. John snapped his fingers and pointed, and the dog looked up at him for a moment as if to say "Aw, do I have to?" before lying down and putting his head on his forepaws with a put-upon sigh so heavy I heard it from across the yard.

Leaving the dog where he was, John trotted down the front steps and across the yard. Dressed in sweats and a T-shirt that hugged his muscular chest in all the right ways, he didn't look like he was going to work anytime soon, but his long dark hair was still damp from a recent shower.

When he got close enough, he pushed the gate open farther and motioned me inside. "Sure, you're welcome to park there anytime. Don't worry about Gus. He talks a good game, but he's pretty friendly."

"And well trained," I said, slipping inside so he could close the gate.

John glanced over his shoulder at the big dog still lying obediently where he'd left him. "He's dying to sniff you. Would you like to come say hello?"

"Sure. I can't stay long, though. I'm on semi-official police business."

He nodded and turned without further ado to lead the way back across the yard to the porch. It stunned me for a moment, probably because I was more accustomed to fending off probing questions from well-meaning but ulti-mately nosey friends. But I picked up my feet and followed him, and by the time we reached the porch the dog was visibly twitching with the urge to stand. A low whine escaped him, and John chuckled.

"Alright, alright." He made an up motion with his hand, and the dog sprang to his feet, rushing over to sniff me everywhere he could reach. Which was more than half my body, for the record.

I stood there stiffly while Gus gave me a once-over. Then a twice-over. "How long does this usually go on?"

"Relax, he won't bite. Not much experience with dogs?"

"Not particularly."

"Oh right, you have a cat. Yeah, this could take a while." His dark eyes twinkled with amusement. "You might be able to distract him with ear rubs. Offer him your hand."

I did as instructed, and Gus snuffled his cold wet nose against my palm before giving it a lick with his large slobbery tongue. I wrinkled my nose and fought the urge to wipe my hand on my jeans, not wanting to offend man or dog. Instead, I turned my hand over and went for the big dog's ears. A few rubs, and he was sitting at my feet, leaning his massive frame against my legs. I had to brace myself a bit to hold him up. "What on earth do you feed him?"

John laughed. "Kibble, same as any dog. He's part mastiff, and those run big."

I found rubbing the dog's soft ears and head much more pleasant than letting him sniff me. There were wet spots on my jeans from his nose, and that was just . . . weird. "He seems like a good companion."

"The best. Can I offer you something to drink? I've still got some coffee in the pot."

"No, I really can't stay. I need to get Kassidy's take on something. Though, now that I think about it, are you busy?"

"Not particularly. I'm off duty today. I was going to spend some time in the studio, but it can wait. Would you like me to accompany you?"

"Yes, I would." The answer surprised me since I'd had every intention of avoiding him entirely when I came out to the Pueblo. But there was more than one type of magic out there, and it would be foolish of me to not tap every resource I could. I just had to put my personal issues aside, though that was difficult with the way he smiled at me just then.

"Let me change real quick and grab my keys. Gus will keep you company."

After watching John head inside, Gus turned his head and gave my hand a lick, then bounded into the yard.

"I thought we were friends," I called after him, chuckling.

Gus disappeared around the corner of the house but returned a few seconds later with a tree branch between his massive jaws. Okay, it was a stick. But it was a really thick stick, and most of the bark had been chewed off it, so it was clear it was a favorite toy. He dropped the stick at my feet and then bounced back a bit, ears perked. I bent and picked up the stick, hefting it to test its weight.

"I'm not sure if I can throw it far, buddy." Nonetheless, I drew it back and gave my best effort. The stick sailed maybe twenty feet, but he was off like a shot before it hit the ground and managed to snatch it from the air.

"I see you two are fast friends," John said, emerging from the house a half dozen throws later. He'd traded his sweats for jeans and thrown on a flannel shirt over his T-shirt.

Gus made a beeline for John, stick in mouth and tail wagging furiously. Chuckling, I wiped my slobbery hand on my pants. "Don't worry, looks like you're still his favorite."

"I'm not worried. Dogs have an enormous capacity to love. Give it." The last was directed at Gus as he held out his hand. The big dog placed the stick in John's hand, then danced back again, clearly ready for another throw. "Sorry, buddy. We'll play later, I promise." He opened the screen door and pointed into the house. "Inside."

Gus hesitated only a moment, then hopped back up onto the porch and trotted past, disappearing into the house. John closed the door behind him and let the screen door swing shut, then turned back to me. "Ready?"

"You're not going to lock up?"

"Just the gate. It deters the casual criminals, and anyone who goes inside will have to get past Gus."

I glanced toward the house. "He doesn't seem like much of a deterrent. Well, ferocious bark aside."

"He's a sweetheart, but make no mistake. He's fiercely protective."

We set off for Kassidy's cabin, a comfortable silence settling between us for the first few minutes. The morning air was crisp and clear, and I allowed myself to relax to the rhythm of my steps on the shoulder of the road. After we turned off onto the faint path leading into the trees, I let the wilderness embrace me and my thoughts scatter until they were little more than background noise. Each step across the rocky terrain seemed to take me farther away from my troubles, and at that moment I understood how some people liked to go camping or hiking or otherwise disappear into the wilds to get away for a while. I'd never been one of those people, always of the mind that getting away from things and people was easy, but getting away from one's thoughts wasn't. Maybe I was wrong, or so it was easy to imagine as a sort of peace wrapped around me.

"Have you found a solution to your problem with the Circle?" John asked eventually, breaking the silence. So much for my peaceful Zen state.

"Nope. Not one I'm happy with, anyway. I mean, there are several potential solutions, just not many desirable outcomes."

"I'm sorry. I wish I could help. If I had a coven, you'd be welcome to join it if that would help."

"At this point, I'm not sure if it would. I tried telling

Adrian—their rep—my story, but he thinks I'm holding something back."

"Are you?"

I snorted. "Of course I am. There's no way I want the Circle or my parents to find out I'm a Conduit."

"Hmm. At the risk of sounding critical, you're not exactly laying low."

He wasn't wrong. I couldn't kid myself about that. "Yeah, I know. But I honestly didn't think my parents were paying that much attention. And now that I know they are . . . ugh." That was something I didn't want to think too hard about. Just how closely were they watching me, and had they been doing so ever since I left Boston a decade ago? Had the independence I'd enjoyed all these years been an illusion? I blew out a sigh. "Anyway, I like working with the police department. And as long as I want to keep working with them, I have to be registered. And I doubt getting out of the registry is as simple as getting in."

"Probably not. I suppose you'll have to convince this representative that you're telling the whole truth, then. Or give him a reason to look the other way."

I stopped short, practically leaving skid marks in the dirt. "What?"

"Well, I suppose seduction is out," he mused, eyes on the canopy above, then glanced at me. "But intimidation, blackmail, bribery?"

"Intimidation didn't work, and I don't have any—wait, why is seduction out?" I glanced down at myself. Sure, I wasn't exactly dressed to impress, but I liked to think I could seduce a man if I set my mind to it. Especially this one. Maybe I'd been reading the signs wrong, and John wasn't attracted to me after all? Why did that fill me with disappointment rather than relief?

John cleared his throat. "Um, that's not to say that—I only meant that you don't seem like the sort of woman to seduce a man for personal gain."

Ego mostly soothed, I swept my eyes over him and smiled. "Ahh. You're right. When I seduce a man, it's definitely for mutual gain." Why was I flirting? I needed to stop that before he got the wrong idea. Or the right one. Clearing my throat, I resumed walking. "My partner said he'd see what he could dig up on the guy. Maybe there's some leverage to be found there. Thanks, you've given me something to think about." Especially since, now that I thought about it, bribery was not off the table. I may not have been eager to use my parents' money to pay my bills, but the idea of using it to pay off the Archon's henchman—excuse me, deputy—had a certain poetry to it.

How much would it take? Five grand? Ten? Twenty? But if I paid him off now, what would stop him from coming back for more down the road? Bribery was a slippery slope. And that was assuming he even could be bribed.

I was so preoccupied with my thoughts that before I knew it we were climbing the front steps of Kassidy's cabin. John rapped sharply on the door, then turned the handle and cracked it open. "Kass, are you decent?"

"Come on in!" Kassidy called from somewhere within.

I followed John inside, shrugging off my coat and glancing around as he shut the door. The interior looked the same as ever, homey and rustic but for the high-tech computer rig in the living room. The only thing missing was Kassidy herself. John took my coat and hung it by the door, then headed into the kitchen to fill the kettle and put it on the stove.

"I hope this isn't a bad time," I said, raising my voice to be heard wherever she was. This main section of the cabin had a door at each end leading into the wings, but they'd always been closed when I visited before, so I had no idea what lay beyond them. You wouldn't think much from the size of the cabin from the outside, but what I could see of the spacious interior was already larger than it should've been, so all bets were off.

The door to the left opened, and Kassidy stepped into the doorway in a blue silk kimono patterned with cherry blossoms. Her long red hair was pinned up atop her head, and her fair skin had a bit of a flush to it, particularly around the edges of the burn scars covering the left side of her face. "Emily! What a pleasant surprise. I'm fresh out of the bath, but make yourself at home. There are some biscuits in a tin on the counter. I'll be right out."

Feeling a little guilty for interrupting her bath, I joined John in the kitchen and found the "biscuit" tin, which contained a batch of biscochitos, tasty anise and cinnamon cookies that are a local favorite and—I kid you not—the New Mexico state cookie. John produced a small serving platter from the cupboard, and I arranged a dozen or so cookies on it to go with the Earl Grey tea.

By the time Kassidy emerged again, this time dressed in a well-worn pair of jeans and a faded gray Rolling Stones T-shirt, John and I had tea, cups, and cookies ready to go on the table. Her blue eyes sparkled with delight as she approached me, leaning in to press an air kiss beside my cheek. It was a little strange, but I went with it. She'd never been anything but friendly to me, but she'd never greeted me like a society matron before.

"It's so good to see you," she said. "What brings you by?"

I held back my wince, but barely. "I'm sorry, I really should come by sometime when I don't need your help with something."

She waved me off and pulled out a chair. "As long as you bring me interesting tidbits, I don't mind."

While John poured the tea, I backtracked to my coat, fetching the little baggie of fairy dust and bringing it to the table. Kassidy's eyes latched onto it as I approached and lingered as I held it out. John stared at it too, long enough to overfill a teacup. He looked away with a quiet curse and grabbed a napkin to mop up the spillage.

"What's this?" Kassidy asked, plucking the bag from my hand. She pinched it between two fingers and held it up for a closer look.

"They call it fairy dust. It's been circulating in Santa Fe for a few months. What do you make of it?" I pulled out a chair and sat, claiming the overfilled teacup for my own. John was too distracted peering at the baggie Kassidy now held to notice or object.

I probably should've objected when Kassidy opened the baggie. Instead, I watched her as I blew across my tea and worked on sipping it down to a less precarious level. She peered into the baggie, then moved her teacup and poured half the contents of the baggie into the little well in the center of the saucer. She set the baggie aside, and John picked it up and pinched the top open to peer inside.

I snagged a cookie from the plate and bit into it, watching with no small amount of amusement. Who needed cable with a show like this at hand? A magical glow wreathed John, the threads of a spell coming together before my eyes. The iridescent powder rose out of the bag in a spiral and danced through the air, reflecting the light in a kaleidoscopic rainbow.

My mouth hung open. The amount of finesse required to accomplish something like that was staggering, and he'd done it so casually—it wasn't like he was showing off; he was studying the floating crystalline powder too closely for that.

When my eyes drifted back to Kassidy, I found she'd produced a pair of half-moon spectacles from somewhere. They sat low on her nose, and she peered down her nose through them to the portion of the drug nestled in her saucer. My eyes gravitated to the arms of her spectacles automatically, looking for glowing sigils, but none appeared.

"Fascinating. What is this?" Kassidy said, finally breaking the silence.

"I was hoping you could tell me," I said, watching John spin another spell to return the drug to the bag. It whirled into a spinning vortex that seemed to be sucked into the bag like a genie returning to its bottle. "I mean, I know the basics. It's a drug, a crystalline powder that boosts a witch's strength, speed, and endurance. What I don't know is how it's been infused with magic, or by whom."

"Some crystals have inherent mystical properties, but this is something different," Kassidy said before moistening a fingertip and poking it into the small pile of powder, collecting some of the crystal dust on her fingertip and peering at it more closely.

"It can't be true crystal," John said, sliding the small baggie back toward me. "Crystal wouldn't dissolve when ingested."

"Some crystals are soluble," Kassidy mused, pinching the powder between her thumb and fingertip and rubbing them together. "Salt, for example."

"Huh. So, someone might've gotten their hands on a big salt rock, cast a spell on it, and ground it down to a powder?"

Kassidy dabbed the tip of her finger to her tongue and made a face. "Theoretically, yes. But that's definitely not salt."

"Are you nuts?" I leaned over and snatched her saucer from her, moving the rest of the fairy dust out of her reach. "One, this is evidence. Two, I repeat, are you nuts?"

She looked at me over the tops of her half-moon glasses and arched a brow. "Do you want to know what this is, or not?"

"Honestly? I wasn't expecting you to identify it—though it'd be great if you could. I was hoping you might know something about how an object might be spelled in such a way that it retains that magic when ground down. Either I slept through that unit in Magic Theory, or we're dealing with something highly unusual."

"Oh, it is unusual. Truly," Kassidy said, eyeing me. "But it seems a number of long-forgotten magics are beginning to surface."

I ignored the look and slid the saucer over to John. "Would you mind putting that back in the bag before she starts rolling dollar bills?"

He chuckled but swept the powder off the saucer with a quick spell, suspending it in the air as he had the rest while he opened the baggie again. I watched more carefully this time, but the spell still came together so fast that I barely glimpsed its unfamiliar runes.

I shifted my attention back to Kassidy, who had lapsed into silence, staring off into space while her fingers toyed with her teacup. I picked up the saucer, blew on it just in case there was any lingering residue, then passed it back to her. "You're not wrong."

"Hmm?" Her blue eyes focused on me after a few seconds' delay.

"What's old is new again. Vintage magic."

"Ah, yes."

I nudged the saucer to get her attention, and she lifted

her cup to slide it underneath. Seconds ticked by with nothing further from her, and a knot of anxiety formed in my stomach. If she clammed up now, I was up shit creek.

"I'm sorry. Sometimes my mouth gets ahead of my brain. I just don't know what effect that stuff might have on you. I mean, it only affects witches as far as we know, and you're not a witch. Right?"

"No, I'm not." She shook her head and tapped a fingertip against the side of her teacup.

I itched to ask her what she was, but since I already felt like I was on thin ice, I held my tongue. If she was merely human, I'd eat my shirt. She gave off absolutely no magical signature, but she lived in a cabin that'd give the Tardis a run for its money, she could perceive magic, and I got the feeling she was way older than she looked. Just a hunch, based on her mannerisms and a few things she'd said in my presence. But asking her age felt just as taboo as asking what she was, even though the suspense was killing me. So to speak. A few more seconds passed in uncomfortable silence.

"You were saying something about a forgotten art?" I prompted.

"Indeed. Magic acts as an amplifier, dialing up the natural properties of whatever it imbues. Imbue a rock, it will become harder than iron. A feather? Lighter than air."

"Wouldn't that mean a magic-imbued crystal would be rather difficult to grind?"

"Yes, if the hardness was what was amplified. But, as I said, some crystals have mystical properties, and with the right technique, the magic could amplify that rather than the crystal's physical attributes."

I thought about what Adrian had said about magically reinforcing the drug's chemical bonds. It sounded like a similar theory. "So, you think we're looking for a magic crystal with a solubility similar to salt which, when amplified, makes witches faster, stronger, better?"

"No, not quite. I think perhaps an experiment is in order."

That certainly piqued my interest. "Oh?"

"You've used your power both ways, yes? Both to draw power from a witch and feed power to a witch?"

"Not sure where you're going with this, but yes."

"Splendid. John, if you would?"

Once more, John was wreathed in a golden glow. This time, rather than casting a spell, he offered me his hand. I took his long, elegant fingers in my own, then looked to Kassidy. "Now what?"

"Tap into his magic, and let it flow into you. See if you can stop it from grounding."

"Is that possible?"

"Try it."

I glanced at John, and he gave me a slight nod of encouragement or permission, it was hard to say. I could feel the magic thrumming in his hand beneath my fingers. Now that I knew how to tap into it, it was fairly easy to do. It rushed into my hand and up my arm, through my torso, and down my legs in a matter of seconds. Before I could even think about stopping it, it hit the floor and began to spread beneath my feet.

"Think about what it feels like to reverse the flow," Kassidy said. "Rather than flipping the switch entirely, see if you can stop it halfway."

"Easy for you to say," I muttered but did my best, seesawing back and forth as I tried to find that elusive middle setting—if one even existed.

Sweat beaded my forehead and my throat went dry. I

really wanted a sip of tea, but I kept trying until I found the sweet spot, a balance point thinner than the edge of a blade, where John's magic filled me but wasn't flowing one direction or the other.

It was freaking amazing. I tingled all over, practically vibrating in my seat as the wild energy hummed beneath my skin. My skin felt almost too tight, and the magical aura that wreathed John when he called upon magic wreathed me as well, no hint of a seam where our hands joined.

"Holy shit." The breathy words escaped me as I looked to Kassidy once more. She sat there with one of those Mona Lisa smiles on her face—a little unnerving given that one-half of her face was covered in scar tissue.

"Good, good. Now, just as you can control the flow of magic between you and John, you can control where you ground it. Put your hand on the table and try grounding it there instead of the floor."

I placed my hand on the table and it felt different, like I could feel every tiny ridge and valley in the woodgrain beneath my palm. I willed the magic out through my hand and she was right; it wasn't much different from pushing magic into a witch. A spiderweb of energy spread out across the table, and the strange sensation of my skin being too tight eased. Reversing it was easy, but stopping it again took a bit of effort to get that delicate balance just right.

"Good, good." Kassidy leaned over and slid my teacup closer. "Now touch the surface and do it again."

"You want me to ground magic into tea?"

"Yes. Just a little, though."

"Just a little." I shook my head but dipped a fingertip into the tea and renewed my focus. It took a few tries, but I was able to let a small burst of magic out. Rather than spreading across the surface of the tea, it swirled around inside the cup. I pulled my finger out and watched as it lingered there the same way it did when I grounded it, pulsing with glittering energy for fifteen seconds or so before fading from sight.

"Well done," Kassidy said. "Now do it again, but this time take a sip of the tea before the magic dissipates."

I probably should've given that request a second thought, but I was riding such a high from accomplishing the tasks she'd set before me that I complied without question. Once more, I let a stream of magic flow from the tip of my finger into the cup, and before it dissipated, I brought the cup to my lips and took a sip. The liquid that spilled over my tongue is difficult to describe. It was tea, but any hint of bitterness was gone, and the notes of bergamot and lavender were amped up considerably. The way it danced across my tongue and filled me with euphoria was definitely different. I felt it all the way down my throat to where it pooled in my stomach, warm and relaxing. But the sensation quickly faded, just as the magic swirling within the cup dissipated.

"That's—What did—Did I—" My eyes darted between John and Kassidy, taking in the open curiosity in his face and the approving smile on hers. "I just imbued the tea, didn't I?"

"Temporarily," Kassidy said. "Was it good?"

"Good god, yes." I licked my lips, but the flavor was but a memory. I wanted more, but I resisted the temptation. Who knew what the long-term effects of ingesting magic might be? It certainly wasn't working out well for the witches doing fairy dust. "Does that work for everyone?"

"Nay. Only a witch can taste the magic."

"But it fades so quickly. How do you make it stick?" My eyes slid to the plastic bag on the table, whose contents still thrummed with magic.

"You're familiar with vessel charms, yes?" Kassidy asked.

"You mean, like, spelled jars for long-term food storage?"

She shook her head. "No, like the amulet you encountered last year, the one the witch was using to store the magic he drained from others."

"Oh! Yeah. Um, why did you ask the question if you already knew the answer?"

There it was again, that faint smile, and she didn't even begin to address the question. "The technique is similar. A cousin, if you will. In order to imbue something with magic, you have to funnel magic into it and create a persistent bond. It will wear off eventually, just as a vessel charm cannot hold magic indefinitely. But it can be made to last quite a while."

"So, it's a spell. Long story short. There's an 'imbue magic' spell."

"A combination of spells, actually. One to funnel the magic, and one to seal it in place."

"But Emily doesn't need the first one, does she?" John said.

Kassidy shook her head. "No, she is essentially a walking magic funnel."

"Thanks," I muttered, reaching for another cookie. "So, unless there's a type of soluble crystal whose 'mystical properties' increase strength, speed, and endurance . . ." Neither of them spoke up, so I continued. "We're dealing with a pharmacological drug with a crystalline structure which, at some point during its production, is being imbued with magic." Why did I suddenly feel like I was back at square one?

"A true blending of magic and science," Kassidy said, flush with wonder. "Remarkable."

Her words struck me like a snowball between the eyes. A

blending of magic and science. Why hadn't I thought of that before? Whoever had created this drug was a witch with a science background. I gulped the rest of my tea and pushed back from the table, snagging the baggie of drugs and a cookie for the road. "I hate to eat and run, but I've got to get back to work."

John stood as well, though at a more measured pace, with cup and saucer in hand. "I'll walk you back." He leaned over to reach for my cup and saucer, but Kassidy waved him off.

"Leave it, dearie. I'll take care of it."

"You're sure?" he asked. I was already halfway to the coat rack.

"Yes. I can see she's had a bit of an epiphany. Best to strike while the iron is hot."

I turned in the process of slipping on my coat, cookie held between my teeth. I removed it long enough to say, "Thanks!" and finished donning my coat in record time.

"But Emily? Do come again soon. There's something I need to discuss with you."

"Oh?" Why was the notion of her wanting to discuss something with me like a wet blanket over my excitement? "Well, I mean, I don't have to run right off if it's important. I really appreciate your help, as always. Oh! That reminds me, I learned something new about my conduit powers. I can absorb spells directed at me and ground them."

"Truly? That is remarkable. I'd love to see a demonstration of that. Next time, of course. I wouldn't want to get in the way of your investigation. But when this case is closed, come see me. And bring John. This matter involves both of you." With that said, she stood and began clearing the table.

John and I exchanged a glance, enough of one that I easily determined he was as clueless as I was about whatever this mysterious matter was. Kassidy sure knew how to leave a girl hanging. But as curious as I was, there was still a part of me that suspected whatever it was, I wasn't going to like it. That more than anything drove me out the door, and a fog of unease lingered with me all the way back to my car.

Sharing everything I learned about my conduit powers was an ongoing condition of Kassidy's help. But the first time she'd helped me, she'd done so in exchange for a favor to be named later. I couldn't help but wonder if that favor was about to come due.

23

Once I got back to the station, it took me and Mike less than an hour to compile a list of every registered practitioner in the county who had a science-y occupation, from doctors to teachers and everything in between.

The list of suspects was slim. Santa Fe is more of an arts town than a science one. We have a community college, a liberal arts college, an acupuncture college, and a few art schools. Our opera house is pretty damn cool, and there is enormous support for all kinds of visual and performing arts, but you won't find any big science initiatives here. Add to that the fact that the witch community only made up a fraction of the population—with the registered witch community an even smaller piece of the pie—and you can do the math. Still, even a short list was more than we'd had for weeks, so I was ridiculously pleased with the breakthrough.

We started with the chemistry teacher—thanks, *Breaking Bad*—but quickly ruled him out. As it turns out, he'd been dead for over a year. That left us with two acupuncturists, which sparked a heated debate between us over whether they'd have the pharmacological knowledge to concoct something like fairy dust. After all, acupuncture is an alternative to pharmacological treatment, and Traditional Chinese Medicine makes use of herbal remedies, not the sorts of compounds that showed up on the tox screens of the deceased witches. In the end, Mike agreed to set them aside for the time being and focus on the other two names on the list: a doctor and a pharmacist.

Yes, that's right, there was a freaking pharmacist on the list, and he wanted to investigate the acupuncturists first. Every now and then, I wondered how he passed his detective exam.

Anyhow, both witches worked at St. Vincent's. Dr. Micah Schwartz worked in pediatrics, so I'd only interacted with him in passing at holiday parties and whatnot. Victor Montenegro, the pharmacist, I was a little more familiar with from years of fetching patient medications. He was a quiet, reserved man who ran his pharmacy like a well-oiled machine. In any other circumstance, he wouldn't have been my first suspect. But he had the knowledge, means, and opportunity to pull off this particular crime. Motive, we were still unsure of. But it definitely merited dropping by the hospital to ask him a few questions.

Fortunately, we went in through the front door this time rather than the ER, so I was spared a lot of curious glances and awkward interactions with my former co-workers. I led the way to the pharmacy, where a short line stretched from the service window. Through the plexiglass, I could see Heather, Montenegro's assistant, rushing to and fro. Her bun was askew with wisps of hair falling out, and I caught a glimpse of a tag on her back—her sweater was on inside out.

Curious what had the usually effervescent woman so

frazzled, I leaned in and asked the unfamiliar nurse in front of us, "What's going on?"

He glanced back at me and shrugged, then resumed burying his nose in his phone while he waited. The device was supposed to be in his locker while he was on duty, but it wasn't any of my business, so I turned back to Mike. "Maybe we should . . ." I trailed off as a familiar figure approached.

It was Steel Wool Wendy, my former supervisor. "Emily, I thought that was you. How are you doing?"

The question had more of a perfunctory air to it than one of genuine concern. "Fine, you?" I responded in kind.

"Fine," she said.

A few beats of awkward silence followed, then I jerked a thumb at Mike. "You remember my partner, I assume."

"Yes." Finally, she cracked a faint smile. "Nice to see you, Detective Escobar."

"Likewise," Mike said, then nudged me to move as the line advanced.

"Here on police business?" Wendy asked.

"Yes," Mike and I said in unison, then chuckled.

"Any idea what's going on in there?" I nodded toward the pharmacy window.

"Victor called in sick, and his backup is running late."

I glanced at my watch. It was past one in the afternoon. "Late? I'll say. Poor Heather."

"Actually, Detective, do you mind if I borrow your partner for a few minutes?"

My eyes locked on Wendy. I blinked slowly, unsure I'd heard that right. What reason could she possibly have to want to talk to me?

"Sure. Looks like this'll be a while," Mike said, indicating the slow-moving line. Either he was playing the reason for our visit super cool, or he wanted to ask Heather some questions in lieu of her boss. Maybe both.

"Great. Emily?" Wendy pivoted and headed back down the hallway. I hastened my steps to catch up.

"What's up?"

"I have something for you in my office. It won't take long."

We walked the rest of the way in silence. I had no idea what to say to her, and the situation was awkward as fuck. I hadn't spoken to Wendy since the day she fired me and figured she hadn't given me a second thought since then. What could she possibly have for me? Exit paperwork? No, that had been delivered along with the contents of my locker the day after I was fired.

Wendy's small office had a big window overlooking the parking lot across from the ER, a large desk with a swivel chair, a visitor's chair, and one of those backless leather sofas with one end slightly raised that you usually see in psychiatrists' offices. I suspected Wendy herself used it more than anyone else since no one came to her office for counseling.

"Open or closed?" I asked, lingering by the door in hopes of a quick exit.

"Closed." She plugged her tablet into the charging cable coiled on her desk, then pulled open the center drawer and took out a file folder.

I shut the door and wandered closer to the desk, doing my best to ignore the knot of unease in my stomach. "Well, you've certainly got my attention."

She let the folder fall to the desktop. It landed with a quiet slap, and she motioned to the chair across from her in silent invitation before sitting in her own. Leaning forward, she laced her fingers together and set them on top of the file. "Are you working with the police full time now?"

I sat. Reluctantly. "For the most part." The fact that I was doing full-time work for part-time pay wasn't something I was keen to advertise.

"Are you still interested in nursing?"

"Yes . . ." What was she fishing for? How was that even a question?

"Good." She picked up the folder again and held it out to me. "This is a copy of your HR file."

I reached for the folder automatically, blinking slowly. "My HR file?"

"Yes. Don't ask me how I got it. If anyone asks, you didn't get it from me, and I'll deny giving it to you with my hand to God. But I think your lawyer will find it very useful."

"What makes you think I have a lawyer?"

She quirked a smile, leaning back in her chair with her elbows planted on the arms and her hands folded across her stomach. "How long did you work in the ER?"

"Seven years."

"Who is the most senior nurse in the ER?"

Was this a trick question? "You are."

She smirked. "Besides me."

"I—I don't know. I guess Gracie, now that I'm gone."

"Exactly." She banged the desk with her fist, and I jumped. "*You* were the most senior nurse in the ER, because more than fifty percent bail in the first year. The rest transfer out within three years to greener pastures. This job is physically and emotionally exhausting, and the burnout rate is high. But every now and then, someone defies the odds. I'm not saying you're a lifer, but I am saying that you loved your job, you were damn good at it, and those records prove it."

Tears sprang to my eyes, and it took me two tries to swallow the lump in my throat. Steel Wool Wendy was not a woman who lavished praise, so hearing her say that meant a lot to me. "Thank you. But if you felt that way, why didn't you fight for me?"

"I did. At least, I tried. I was sure there had to be some misunderstanding, and I lobbied with HR for a hearing so you could at least tell your side of the story. The next thing I knew, legal was breathing down my neck. It was obvious there was pressure from high up in the chain of command to make your dismissal happen."

"How high up?"

"I appealed all the way up to the Director of Nursing, and he said his hands were tied. That means the Executive Director, or maybe even the board."

"The board?" I really needed to stop parroting things she said, but I couldn't help myself. I'd never met a single member of the board of directors. Hell, I couldn't have so much as named one of them if a gun was held to my head.

"Yeah, you know. The board of directors. The stuffy guys in suits who—"

"I know what the board of directors is." The words came out more snappish than intended, and I winced. "Sorry. This is just all a little . . . intense. But why are you just now telling me this?"

"Honestly? I thought they were kicking a hornet nest. I didn't expect you to take it lying down."

"I'm not. It took me a while to find an attorney, but I've been working on it."

"You don't need an attorney. Do you know what hospital administrators fear more than lawyers?"

"Universal healthcare?"

She snorted. "I was thinking bad publicity, but you're not wrong."

"You think I should go to the media?" The idea was almost as unappealing as being at the center of a potentially landmark witch civil rights case. Sometimes it seemed like the universe was conspiring against my desire to live a quiet, ordinary life.

"Maybe. Hell, even social media could be something if you use the right hashtags."

I thought about my dormant social media accounts, which had been gathering digital dust for months, ever since Matt had made me watch a documentary on the insidious nature of social media and its harmful impacts on mental and emotional health.

When I didn't answer after a few seconds, Wendy shifted in her chair. "Something to think about."

"Yeah, definitely. Thanks." I looked down at the folder in my hands and opened it, flipping through the pages inside. "Hey, is my new-hire paperwork in here?"

"It should be."

I found it at the back, which I suppose should've been expected for a largely chronological file. Sifting through the pages, I thought about the meeting with the AWL attorney and the question he'd asked about whether I'd signed anything specifically stating I was a witch besides my employment application and its ubiquitous checkbox. There was nothing. I flipped to the very last page of my employment application, and my eyes caught on the fine print above my signature.

I affirm that all the information contained herein is accurate to the best of my knowledge . . .

I stood abruptly. "I've got to go."

"Of course." Wendy joined me in standing but lingered

behind her desk. "Remember, that didn't come from me. But I hope it helps."

"Oh, it does. More than you know. Thanks, Wendy."

I lit out of there like the floor was on fire and headed for the admin wing. I was done licking my wounds and weighing my options. I had the truth on my side. I hadn't lied on my application.

When I'd signed it seven years ago, I hadn't hesitated to check the non-witch box. I'd believed it to be true. I was a null, not a witch by anyone's definition—least of all my own.

24

I at least had the presence of mind to text Mike before enacting my half-assed plan. He was still in line waiting to talk to Heather, so I told him I had something to take care of and I'd catch up with him afterward. I had approximately two minutes—the time it took to walk from Wendy's office to HR—to figure out what I wanted to do when I got there.

I changed course along the way. HR couldn't help me. If the order had come down from above, I needed to go to the top. I paused outside the Executive Director's office to check my reflection in the window beside the door, mostly to make sure I didn't look as crazy as I felt. Reassured, I hauled open the door and stalked inside, doing my best not to glower as I approached Director Mayhew's assistant's desk.

The forty-something mother of twelve—or so I assumed from the massive collection of family photos on the credenza behind her—looked up from her computer and turned a polite smile upon me. "Can I help you?"

"Is Director Mayhew in?"

"Do you have an appointment?" Her smile faded a touch, wariness entering her expression.

"No. Tell him Emily Davenport is here to see him."

Her brow furrowed. "I'm sorry, but if you don't have a—where do you think you're going?"

I marched past her desk toward the big wooden door, my resolve firming with each footstep. Mayhew's assistant rocketed to her feet and hurried after me, but my legs were longer and I had a head start. I reached the door first and opened it before she could stop me.

The office beyond was about what I'd expected—lots of dark wood and a giant window with a gorgeous view of the mountains. The remains of the director's lunch were spread out on the desk in front of him, a mostly eaten sandwich sitting on a curling slab of paper and a cup bearing a logo I recognized from a nearby deli. The man behind the desk, on the other hand, was not what I expected at all. I don't know why I expected some sort of balding overweight bureaucrat, but nothing could've been further from the truth. He had a full head of dark hair peppered with silver and a likewise silver-threaded close-trimmed beard, to start with. His suit coat hung on the back of his chair, and his tie was tucked into a matching vest worn over his crisp white dress shirt.

But the most startling thing of all? He was absolutely, positively, unmistakably a witch, and he had not come up on our registry search for local witches in science and health-care fields.

The director looked up from his lunch and arched a brow as I stalked in, his assistant trailing in my wake.

"I'm so sorry, sir. I told her she needed an appointment, but she wouldn't listen."

The director dabbed at his mouth with a paper napkin. "It's okay, Linda. I believe I have an hour or so until my next meeting, yes?"

"Yes, sir."

"Would you like something to drink, Ms. . . .?"

"Davenport." I watched his eyes for any trace of recognition and was rewarded by a slight twitch of his brows. "And no, thank you."

"Very well, Ms. Davenport. Linda, please hold my calls until we're finished."

"Yes, sir." Linda shot eye daggers my way as she brushed past me to exit the office, pulling the door shut behind her.

I ignored her. My thoughts were spinning a mile a minute, my half-assed plan failing me as I struggled to process the implications of the kernel of magic pulsing inside the man behind the desk like a goddamn beacon. The director was a witch, and I was 99.9% sure that was not public knowledge.

When silence stretched between us, the director grabbed his soft drink and leaned back in his chair, sipping it while watching me with curious blue eyes. "You have my attention, Ms. Davenport. Emily Davenport, yes?"

"You know very well who I am." It was a guess, but he didn't deny it. I drifted closer to his desk, my file tucked under my arm. "I want my job back."

"I want a lot of things. A Tesla, for example. Did you know state law prohibits them from opening a dealership or service center in New Mexico because they sell direct to consumers online? I mean, I could still buy one but it seems like such a hassle."

I blinked slowly and counted to ten, drawing a deep breath and letting it out. "Wow, that really sucks for you." The sarcasm couldn't have been thicker if I'd poured it from a bucket.

He chuckled, though there seemed to be little mirth in it. His expression quickly sobered, and he rocked forward to set his cup back on his desk. "If you have an issue with your termination, I suggest you take it up with HR. But the facts, as I see them, are plain enough."

"Oh, I dunno. They seem to be getting more complicated by the minute." I dropped the file folder on the edge of the desk and took out my phone.

"What's that?"

"My employee file." I unlocked my phone and brought up the web browser. "You know, performance reviews, onboarding paperwork, that sort of thing." He leaned over and reached for it, but I slapped a hand down on the file and moved it from the desk to the armchair to my left. "Get your own copy. I'm sure Linda would be happy to oblige." I went back to my phone.

He studied me from the other side of the desk, forehead wrinkling and fingers toying with the edge of his sandwich's wrapper. "What are you doing?"

"Checking to see if you're in the registry." I glanced up from my phone in time to see him stiffen, though he still maintained a heck of a poker face.

"Why on earth would I be in the registry?"

I met his eyes. "Oh, come on. We both know why."

"Don't be ridiculous."

"Ridiculous?" I laughed. "Wow, that's rich coming from you." I plugged his name into the web portal and started the search, then wandered around the desk to half-sit on one corner. "You know, the funny thing is, I came in here ready to threaten to light up social media with my story, maybe even suggest an AWL-backed lawsuit. They reached out to me, you know. The offer is on the table. As much as the Davenport name has worked against me in my life, it at least opened that door. But this hospital and the community it serves are important to me, you know? The thought of my actions resulting in an expensive lawsuit, probably leading to budget cuts and impacting patient care, it eats me up inside." I glanced down at my phone, which had brought up zero results from the registry search. I tossed it down on the desk in front of him so he could see for himself. "But I don't give a single fuck about you."

He glanced at the phone, frowned, and rolled his chair farther away from me. "You can accuse me all you want. That doesn't make it true."

"No, it being true makes it true. You're a witch." I paused a beat to let it sink in, smirking. "It takes one to know one."

He narrowed his eyes at me, lips pressed together so hard that they twitched.

"It's not a good look for you, having me fired for failing to disclose my practitioner status when you, yourself, are hiding yours."

"You're just fishing. You can't prove anything."

"Can't I?" I shifted back to my feet and advanced on him, considering my options.

He stood so quickly his chair went rolling back a few feet and held up a hand, palm out. "You have ten seconds to leave before I have security escort you out."

I glanced over my shoulder at the phone on his desk, then back at him. Unless he had the number for security handy on his mobile, it was a hollow threat at best. I made a grab for his hand, but he yanked it away and kept backing up until the backs of his legs hit his chair and he fell into it. The chair fetched up against the wall as I continued to advance. I still wasn't sure what I'd do when I got there. I hesitated to demonstrate my own power, not wanting to give him any more ammunition to use against me. But my intimidation wasn't making him lash out with magic as I'd hoped.

Had I encountered yet another witch who didn't know what he was? Two in one month would be utterly bizarre.

No sooner had the thought occurred to me than a golden glow wreathed him and his eyes shifted to my left. I ducked just in time for the paperweight from his desk to sail past where my head had been. It hit the window and bounced off without so much as scratching it—that was some pretty impressive security glass—then dropped to the carpeted floor with a dull thud.

"That wasn't very nice. Whatever would you have told Linda?"

He sprang to his feet and got in my face, still wreathed in power. He had a couple of inches on me, and miles more magic power, but I still had plenty of tricks up my sleeve. I met his gaze evenly and held my ground.

"It'll be your word against mine, you bitchy little witch. And in case you hadn't noticed, you're a disgruntled former employee with a history of lying."

"Was it you who got me canned, or did it come down from the board?"

"Why does it matter? The result is the same."

"Because I want to know."

He ground his teeth, the glow of magic around him intensifying. "It was me. Is that what you want to hear? I found out about your registration, and I initiated your dismissal to protect the hospital."

"How?"

His brows drew together. "By removing you from the equation before our insurance provider found out—"

"No, no. How did you find out?"

"A private investigator."

"You were having me investigated?"

"What? No." He shook his head and stepped back, and

the aura around him began to fade. "He didn't tell me who his employer was—and I guess I didn't ask."

"I'm going to need his name." It's a wonder I managed to form a coherent sentence at that point. His revelation had my thoughts spinning like a whirlpool. I'd always assumed it was one of the registry watchdogs who delighted in harassing witches who'd outed me to the hospital. The incident had come at the height of my post-registration harassment, after all.

The director stepped around me and approached his desk, bending to open the center drawer. He rummaged around a bit before producing a business card. Turning back to me, he held it out, but when I reached for it, he flicked his fingers up, moving it out of reach. "I give you this, and we're even."

I laughed and shook my head. "As if. We're not even remotely even, director."

"I figured as much." He gave me the card anyway, then folded his arms. "You may as well call me Kurt."

The name on the card, Henry St. John, was unfamiliar to me. The phone listed had a local area code, but since said code was one of two assigned to the entire state of New Mexico, the definition of local was rather broad. "Thanks." I tucked the card in my pocket and turned my attention back to him. "Look, I'm not on any sort of crusade here. I'm sure you have your reasons for being unregistered, just like I did. I'm not going to report you."

He arched a brow. "But?"

"But can I please have my job back? You didn't give me a chance to explain myself or correct the situation. I registered barely two months ago. It was new. I honestly didn't realize it was such a big deal, or I would have told HR and gotten things straightened out."

Calculating blue eyes studied me for a long moment. Long enough that I had to fight the urge not to fidget and began wondering if I'd made the wrong decision by declaring I wouldn't report him. Then he breathed a heavy sigh. "Alright, Nurse Davenport. Provided legal signs off on it and all the paperwork is filed correctly this time, yes. You can have your job back."

My heart stuttered and I nearly whooped with joy, but something about the delivery made me hesitate. "But?"

"But I will remind you that New Mexico is an at-will employment state, and if you ever try to blackmail me or break the hospital's Magic Use in Patient Care policy, you'll be back on the unemployment line faster than you can say unregistered witch."

I put out a hand. "Consider us even, direc—Kurt."

He shook my hand, then retrieved his chair and wheeled it back to his desk. "Here." He thrust a notepad and pen at me. "Write down your current phone number and email address. HR will be in touch."

I complied, scribbling my name as well. It seemed a good policy, though I doubted he had meetings quite like this every day. I passed the notepad back with a hundred-watt smile. "Thanks."

He tossed the notepad down on the desk and resumed his seat. "Don't make me regret it."

I headed for the door with a bounce in my step—and a brief detour to collect my file folder—and let myself out. In the outer office, I breezed past the director's assistant with a smile. "Have a great day, Linda!"

She gave me a wary look and a tight nod. It would've taken way more than that to dampen my mood at that point. I left the director's office behind and breezed down the hallway, walking on air. I'd done it. I'd gotten my job back. Sure, legal still needed to sign off, but that was a formality. I glanced up and down the hallway to make sure no one was looking and did a quick victory dance.

A grueling swing shift in the ER had never sounded so good.

25

B y the time I got back to Mike, he was finishing up his chat with Heather. I lurked unobtrusively while he wrapped things up and slid his card through the slot under the window for her, but I must've been a bit quiet in my approach because when Mike turned from the window and saw me standing behind him he gave a start.

"Jesus, Davenport. Wear a bell or something."

I grinned. "Sorry-not-sorry. I've got good news."

"You can tell me on the way to the car."

He set off down the hall, and I matched his pace. "We're not going to talk to Dr. Schwartz?"

"Maybe later. But for now, I want to follow up on this. Ms. Friedman said her boss has been acting strangely the last few weeks." He took out his phone and punched numbers into it from a business card, then lifted it to his ear.

"Strangely how?"

"Absent-minded, making simple errors, snappish. Something's fishy."

"Maybe he's got a newborn at home."

"Maybe." He was quiet a moment, then disconnected the

call. "No answer. We can swing by his residence and see if he's there. He should be, if he's really sick."

Pharmacists making errors was a big red flag, especially ones like Montenegro, who did custom compounding on the regular. It was a good thing Heather had caught at least some of his errors. Hell. It was a good thing he hadn't made one bad enough to hurt someone. Anger stirred in my belly, but I told myself not to think the worst when there was no real proof. For all we knew, there was a perfectly reasonable explanation for all this.

"How'd the meeting with Wendy go?" Mike asked as we exited the building.

I glanced at the file still tucked under my arm. "Great, actually. Apparently, she misses me and valued my contributions to the team. She gave me a copy of my HR file. I can't wait to see all the nice things she's said about me in my evals. But that's only half the story. I got my job back."

"Really? That's great, Em. Congratulations." He clapped me on the shoulder.

"There's still some legal stuff involved, so it's not totally final. But I'm confident. I'll be back in the ER soon—and not as a patient. I hope."

"I bet that's a huge relief."

"Seriously." I was going to have to get in touch with Gordon McAllister and let him know I wouldn't be needing their services after all, but I'd wait to make sure everything was final first. There was no sense jumping the gun and burning a bridge. "Now I just have to figure out what to do about the Circle."

"We'll figure that out together," Mike said, leaving me feeling all warm and fuzzy inside. Damn, it was nice to have a partner.

The drive from the hospital to Montenegro's house was

short, only a few minutes really. He lived in the "triangle" formed by three of Santa Fe's main arteries, Cerillos Rd., St Francis Dr., and St Michaels Dr. The area is primarily a mix of single-family homes and condos and has remained fairly affordable—compared to the million-dollar real estate so common in the area, anyway. Part of that is probably because you'll rarely find anything for sale in the area, particularly on the west side of the railroad tracks. I've heard a lot of the modest adobe homes there are still inhabited by their original builders. I guess some people know how to hold onto a good thing while they've got it.

Montenegro's one-story adobe home turned out to be on the west side of the triangle. He wasn't old enough to be an original owner—this neighborhood went up in the sixties at the latest—so he'd either lucked out or inherited the property. It was the only home on the block without a tin roof, marking it as an older construction. But the adobe was well maintained, its packed-dirt yard fenced by a low brick wall. A scraggly cypress tree grew beside the empty driveway, which lay behind a metal gate.

"Looks like no one's home," I said as Mike pulled up to the curb.

"We should knock anyway, just in case."

So we did. No one answered.

We grabbed a late lunch, parking on the other side of the street when we got back. Nothing had changed outside, but we knocked again anyway. Still no answer, nor any hint of movement of the blinds covering the windows.

When we got back to the car, Mike put out an APB on Montenegro's car.

"Now what?" I asked.

"Now we wait."

"If I'd known we were headed for a stakeout, I would've saved some of my lunch."

He chuckled and adjusted the tilt on his seat to lean back a bit. "How are you hungry again already? I think there's a power bar in the glove compartment if you want it."

"Mmm, warm and toasty power bar," I said, though my stomach rolled over at the thought. Who knew how long the thing had been in there, for starters. "But no, I'm not hungry again. I'm just remembering our last stakeout and antici- pating future hunger. Stakeouts without snacks are a drag."

"Boredom eating isn't good for you anyway."

"What are you, the FDA chairman now?" I teased, reclining my own seat a bit and staring up at the ceiling, leaving Mike to watch the house for the moment. Silence settled between us. Mike and I were comfortable existing in the same space without having to fill it with constant conversation. It was one of the things that made us a great team. But I had a lot on my mind, between the Circle and, well, the Circle. To distract myself, I asked, "Have you heard from Dan at all?"

"Not a peep."

"Me neither. I'm not sure if that's a good thing or a bad thing."

"It's only been five days. I'm sure he's fine. The first few days of the academy are intense."

"Did you go to the Santa Fe academy?"

"No, I started out in Albuquerque and transferred here a few years after I made detective."

"What made you decide to relocate?"

He was quiet long enough that I glanced over at him, observing the back of his head as he gazed out the side window. "Xavier."

Oops. Land mine. I wondered how many of those were

buried around my partner, how long I'd need to tiptoe to avoid bringing up a painful subject. Then again, I'd worked with Mike two months before I even met the guy.

Silence stretched between us again, but this time it was less comfortable. The air felt heavy somehow, and I stretched my fingers out to crack the window, barely able to reach the controls on the door with my seat leaned back. As the cool, faintly woodsmoke-scented air wafted into the car, I closed my eyes and settled in to ride it out.

"We met in the academy," Mike said eventually. My eyes popped open in surprise, but I didn't dare interrupt, holding out hope he'd keep going. He did. "I can't say we were fast friends. He had a chip on his shoulder, and I—well, I probably did too. We were both so young. Barely out of high school. But we found common ground along the way, though it's a miracle we didn't get kicked out after some of the pranks we pulled." He turned his head, eyes scanning the street, and his face became visible to me in profile. A faint smile tugged briefly at the corner of his mouth. "We kept in touch after graduation, but our lives went in different directions. He got married and ended up moving to Santa Fe so his wife could be closer to her family. I didn't hear from him for years, and then one day he called out of the blue and said his partner was retiring and I should apply for his job. I didn't know until then that we'd both ended up in Narcotics, but I guess it shouldn't have been too surprising. We'd talked about it in the academy, but . . . You never know where life is going to take you."

He went quiet again, and I held my breath for fear he'd stop. After a few seconds, I emitted a quiet "mmm-hmm" to let him know I was listening.

"I turned him down, but he was persistent. Called me every day for a week and then one day showed up in person to take me to lunch. It was good to see him again. You ever have one of those friends who you can go without speaking to for years, and then you reconnect one day and it's like no time had passed at all? That was us. By the time he dropped me back off at HQ, I was already mentally polishing my resumé. I got the job. And you know the rest, I suppose. I just keep wondering how far back his bullshit went. Did he recruit me just so he could have a partner who'd be easy to fool? Or did the change happen right under my nose, and I didn't notice?" He snorted. "Some detective I am."

"Hey, don't say that. You're a great detective."

His jaw tightened and he shook his head. "My partner was in bed with the bad guys, Emily. He killed the woman I loved. I had no idea about either until you told me, and even then my first instinct was denial. How could I be so blind?"

"Because he's your friend, Mike." I reached across the console to put a hand on his arm. "No one wants to think the worst of their friends. That's called being human. Besides, it's entirely possible that he didn't go full Voldemort until after you left for Magic Crimes. Maybe his new partner corrupted him."

"Great, so now it's my fault for not being there for him? You suck at this."

I rolled my eyes and punched his arm. He grabbed it reflexively and looked over at me with a frown. I caught his eyes and held them. "Don't even try to turn it around on me. You're hell-bent on blaming yourself right now, and I get why. I do. I'm the queen of the self-blame game. The truth is, Xavier went over to the dark side. When, how, why, we don't know. He did some terrible things, and he's going to pay the price. No one is to blame for that but him. He is a grown-ass man, and he made his own decisions."

His gaze lingered on mine, flicking back and forth

between my eyes. "I'm sorry he hurt you. Normally, I'd wish our positions had been reversed, but this time . . . Christ, Emily. If it'd been me, I would've killed him."

"No, you wouldn't have. I mean, you would've wanted to. I'm sure you would've felt extremely conflicted about it, but your first instinct is always to uphold the law. To bring them in. To see justice served. That's just who you are, and that's—"

"Weak."

"I was going to say 'okay,' but now I'm upgrading it to wonderful. The world needs more men like you, Michael Escobar. Don't wish yourself into something you're not. If you do, evil wins."

His nostrils flared and his eyes grew moist before he looked away. I left him to his thoughts, turning my eyes back to the roof.

"I was wrong," he said after a moment, his voice a quiet rumble I had to strain to hear.

"Hmm?"

"You're actually pretty good at this."

"Damn right I am."

The silence went back to being comfortable after that, and for the next few hours, we kept what conversation did occur lighter. There were no hits on the APB and no sign of Montenegro at his house. As the sun began to set, I wondered just how long we were going to sit out here.

"One more hour," Mike replied. Oops, I guess that had been out loud.

Our persistence was rewarded when a car pulled up alongside ours about twenty minutes later. It wasn't Montenegro's, but the passenger climbed out to open the gate at the foot of his driveway, and the driver pulled in once the path was clear. After parking, the driver got out and met the passenger on the other side of the car. They were both youngish Hispanic men with tattoos on their hands and thick chains around their necks.

"Either of them familiar?"

"The driver, yeah. That's one of Big G's crew."

We watched as the men crossed the yard and stepped onto the porch, where they collected a hidden spare key and let themselves in.

"So . . . now what?" I asked. "Do we go knock, ask some questions about what they're doing in Montenegro's house?"

"They didn't break in, and there's no other evidence of a crime," Mike said, but he did aim his phone out the window. The camera shutter sound effect went off as he snapped a picture of the guys' license plate. "But I can run the plate, see if there are any outstanding warrants."

Running the plate didn't take long. It was clean, so we resigned ourselves to wait longer. The pair exited the house about ten minutes later, one of them carrying a green duffel bag. While he headed for the car, the other guy locked up and returned the key to its hiding spot.

"Please tell me we're going to follow them. They could lead us straight to Montenegro," I said, returning my seat back to its full upright position.

Mike followed suit. "Great minds think alike. Buckle up."

26

B y the time the troublesome twosome pulled down a private drive some fifteen minutes outside the city proper, I was glad they hadn't waited until dark to drop by Montenegro's house. We would've been a lot more conspicuous following them down the remote road if headlights had been required. As it was, Mike gave them enough distance to fade into the background, but not enough that we couldn't keep an eye on them.

A single-wide trailer stood in the distance, and we watched from the road as the car traversed the dirt driveway and parked beside a white car outside.

"Is that Montenegro's car?" I asked.

"Could be," Mike said, leaning toward me to peer out the passenger window. "I can't make out the plates from here. Try zooming in with your phone."

I tried, but it was too far off for the phone's lens to help, even as high-tech as smartphone cameras had become. Meanwhile, one of the two thugs got out of the car and fetched the duffel from the back seat, then walked it up to the front door and knocked. Someone answered, but again . . . too far to see much. The duffel exchanged hands, and then the delivery boy went back to the car and climbed inside. As the car turned around to head back down the drive, Mike pulled the car down the road a ways and back off onto the shoulder.

"Get down," he said, killing the engine and unbuckling to follow his own advice.

I did so, sinking down into the wheel well and leaning over the seat. "Why? They came from the other direction."

"They won't necessarily leave the same way, and two people sitting in a parked car are enough to draw notice. No one cares about an abandoned car, though."

I'm not sure how long we waited, only that after a time Mike poked his head up and declared the coast clear. I climbed back into the passenger seat and looked around, seeing no sign of the car we'd followed out into the sticks.

Mike started the car back up and reversed down the shoulder back to where we'd started.

"I hope the department has a road hazard warranty on these tires," I mumbled, mostly to myself.

"Hm?"

I motioned out the window. "Want me to go take a closer look? Get that license plate?"

"Let's wait until it gets a little darker. There's nowhere for me to hide out there if someone looks out the window."

I noted the way he turned it around so he'd be the one doing the snooping and I blew out an annoyed breath. "We could both go."

"No, I need you to stay here and keep watch in case something needs to be called in."

"You're the one that knows all the fancy radio shit."

He paused, glancing between the distant trailer and me a few times. "Fine. But call me, and keep the line open and your phone in your pocket the whole time."

A small victory, but a victory nonetheless. "Will do."

Twenty minutes later, I exited the vehicle under cover of dusk and crossed the street to approach the house. The driveway was softer on the shoulder than the harder-packed earth down the middle, so my feet kicked up little clouds of dust as I went. I kept one eye on the terrain and the other on the two windows with lights in them, watching for any flicker of movement of the curtains, but all remained quiet and still.

When I got close enough to make out the license plate, I slipped my phone from my pocket and read it off to Mike.

"It's a match," he said. "Get back here."

But it felt good to finally be doing something besides sitting and waiting, and I wasn't ready to go back. "I'm just going to take a quick peek around back, see if there's another exit."

I dropped my phone back in my pocket before he could reply and hurried toward the end of the trailer, ducking to stay below the line of the windows, even though there were no lights on behind them. As I neared the back corner, a familiar clipped voice drifted to me on the evening breeze.

". . . the best I can, but proper safety protocols must be observed."

It was Montenegro. I dared to peek around the corner and found him standing on a back porch, his phone to his ear. His other hand held a cigarette, its faintly glowing cherry bobbing with his every movement.

"It's not my fault your incompetent distributor lost what was left of the last four batches to the cops, is it?" he said, making me really wish I could hear the other side of the conversation. If only I'd had a little magic to eavesdrop properly—but no, it wouldn't have done me any good in this case. Montenegro was a witch. He couldn't sense me the way I could him, but even the slightest bit of magic use would've alerted him to my presence.

"I can't change the timetable. I'll be working through the night as it is . . . Yes . . . No . . . Uh-huh . . . Nine at the earliest, and I'll expect double the usual payment." He lifted the cigarette to his lips and took a deep drag, then flicked the rest of it into the darkness. Sparks flew as it bounced off the ground and rolled a few inches before coming to rest. Then he turned to head for the back door.

I ducked my head back around the corner, pressing my back to the wall and hoping he hadn't seen me. A few seconds later, I heard the door open and shut, and the trailer creaked as he moved around inside. The coast seemed clear, so I counted to ten and then hoofed it back to the car.

When I opened the passenger door, the dome light briefly illuminated Mike's angry face before he reached up and slapped the button to turn it off. "You like to think you're the steady, responsible one, but when it comes to reckless impulses, you and your brother are a matched set."

"Ouch. Low blow, partner."

"Well? Was it worth it?"

"Actually, yeah." I shifted in my seat to wedge my fingers in my coat pocket and extract my phone to hang up the still-open call. "There is a back door, and Montenegro is definitely here. I overheard him talking to someone on the phone. Whoever is buying the drug from him, it sounded like. He's making a batch tonight for pickup in the morning."

"That's great. We can grab him tonight and pick up the

courier in the morning, keep working our way up the chain." He reached for the radio handset. I expected him to call in backup, but instead, he reported our location and that he was leaving his car to pursue a suspect on foot.

"What's the rush?" I asked. "We should wait for backup."

"If we want to set up a sting, we need to be quiet about it. A caravan of black and whites out here is the opposite of discreet. Besides, it's just one guy. And he's a pharmacist. How much trouble could he be?"

"A whole hell of a lot. He's a witch, remember?"

Mike looked past me to the trailer, his forehead wrinkling in thought. "If he uses magic against me, he'll be in big trouble."

"He's cooking illegal narcotics. He's already in big trouble."

"Bigger trouble, then. Look, everything we know about this guy says he's a scientist, not a hardened criminal. He'll put his hands up and surrender as soon as I flash my badge." His warm fingers curled around mine, and I studied his face in the near-darkness, uncertain of his motive. "But just in case, if it makes you feel better, you can wait here and call for backup if we need it."

"What? You're not leaving me here!" I tried to yank my hand away, but he tightened his grip.

"I was afraid you'd say that."

The next thing I knew, my wrist was handcuffed to the steering wheel, and the apology in his eyes did nothing to soothe the anger that surged in my chest.

"You son of a bitch!"

Mike opened his door and slid out of the car before I could reach him with my free hand, which only proved he did have at least some hint of a self-preservation instinct.

Bending down, he looked into the car where I yanked on the cuffs and fumed. "I'll be right back."

"If you think HR won't hear about this, you've got another think coming!"

He chuckled and shut the door, then ambled off across the street and down the driveway, leaving me stewing in frustrated silence. My phone rang in my lap, Mike's contact photo showing on the screen. I jabbed the screen with my thumb to answer, then put the phone to my ear.

"Fuck you."

"I'm putting you in my pocket on speaker. Yell at me later."

I ground my teeth in frustration. "Fine." Then I muted myself and tossed the phone onto the dash, the better to dig half-moons into my palm while I waited, listening to the scratchy pocket noise and cussing him out under my breath.

Mike bypassed the front steps at first, heading for Montenegro's car. He walked the length of the driver's side, bending down briefly at the front and back, but whatever he did was blocked from my view since he was on the opposite side of the car. Then he approached the trailer, climbed the front steps, and knocked on the front door. The curtains in the window nearest the door twitched briefly, then the door opened.

"I'm sorry, I must have the wrong address," Mike said, putting up his hands.

Shit. He was blocking my view of Montenegro, but he must've had a weapon of some sort.

"Not a hardened criminal my ass," I muttered and yanked on the cuffs again, but all it did was make the metal dig uncomfortably into my wrist.

I heard a faint reply but couldn't quite make out what was said. Then Mike stumbled forward as if dragged inside, and the door slammed shut behind him. Cursing a blue streak, I scrambled for the radio.

"This is Santa Fe Unit 125, requesting backup. Officer needs assistance at last reported location. Suspect has grabbed officer and retreated into a domicile."

27

I sat there in the gathering darkness, watching the trailer like a hawk, calculating how long it would take the cavalry to arrive, and plotting my partner's murder. Okay, not his literal murder, but I was fairly keen to eviscerate him with razor-sharp looks and lash him with a barbed tongue. He was going to get a piece of my mind when all this was over.

My only consolation was that Mike's phone was still live, so I could at least hear a little of what was going on. Two things became clear right away. He knew the person who'd answered the door—someone named Pablo—and that meant Montenegro wasn't alone. Mike tried to talk to this Pablo person, who mostly yelled at him to shut up, and after thirty seconds or so there was a bunch of pocket noise before the line went largely quiet. Still connected, but quiet.

As the minutes ticked by, worry supplanted rage, and I was so focused on the distant trailer that I lost track of my immediate surroundings. When the driver's door opened, I all but levitated in my seat as I whirled to face the man who slid behind the wheel.

"Well, this is—how is it you Americans say—quite the pickle?"

"Jesus, Volkov. You about gave me a heart attack." My racing heart was slower to settle than it had been to ramp up, only to get another jolt when I realized my salvation was sitting less than a foot away. "Get me out of these cuffs, would you?"

He cocked his head. "Why should I, hmm? It will save me the trouble of using my own."

"I hope you're joking. Because my partner's just been taken hostage, and even though it kind of serves him right for leaving me here like this, I'd like to kick his ass myself."

"What's your plan?"

"What?"

He motioned in the general direction of the trailer. "To rescue him. If I set you loose, what are you going to do?"

He had a good point. "I—I hadn't gotten that far. But I'll think of something. Backup is at least twenty minutes out. He might not have that kind of—wait, how did you find me? You didn't follow us out here. Mike would've noticed."

"Would he?" His shoulder rose and fell.

I narrowed my eyes. "Out with it."

He slid a hand into his jacket pocket and removed a small vial, holding it up in silence. A faintly glowing sigil marked the stopper. I watched as he tilted the vial and the dark liquid within spilled from one end to the other.

"Is that my blood?" I lunged at him and made a grab for it, but he evaded me easily since I had to reach across my body and I remained cuffed to the steering wheel. "How did you—You took my blood at the hospital. Son of a bitch!"

"An unfortunate necessity, I'm afraid." He rolled the vial between his fingers. "I'd hoped you'd be more forthcoming and I wouldn't need it. But as they say, desperate times call for disparate measures." He met my eyes, an utter lack of apology in his gaze.

"Desperate. Desperate measures," I muttered, then fell back in my seat with a growl and looked out the window again at the trailer. As if this night couldn't possibly get any worse, now the Circle could find me anywhere, at any time. "If all you came here to do was gloat, you can fuck right off."

"Oh, no. I came to help. The gloating was just a bonus." He tucked the vial away in his jacket again. "So, here's what I'm thinking—"

"I don't need your help," I snapped, throwing him a glare for good measure. Then I remembered my predicament and sighed. "Okay, I do need your help. But I don't think I can afford your price."

"Price? Who said anything about price?"

I arched a skeptical brow. "You expect me to believe that you're going to help me out of the kindness of your icy, Circle-issued heart and ask nothing in return? I wasn't born yesterday, you know."

Adrian sighed, and magic flared briefly around him. Both sides of the handcuffs unlocked simultaneously and fell, clanging off the gear shift and sliding down the console to land on the floor. I pulled my hand close and rubbed my wrist but kept my eyes on Adrian.

"Thanks," I said.

"You're welcome. Now, as I was about to say, we need a diversion. Something to attract the attention of the two men inside so we can slip in and get your partner out."

"There is no we. Wait, how did you know there's two men?"

"Three, counting the detective."

"Fine. Keep it to yourself." I checked Mike's glove compartment, hoping for a backup pistol, but even before I looked, I knew he was way too responsible to carry a spare gun in an unlocked compartment. Kind of like he was too responsible to let me carry my own gun while on duty, so I didn't have that either. My shield charm was depleted, so I had left it at home along with the rest, not thinking I'd need them when I left the house this morning. I needed to rethink the essentials of my daily kit. You never knew what might happen. As it stood, I had no weapons. Every tool in my arsenal was defensive, unless I could get my hands on Montenegro and drain his magic.

"Are you carrying this time?" I asked, glancing Adrian's way.

"Yes, of course."

"I don't suppose I could borrow your gun?" His stone-faced reply was all the nope I needed. I sighed and rubbed my temples. A diversion. Yes, I needed a diversion. The answer came to me in a flash, accompanied by the memory of Montenegro's cigarette butt sailing into the night. "What about a lighter? Do you have one of those?"

"I don't smoke."

I riffled the glove compartment again but came up empty. Throwing myself back in my seat, I tipped my head back and stared up at the ceiling. What were the odds that the cigarette was still lit? Not very good.

Adrian opened the door and got out of the car. Blinking, I called after him, "Where are you going?"

"To create a diversion."

The door swung shut with finality, so I had to open my own and climb out to respond. I rounded the front of the car for good measure and jabbed a finger into his chest. "Stay out of this. I don't need your help. I don't *want* your help. I can do this."

"I believe you. But I'm not letting you do it alone. So you

might as well get used to the idea and make the most of it." He placed one foot on the bumper and tugged up his pant leg, revealing an ankle holster. He pulled the small revolver free and slid the cylinder open to show me it was loaded, then slapped it back in place and offered it to me handle-first. To his credit, he didn't ask if I knew how to use it.

Pride made me hesitate a few seconds more before I grabbed the gun. "Start a fire around the back, a little ways from the porch. The dry grass should light easily, and one of them tossed a cigarette out there not long ago, so it won't strike them as immediately odd. Once you draw them out, I'll go in the front and get Mike."

Adrian nodded and put a hand on my shoulder, squeezing. "Get him out and go. I can take care of myself."

"Whatever." I shrugged off his hand, looked both ways, and headed across the deserted road toward the target.

I shouldn't have agreed to that. Never leave a man behind, right? And he was trying to help me. Not my best moment. I muttered to myself all the way down the driveway. By the time I crouched beside Montenegro's car, hidden from the front of the trailer should anyone open the door or look out, I'd resolved to make sure Adrian did in fact make it out. It was the right thing to do. And besides, a Circle rep disappearing—or worse—while investigating me was just as incriminating as any other scenario I'd come up with.

I squinted in the darkness but didn't catch a glimpse of Adrian moving across the darkened landscape, so I cocked the borrowed revolver and settled in to wait.

28

It felt like forever before I caught the first whiff of smoke, but it only grew stronger as the seconds ticked by. Somewhat belatedly, I realized the folly of setting a grassfire out here where there was a whole lot of available tinder to feed it. I hoped Adrian could keep it under control. At least it wasn't fire season, so we had that going for us.

Us. I shook my head at the thought, briefly wondering how I'd gotten myself into this predicament. Then I remembered it wasn't my fault at all. It was Mike's. So, I guess there was that.

As the smoke smell grew more intense, I kept my ears peeled. Was that the crackle of fire? Or was I hearing things because I knew it was out there? It wasn't too much longer before I heard heavy footsteps moving swiftly through the trailer and the distant sound of the back door flying open to slam against the wall. Raised voices drifted my way on the wind. I couldn't make out what they were saying, but that was my cue.

I ran for the front door, hoping it was unlocked. The handle turned without resistance. Finally, something was going my way! I cracked it open to peek inside. The shabby living room was empty, so I slipped inside as swiftly and quietly as possible, scanning the room for any sign of my partner. A gun that looked like his lay on the coffee table beside a few empty beer bottles. I grabbed it and dropped it in my coat pocket, where it sat heavily as I considered my options. To the left was the kitchen, which looked more like a laboratory with all the beakers, flasks, and tubes set up. That must've been where Montenegro was working. The still-open back door was also off the kitchen, so I decided to go down the hallway to my right first.

The first door opened on a grungy bathroom—seriously, how do people live like that? The second was a bedroom, and that's where I hit pay dirt. Mike lay on the floor, curled on his side, his wrists and ankles bound with electrical cords.

"Mike!" I rushed over to crouch beside him, but he didn't stir. Unconscious was never a good sign. I checked for a pulse, then chided myself. Why would they tie him up if he was dead? Still, it was a comfort to feel his steady heartbeat under my fingers. "You're gonna owe me so big when this is all done," I muttered, tucking Adrian's revolver in my other pocket to free both hands so I could loosen the bindings.

I worked as quickly as I could, but picking at the stiff knots took longer than I would've liked. I expected Mike to come to while I was at it, but he remained still. The longer he stayed unconscious, the more it worried me. Any loss of consciousness was troubling, but the longer a person was out, the worse off they generally were. I hoped they hadn't knocked him upside the head too hard. If anyone was going to give him a concussion at this point, I wanted it to be me.

When he didn't stir, I was left with little choice but to grab his ankles and start dragging him toward the door. It's harder than you might think to drag an unconscious body, especially one that weighs significantly more than you do. I strained and grunted, the tender muscles in my torso twinging in protest, getting him halfway out the door before my back hit the wall. Oh right, it wasn't a straight shot to the door. And how was I going to get him down the front steps without his head banging every one on the way down?

Tears of pain and frustration welled in my eyes—or maybe it was the smoke wafting in through the back door making them sting and burn—but I refused to give up. We inched down the hall at what felt like a snail's pace, urgency bubbling beneath the surface of my skin as I took one difficult step after another, willing him to wake up so he could help me help him. When I reached the living room, the loud crack of a gunshot froze me in place. It took me a moment to realize it was outside.

"Don't waste your bullets. I told you I'd handle this. Go back inside and check the temp on the digital thermometer. It can't go above two-twenty-five." Montenegro's raised voice drifted in from the back porch, raising my heart rate another notch.

"Fuck you! I ain't your lab assistant. We need to get out of here before more cops show up."

"If that solution gets too hot, there won't be enough of us left for the cops to arrest. Go check the temperature!"

I dragged Mike approximately two more feet with a sudden burst of adrenaline, but it wasn't enough to get us out of the line of sight before a man's figure darkened the doorway. He got halfway across the kitchen, gun still in hand, before glancing into the living room. His eyes widened and he halted abruptly.

I dropped Mike's feet and went for one of the guns weighing down my pockets but froze when the guy in the kitchen pointed his at me. He was younger than I'd expected. Probably old enough to vote, but not to buy booze. Not legally, anyway.

"What the hell, how many of you are there?" He turned his head slightly to yell toward the open door. "There's another one in here!"

"What's. The. Temp?" Montenegro called back. His preoccupation with the temperature of the chemicals he was cooking made it one of my priorities too. What exactly would happen if it went above two-twenty-five? He'd made it sound like it might explode.

"Go ahead and check it," I said, now-sweaty hands raised. "I'll wait here."

He advanced a step and turned the gun sideways, like that might make it more intimidating. "Shut the fuck up!"

I flinched and lifted my hands a little higher. Okay, so maybe it was a little more intimidating. Keeping the gun on me, the guy side-stepped across the kitchen, moving closer to where the range presumably sat, out of my line of sight. He squinted, then hollered, "It's good. Only two-fifteen. You want me to turn it down?"

There was a delay before Montenegro answered, and a flare of magic from that direction suggested he was still preoccupied with Adrian. Good.

"No! It can't go below two hundred or I'll have to start over."

A groan from the floor drew my attention before I could point out that the impending arrival of Santa Fe's finest meant this batch wasn't going to be finished regardless. Mike's eyes fluttered open and he reached for his head.

I pointed down at him for the young thug's benefit, then slowly dropped to one knee beside him. "Hey, buddy, welcome back. How many fingers am I holding up?" I wiggled all eight, plus thumbs.

"Emily?" He blinked and stared at me for a few seconds. The moment when everything clicked was easy to see. He started to sit up, but I put a staying palm on his chest.

"Just stay there for a minute, okay? You've been out cold for a few minutes at least. You're probably going to be dizzy, and you might be concussed."

The guy in the kitchen—Pablo, presumably—walked forward, crossing into the living room, keeping his gun on us and radiating menace. "I told you to shut the fuck up." Gold flashed between his lips. Now that he was closer, I could make out the half-grill he sported along with the dark fuzz on his upper lip.

"Aren't you supposed to be keeping an eye on the stove?" I couldn't help but ask, uncertain what the more immediate threat was, the volatile concoction simmering away in the kitchen or the agitated man in front of me with a gun in his hand.

I soon had my answer. The gun went off with a loud bang, and my heart damn near stopped. It took me several seconds of furious self-assessment to register that I wasn't actually hit, and then my eyes cast a wider net, first scouring Mike before eventually finding a gouge in the carpet a foot or so to my left. A warning shot. My mouth went dry and fear lodged in my throat. I only realized I was shaking when Mike lay a steady hand over the one that was still on his chest. I envied his calm.

Gently, he removed my hand and sat up, twisting to look over his shoulder at the shooter before reaching for his head again. He winced, fingers probing an obviously sore spot on the back. "Give the girl a break, Pablo. She's a civilian."

"Shut up, cop, or I'll put your lights out again. Permanently this time."

"That's no way to talk to an old friend," Mike said.

"I ain't your friend, pig!" The hand holding the gun began to shake, and I couldn't decide what was scarier, watching it or taking my eyes off it.

"That's not what you said when I kept you out of juvie. You swore you were turning over a new leaf, that you weren't going to follow your dad into this life. What changed?"

Puzzle pieces clicked into place. This was Big G's kid. Guillermo Ochoa the crime boss's kid. Pablo stood there glaring daggers for a few moments more, hand still shaking, then heaved a heavy sigh and lifted the gun to his stubbly head. Not pointing at it, just laying it across it as he rubbed a tattooed hand down his face. "Fuck, *ese*, I dunno. Nothing. Everything. Fucking life, man. I told the old man getting in bed with these people was a bad idea, but did he listen? Of course fucking not. All he could see was the green."

These people. That was interesting. My eyes slid to my partner, but otherwise, I dared not move. Pablo wasn't just talking about Montenegro—but speaking of which . . . "There's something on the stove," I whispered while Pablo was distracted. "If it gets too hot, kaboom."

Mike gave me a slight nod but kept his eyes on Pablo. "Well, let me do you one more favor. I called in backup before I came in here. I'm not sure how long I was out—" He winced again, rubbing the back of his head. "—but I'd say you've got a few minutes, tops, before the cops swarm this place. There's still time to beat feet, but not much."

"What good is that gonna do me? You already know I was here. Unless . . ." He pointed the gun at us again, the answer to his dilemma shining in his tired brown eyes.

Mike got his feet under him and hauled himself into a

standing position. He swayed a little, so I quickly joined him, reaching for his arm to steady him. He turned to face Pablo and pushed me behind him. Indignation rose, but the heavy weight of his gun in my coat pocket bumped my leg as it swayed with the movement, and an idea struck. Using Mike's body as cover, I slipped my hand into the pocket and curled my fingers around the gun's thick, textured grip.

"It doesn't have to end like this," Mike said. "You're Big G's son. His number two. I'll bet you know more than enough to take his whole operation down. The DA would do a lot of favors for your cooperation."

"You really think I'm gonna turn against my pops? My boys? You're dumber than you look, *ese*."

"I think you play the thug because it makes him happy," Mike said, the words hanging in the air like the growing haze of smoke.

I drew the gun from my pocket. It felt heavier in my hand somehow than it had in my pocket. I'd fired Mike's pistol at the range once, but I wasn't used to its weight, and I'd sure as shit never fired at a living target. After a moment's hesitation, I adjusted my grip and pressed the gun length-wise against the small of Mike's back, hoping he'd get the hint.

Slowly, he moved his hand behind his leg. "You wanted to go to college, Pablo. To make something of yourself. You still can."

"Keep your motherfucking hands where I can fucking see them!" Pablo shouted. Mike lifted both hands, but Pablo wasn't satisfied. "You too, Goldilocks!"

I swallowed, still holding the gun against Mike's back. Then, suddenly, a shrill alarm pierced the silence. There was finally enough smoke in the house to trigger the smoke detector. In the ensuing confusion, I shifted my grip on the gun to hold it properly once more and stepped out from behind Mike with it raised in a two-handed grip. Pablo was covering his ears with one hand and one hand-plus-pistol, eyes scanning the ceiling in search of the source of the racket. His eyes widened when he noticed me and the gun, but before I could make up my mind to squeeze the trigger, magic surged on the other side of the wall and the world tilted on its axis.

29

The floor beneath me tipped suddenly and sharply as if a giant were deadlifting the back of the trailer. The floor rushed up at me, and I barely kept my feet under myself by adjusting my stance to ride it like a surfboard. Already unsteady on his feet, Mike wasn't so lucky. He fell backward on his ass, landing with a noisy thud. Pablo managed to fling himself at the nearby kitchen counter for something to hold onto, but everything in the trailer not nailed down went sliding.

As the trailer tipped farther and farther, I began to worry it was going to end up on its side. But then my stomach bottomed out as it slammed back down onto its foundation, rattling the windows in their panes and the glassware in the kitchen, not to mention the teeth in my jaw. I returned both hands to Mike's gun and leveled it on Pablo once more, but his eyes were wide with panic.

"Fuck this shit!" he said and ran out the back door.

I took off after him but came to a screeching halt on the porch at the sight of a ten-foot-high wall of flame not twenty feet away. Whipping my head left and right, I caught a glimpse of Pablo disappearing around the corner of the trailer, but I doubted he'd get far. The blazing firestorm wrapped around both ends of the trailer in a ring of fire. Suzi's vision flashed in my mind and I almost laughed. Who would've thought I'd end up in the center of a literal ring of fire? Well, I'd asked for a distraction, and Adrian had certainly given me one. A groan drew my attention to the edge of the porch, where the man of the hour, Victor Montenegro, climbed up over the railing, tumbling the last few feet to land on his side with a thud.

I pointed the gun at him while he pushed himself up with both hands. "Hello, Victor."

He lifted his eyes to me, brow furrowed in obvious confusion. Seeing me out of context must've thrown him for a loop. "Have we met?" Magic flared weakly around him, a faintly glowing nimbus that suggested he was either a weak witch or he was pushing his limits. I'd felt the surge of magic earlier when he'd sparred with Adrian, so my money was on the latter.

"Emily Davenport, SFPD. Stop casting right now. This is your only warning." I held the gun firmly in both hands and sighted down the barrel, resolve firming up in my stomach. I didn't want to shoot him, but at that moment I knew if it came down to it I would.

Mike stumbled out the door behind me and reached for the gun. "I've got this," he said, but I made sure he was steady on his feet before I let him take over. "Victor Montenegro, you're under arrest for the manufacture of illegal narcotics. Hands up, please and thank you."

Montenegro put his hands up, but the faint glow around him lingered. I wondered if he was going to make me get out the blindfold.

"Bet you wish you had a pair of handcuffs right about

now," I stage-whispered, earning a glare from my partner. I smirked in response and put my thumb and index finger in my mouth to whistle sharply.

The crackling flames parted like a curtain a few moments later, and Adrian stepped through. Not a hair was out of place, in sharp contrast to the rumpled witch kneeling on the porch with his hands in the air. Still wreathed in a magical glow, Adrian cast a spell as he walked, air and water sigils floating just in front of him and then zipping through the air toward the wall of fire at his back. He snapped his fingers—a bit of a showman, apparently—and the flames parted again, this time extinguishing in a cascade spreading in both directions, leaving behind a black ring of charred grass and earth. It was an impressive feat of spellcasting, honestly. Finesse, rather than raw power.

"Who's that?" Mike asked, still keeping an eye on Montenegro.

"Adrian Volkov," I said.

Montenegro paled suddenly and twisted to look behind him, peering between the porch rails at the man striding across the yard toward us. Then he scrambled to his feet and crossed the porch in two strides, vaulting over the side to make a break for it before Mike or I could stop him. Adrian followed him with his eyes and flung a spell at his retreating form that tangled around his ankles and brought him down.

The porch steps creaked as Adrian climbed them, still wreathed in pulsing, golden energy. He pulled a set of zip-tie handcuffs from his coat pocket and offered them to me. "Put these on him. They'll keep him out of trouble."

I'd thought he was joking about having his own cuffs. Apparently not. I took them, surprised by the cool feel of metal on the inside. I took a closer look, discovering that while the zip ties were plastic on the outside, the inside housed a thin, flexible piece of metal onto which familiar runes of binding were etched. A faint sheen of magic glimmered across the silvery band.

"Binding cuffs? Clever. Do they require magic to activate?"

"No, just contact with skin."

"Sweet."

Mike swiped the cuffs from me and trotted off to secure the prisoner.

"Should one of us go after Pablo?" I called after him. The smoke detector continued to wail in the background, but at least it was quieter out here than it was inside.

"He won't get far," Mike replied. "I disabled the vehicle."

Adrian peered into the trailer through the back door. "What's going on in there?"

"Smoke alarm," I said. "It should stop once the smoke clears enough."

Adrian shook his head. "No, I mean what's *going on* in there?"

Frowning, I turned back toward the door, and that's when I noticed magic emanating from somewhere inside in pulses, each one slightly stronger than the last. "Um . . . I'm not sure." I glanced at Mike but he seemed to have things under control. Thanks to Adrian's fancy zip cuffs, Montenegro was no longer a magical threat. "Let's check it out. Be right back, Mike."

I stepped back inside, wincing at the continued piercing shriek of the smoke alarm. Just as in the living room, the contents of the kitchen had slid toward the front wall, and a table and chairs blocked the path to the stove where a burner remained lit and merrily burning. It was hard to say what had been on it, as there were several overturned flasks present, their contents leaking from their narrow mouths and mingling on the stove and counter. The heavy scent of chemicals lingered in the air, a sharp odor that made my nostrils and throat sting enough that I coughed into a hand and held each breath a little longer than necessary. The magic I sensed emanated from two flasks in particular, their enchanted contents now co-mingling and pulsing with vibrant mystical energy.

Adrian began clearing a path to the stove, but I grabbed his arm and pulled him back. "We need to get out of here," I shouted to be heard over the shrieking alarm. "There's no telling what those mixtures are going to do. Toxic fumes are a real possibility, and they could be flammable."

Adrian spared the alarm an annoyed glance. A burst of magic flew from him and the alarm went silent. Some of the tension smoothed from his face, and he turned his attention back to me. "The way the magic is growing? It's essentially a bomb waiting to happen. All it needs is a catalyst."

I stared at the ring of blue flame on the stove. Miraculously, none of the liquid had encroached on it yet, but with the magic within the solutions taking on a life of its own, it was only a matter of time. Was that the catalyst it needed?

I released Adrian's arm and we both worked to clear the debris from in front of the stove. As soon as I could reach, I twisted the knob to turn the burner off. Any relief I may have felt was short-lived, as now I had a front-row seat to what was happening. Swirls of pulsing magic decorated the counter as well as the stovetop, and a faint sheen rose from the puddling liquid.

"We have to nullify the magic somehow," I said, glancing at Adrian. "Have any more tricks up your sleeve?"

He spread his hands and I grimaced. We were running out of time. There was no telling what those enhanced mixtures would do if left unchecked. I thought about the tea experiment, how with Kassidy's help I'd managed to imbue it with magic, albeit temporarily. I wondered if this aspect of my powers worked two ways as well. I already knew I could intercept and ground spells flung at me and suck the magic out of witches. Could I draw this imbued energy out and ground it as well?

I reached out without thinking and touched a fingertip to the glowing, pulsing puddle of magic-imbued liquid on the stove. Adrian threw an arm across my chest and yanked me back, swiftly breaking the contact—but the damage was already done. My fingertip began to burn before I could yell at him for interrupting, and I glanced down at it to see my still-wet skin redden and sizzle. With a yelp, I rushed for the sink and ran some cold water over it, but even as I did so I was keenly aware of the noxious steam that rose as the water came into contact with spilled chemicals in the sink. I held my breath, but not before I'd already sucked in a lungful of it.

Adrian pulled me back again, this time keeping a firm hold of my arm and hauling me several feet back toward the door. My fingertip still burned, but now so did my lungs. Tears sprang to my eyes, but I fought them off as best I could.

"Good idea, Emily. Let's touch the unknown chemicals bristling with magic," he muttered even as he cast a healing spell that washed over my entire hand, providing instant cooling relief. The magic traveled up my arm from there, seeking and soothing the agitated bronchioles in my lungs, then spreading down my torso as well. The dull ache in my stomach faded, and I didn't have to lift my shirt to know that the bruising there was gone as well. A wave of fatigue followed in its wake, and I caught the doorframe with one hand to steady myself.

"It made sense in my head," I replied, unprepared to offer any more explanation than that as I darted a glance at the still-running tap and the steam rising from the sink. Steam which, as I studied it more carefully, bore a sheen of magic. "Um, remember that catalyst you mentioned?"

"Yes."

I pointed my healed finger at the sink as the billowing steam cascaded over the countertop like it had a mind of its own. As it passed over the magic-imbued liquids on the counter, the magic within them rose and merged with the cloud, which began to flicker with golden light like a miniature storm cloud.

Adrian dragged me out the back door in response. I went with him, my self-preservation instinct overruling my curiosity over what would happen next. We found Mike climbing the steps, guiding Victor ahead of him. Victor stalled on the next-to-last step, eyes wide as they caught sight of Adrian.

"Mr. Volkov. I'm so sorry, sir. I had no idea—"

"No time," I said. "We've got to vamoose."

Frown lines stretched across Mike's brow as he lingered on the steps. "What's up?"

"Magic bomb."

"Say no more." Mike grabbed Victor's arm, prepared to haul him away, but the pharmacist's feet remained glued to the steps, eyes locked on Adrian like he wasn't going anywhere without permission.

Adrian crossed the small porch in two strides and got in Victor's face. "Run."

That was an order Victor was more than willing to obey. He

fled like the hounds of hell were after him, down the stairs and away from all of us and the trailer as fast as his skinny legs could carry him. Mike followed him, though the glance he shot me along the way said we'd be having a talk later. I wasn't sure why Volkov scared the piss out of Victor or how they knew each other, but maybe I'd find out sometime between now and then.

In the meantime, I turned to Adrian. "Is there anything you can do to, I dunno, contain it?"

"I'm not tapped, but even if I were at full strength, I'm not sure that'd be enough."

I glanced into the kitchen once more. The cloud had grown exponentially in the few seconds we'd been outside. How much bigger would it get? Would we even be able to get out of the blast radius before it went nova? And even if, in the best-case scenario, we did . . . it would still take all of our evidence with it.

"If you had the juice, could you do it?"

"Theoretically? Yes."

I could give him whatever power he needed, but the cost could be my . . . everything. I still didn't completely trust him, but I trusted the undulating mass of power radiating from the kitchen even less. Flush with resignation—and no small amount of adrenaline—I grabbed Adrian's hand and tugged him to stand at the edge of the porch. The rail was at our backs, but we had a clear line of sight through the open door.

"Do it," I said.

He tried to pull his hand away. "I told you, I—"

"Just do it!" I snapped, gripping his fingers tighter but not taking my eyes off the billowing magical storm cloud that hovered in the kitchen.

I opened the floodgates and pushed everything I could into him. He gasped, his fingers gripping mine now rather than simply allowing me to hold them. I felt his eyes on me but refused to look his way. The cloud before us undulated, pulsing stronger, the golden energy within it flickering faster by the second. It was beautiful in the same way storms rolling down across the mountains are. Raw, untamed, and potentially destructive. We were running out of time.

"Now, Adrian. Please."

My words spurred him into action and he began to cast the spell. Within seconds, a glimmering rune-laden hardened magic shell spread around the cloud. It was a thing of beauty, and I wish I'd had more time to marvel at the intricacies of the spell.

The cloud continued to billow and grow until it couldn't anymore. Then it buffeted the shell with increasing fury like a fist beating at a locked door. But the shield held. There was nowhere to go. Then a second shield sprang up before me. It took me a moment to figure out that Adrian had put a shield up around the two of us, surrounding us in a protective bubble. This one was more physical than magical, and I knew if I put my hand to it, I would encounter hardened air. A backup shield, just in case. I appreciated that and kept the magic flowing between us. Again, just in case.

A flash of light lit the inside of the trailer like a miniature sun, temporarily blinding me. I threw up my free hand automatically to shield my eyes, but it was no use. As quickly as the light had come, it vanished. By the time my eyes readjusted, all was dark again. Both of Adrian's shields had held, but the one in the kitchen was empty.

After heaving a gargantuan sigh of relief, I risked a glance at Adrian. He regarded me for a long, thoughtful moment from within our magic cocoon—long enough that I had to fight the urge to squirm beneath the intensity of his gaze. Then he dropped the shield around us. I released his hand, severing the flow of magic between us. What remained inside me swiftly drained back out into the weathered wood beneath my feet on its way to the earth.

The moment felt heavy, and my heart thumped against my ribs as the enormity of what I'd done caught up with me. Adrian had finally gotten the truth out of me, that was for sure. The question was, what would he do with it?

30

The answer to my unspoken question wasn't immediately forthcoming. After suggesting I recall my partner, Adrian withdrew to check the kitchen for any lingering rogue magic. There wasn't any. He stuck around to answer Mike's questions about his involvement and agreed to come to the station to make a formal statement, but he didn't say another word to me before driving off in his black SUV.

I didn't hear from him for two nerve-wracking days. I'd like to say I was so busy dealing with the aftermath of the big bust and the flurry of arrests that followed as we dismantled Big G's distribution ring with Pablo's help that I didn't spare it a thought, but that'd be a lie. I was busy with those things, but my unfinished business with Adrian was a near-constant hum in the back of my mind. He finally caught up with me in the parking lot of the grocery store where I was transferring two weeks' worth of groceries—I hate grocery shopping, so I try to do it as infrequently as possible—from cart to trunk.

Even when he did appear, he was maddeningly silent,

merely falling in on the other side of the cart and helping me unload. Every rustle of the paper bags put me more and more on edge until I couldn't take anymore. After slinging a bag of frozen goods into the trunk with unnecessary force, I straightened and curled my fingers around the top of the cart.

"Look, I don't know what kind of game you're playing here, but I've had enough."

He paused with a bag in hand. "I don't know what you mean."

I leaned across the cart to jab him in the chest. "Where have you been? Why the radio silence?"

"Keeping my distance, as you asked. You had two more days left." He placed the bag in the trunk.

"Two more—" I sputtered, then grabbed the last bag—the one with the bread and eggs—from the basket. "Seriously?"

He cracked a smile. He was actually kind of handsome when he smiled. It softened his sharp edges. But I still hated him a bit. "I'll admit, I needed to do some thinking. It was a convenient excuse."

"And?"

He leaned across the cart and gently took the bag from me before I could anxiety-squish the bread into oblivion. "I understand why you didn't want to tell me. If the Circle finds out what you can do, they will not rest until you are firmly under their thumb."

"You said 'if.' Does that mean you're not going to tell your boss?" Hope dared to flare within me.

"My task was to determine whether you were masquerading as a witch—a Circle witch, specifically. There's no question in my mind now that you are a witch. And other than using the Davenport name—which you are legally entitled to do, as it is your name by birth—I've found no evidence that you lay any claim to Circle membership. With that said, I would advise you to join a coven to give your mother less ground to stand on."

His words should have thrilled me, but I couldn't quite shake the lingering dread weighing my stomach down like a bad burrito. "You think my mother will let it rest at that? She knows all too well that magic never manifested in me as a child."

"I guess that makes you a late bloomer." He held up the bag containing my eggs and bread. "You want this up front or in the back?"

"The back is fine," I said absently, still mulling over what he'd said while he placed the final sack carefully atop the rest. "Why, though? Why are you willing to lie for me?"

"It's not a lie, merely an omission. I've witnessed your power with my own eyes. That's all he needs to know."

"That simple, eh?"

He shut the trunk lid. "That simple."

"Still, why?" Not knowing was like an itchy scab. I couldn't help but pick at it.

"Because you're one of the good ones," he said, turning toward me and putting a hand on my shoulder. "Keep fighting the good fight." His hand fell away. "How did it go, anyway? With the drug dealers."

I studied his face but picked up no trace of dishonesty. The knot of unease in my stomach began to loosen. "With Montenegro behind bars, their manufacturing arm has been shut down entirely. We still don't know who was bankrolling him, but we've shut down the dealers too. Mike's hopeful he can secure Montenegro's cooperation so we can go after his boss. Time will tell. But that reminds me.

Why was Montenegro so scared of you? Do you two have history?"

"I assume it's because he recognized my name and thought I was there for him. He's lucky I wasn't. The Circle has a zero-tolerance policy for involvement with criminal organizations, and if word had gotten back to the Archon about what he was actually up to . . ."

"Montenegro is a Circle witch?" Wheels started turning. If one Circle witch was involved in this operation, could there be others?

"He is—well, was. After I filed my report, I'm sure actions were taken to scrub any association from the official record."

"It's that easy, eh? Guess it's a good thing he didn't list the Circle on his state registration."

"Even if he had, that would not be a great obstacle."

I blinked. "The Circle has a way to make changes in the registry outside official channels?"

"I didn't say that." His lips quirked in a small smile. "Regardless, my time in Santa Fe is done for now."

"I'm sorry I wasn't a very good hostess." Strangely, it was true. After all, the guy wasn't that bad. Though I'd had no way of knowing it at the start. Plus, he'd done the city—and me—a great service. Several times. I stuck a hand out across the cart between us. "Thanks for your help, Adrian. And if you find yourself out this way again, let me know. I can go out for dinner and you can sit in the parking lot for old time's sake."

He laughed and shook my hand. "Will do. Take care of yourself, Emily."

"You too."

Adrian turned to go, but got no more than a step away

before he pivoted back around, reaching a hand into his suit coat. "I almost forgot."

Wariness must have crept into my expression because he chuckled as he pulled the spelled vial of my blood from the inner pocket and held it out to me. Or, at least I assumed it was mine. I couldn't fathom why he'd be giving me someone else's. I took the vial from him. It was cool to the touch despite being tucked against his chest, on account of the spell cast on it to keep the blood from spoiling. Yeah, he really did seem like a decent guy in the end.

"Thanks. You know what? Forget what I said about the parking lot. You can definitely come inside and watch."

He laughed again, this time a full-throated laugh that brightened his eyes and brought a smile to my face as well. "Sounds good."

I tucked the vial in my coat pocket, because standing there holding a vial of blood might draw unwanted attention, and watched him as he walked to his nearby car, marveling at what a strange week it had been. Then I shook myself and wheeled the cart to the corral so I could get my groceries home before my ice cream became mint chip soup.

31

When you live alone, there are few surprises more pleasant than an unexpected visitor when you have a trunk full of groceries to unload and cart upstairs. Still, I couldn't help but give my partner a little shit when I saw him loitering outside my door.

"You know, there's this miraculous modern invention called a mobile phone. I've heard that civilized people call or text before dropping by."

Mike chuckled and detached from the wall and relieved me of my burdens. "You calling me a savage? I'm half Native, you know. That's pretty offensive."

"Yeah, right." I unlocked the door and held it open for him. "Just put those on the counter and you can help me with the next load."

He did as instructed and headed back downstairs with me without comment. Until we got to the car, that is. "I am, you know."

"Hmm?"

"Half Native. My mom's Hopi."

"Really? Huh. Why haven't you mentioned it before?"

He shrugged. "Didn't seem important. She's not from around here or anything. Her family's mostly on the rez in Arizona. We used to visit a couple times a year when I was a kid, but she had a falling out with her brother after—well, family drama. You know how that goes."

"Intimately." I passed him a couple of the heavier bags and hoisted the last two lighter ones myself. It took a little juggling to get the trunk closed and locked, but we were soon headed back for the stairs.

"I called a buddy of mine at the academy to check on Dan," he commented as we walked. "He's doing fine."

My brows shot up. "Fine?"

"I believe his exact words were 'sarcastic smart-mouthed prima donna prankster.'" He chuckled.

"That sounds like my brother. But how does that translate as 'fine?'"

"It's week one. Everyone is a 'sarcastic smart-mouthed prima donna' as far as instructors are concerned. The prankster addition just means he's making friends."

"Or enemies."

"If I didn't know better, I'd think you were worried about him."

"Worried he's going to end up back on my couch, maybe." But for all my gruff talk, I was glad he wasn't showing signs of cracking under the pressure after one week. I wanted him to succeed, really. And not just so he'd stay off my couch.

We lapsed into silence after that, and once everything was brought in, he helped me unload the bags. Then he leaned against the counter while I finished putting things away, self-conscious about every little-to-no-cooking-skill-required processed convenience food that I tucked into the fridge or pantry.

"Don't judge me," I said eventually. "I can feel you judging me with your judgy eyes."

"I'm not judging you. But for a healthcare professional, I expected better."

"See? Judgery." I slid a fresh box of sugary breakfast cereal onto its shelf and shut the pantry door with finality.

"Speaking of which, when do you start back at the hospital?"

"Not sure. I thought I'd hear back from legal by now, but it's a weekend. So, tomorrow probably." I tugged open the fridge and grabbed two bottles of water, tossing him one.

"You going back full-time?"

"I assume so. Why?"

He twisted the lid off the bottle in his hands and took a sip before answering. "Just wondering."

I eyed him as I moved past him into the living room. Just wondering my ass. "Might as well be out with it."

"I just wonder if that's the best thing for you."

"Oh? And let me guess. You know what's best for me?" I couldn't help but bristle at that as I flopped on the couch and put my feet up on the coffee table. He'd followed me out into the living room but paused a few feet away. Barrington hopped off the back of the sofa and trotted over to sniff his shoes and rub against his ankles.

"That's not what I meant."

"What did you mean, then?"

"Sometimes I wonder if pulling you into Magic Crimes was a bad idea." He held up a hand to forestall the scathing objection on the tip of my tongue. "You've been a godsend, and we work well together. But you already had a full-time job when I brought you on, and I didn't really think about what that might mean, putting in ten to twenty hours of consulting a week on top of that. I mean, you're a grown-ass woman and are fully capable of making your own decisions. I'm not saying you aren't. But I watched the demands on your time wear you down over the course of the first two months. And while I wouldn't ever say that I was glad you were let go—I saw how that affected you, how much stress and turmoil it caused—I've also seen what you were like when you were actually getting a decent night's sleep regularly. And I know you're excited to get back to work in the ER, but Em, you can only burn the candle at both ends for so long before you get burned."

I wasn't sure how to feel about this outpouring of concern from him. Annoyance lurked beneath the surface because he was right—I was a grown-ass woman capable of making my own decisions. But he was also right about the schedule being killer, and even in the middle of it all, I'd wondered if it were truly sustainable in the long run. I'd just been so consumed by the need to get my job back ever since it was yanked away that I hadn't really thought about the full implications of what getting it back meant. But did that mean I didn't want it? No. Did that mean I wanted to give up working with Mike instead? Hell no.

"I can't turn it down, Mike. Not if the department won't pay me a full-time salary. Hell, not even then, really. There's a hole in my heart where only nursing fits. I'm not saying our work together isn't rewarding, but it's like apples and oranges."

"An apple a day keeps the doctor away," he said, bobbing his head, "but oranges have more vitamin C."

I blinked slowly at him. "Uh, right. Anyway, I hear you. And I'll think about it."

"That's all I ask." He picked at the label on his water bottle. "So, uh, we good?"

"Yeah, we—actually, there is one thing."

He ambled over to the sofa and dropped onto the opposite end. "I'm all ears."

"You like working with me, right?"

"Of course. You're doing a great job. I hope you don't think that I was encouraging you to leave the department with all that."

"I like working with you too. Like I said, it's rewarding." I turned my head to meet his eyes and held them. "But I promise you this: If you ever handcuff me to anything again, we're done."

The words hung heavy in the air after I spoke them, several seconds passing before he nodded. "That's fair. It was a dumb move, for any number of reasons. For what it's worth, I'm sorry."

"It's not worth much, but it's enough. I forgive you. Just don't do it again."

He scooted to the edge of the couch and leaned over to put his water on the coffee table, then fished his keys out of his pocket and worked to free one from the key ring. Only when he dropped it in my hand did I realize what it was. A handcuff key. I accepted it as the peace offering it was and added it to my own key ring.

"What do you think the odds are that we can get some more of those fancy zip ties Volkov had?" he asked, sitting back again. Barrington hopped up in his lap, and he rubbed behind the tabby's orange-striped ears absently. "Not for you. I mean, for perps."

"Hmm. You're right, those would be handy. Volkov's gone, but I have his number."

"Does that mean you're square with the Circle?" He chuckled. "Square with the Circle. Funny."

I smirked. "Yeah, actually." I gave him the brief rundown of my encounter with Adrian outside the grocery store.

"Hmm." Mike scratched at his jaw. "So, Montenegro's a Circle witch. I wonder if there are others involved in this."

"That's exactly what I thought when he told me. We still don't know who Montenegro and Ochoa were working for."

"Or Xavier, for that matter."

I stared at him for a moment, blinking. "I assumed he was on Ochoa's payroll."

"Unlikely. Xavier was scared—is scared—for his family. Ochoa's a brute, but he's not a monster. My gut tells me all three were working for this third party, and if we don't figure out who it is, in another six months or a year we'll be right back where we started."

"People keep telling me to trust my instincts, so that's what I'm going to tell you. We'll figure it out. As for the cuffs, Dan or Prince Charming might be able to put something together for us. I saw the spell, and I understand how it works in theory. I think we could reconstruct it, and we still have the pair we used on Montenegro to work with."

"Didn't cutting them nullify the spellwork?"

"Yeah, but the etchings are still there. It's better than nothing. The only catch would be that the cuffs' effectiveness may vary depending on how much mojo the witch we're cuffing has."

"Gotcha. Also, zip ties are great, but it'd be even better if we can etch a standard pair of cuffs. Even better than that if they can be reused a few times before needing recharging."

I wondered if my newfound ability to transfer magic could be used to recharge charms and made a note to experiment with that. "If the department can spare a pair for us to work with, I'll see what I can do."

"Sounds good. But don't use Charming. There's no way he'll agree not to reproduce them for the market, and I don't know how I feel about something like this hitting the streets. Let's keep this one in-house."

He had a point. "Our options are pretty limited for in-house witchery while Dan's in the academy."

"What about the state's witch? Seaver."

I winced. "We didn't exactly part on good terms. But it's a thought. I mean, they'd be as valuable to the State Police as they would be to us. There's something to be gained from collaboration. But she might want to know why I can't just do it myself. I'd like to know her a little better before I open that can of worms." I held a hand out to Barrington, and he eyed me for a moment before miraculously leaving Mike's lap to cross the couch for some pets from me. "What if I found another trustworthy witch to help? Someone who isn't in the charm business."

"Yeah, that's fine. I trust you."

Having his trust meant a lot to me because I knew how hard it was for him to give after Xavier's betrayal. Still, I couldn't resist teasing him a little. I pressed a hand to my chest, gasping softly for effect. "You have no idea how long I've waited to hear those three little words."

"At the rate you're going, it'll be a while before you hear them again," he groused, but with a small smile.

I grinned at him and scooted over, sending the cat running, to plant a smacking kiss on his cheek while he screwed his face up like he'd sucked on a lemon.

"Gah. Witch cooties." He shoved me away and I fell backward, but my laughter was short-lived as I also spilled ice-cold water on myself. Yeah, I deserved it, but I regretted nothing.

32

I didn't have long to mull over my nursing vs police work dilemma. By noon the next day, I was in a conference room sitting across the table from a lawyer and a daunting stack of paperwork. The lawyer, who'd introduced herself simply as Lindsey, didn't look much older than me. Maybe healthcare and hospital law was less competitive than other specialties. Or, more likely, I didn't merit the attention of someone more senior.

Inside, I was a mess. Here I was, on the cusp of getting everything I'd wanted, but suddenly I wasn't sure if I wanted it anymore. Or, at least not the way I'd had it.

"Thanks for coming by," Lindsey said, pinching her tablet's stylus between two fingers like a cigarette. I wondered if she still smoked. Non-smokers rarely developed the habit of holding objects that way. "I'm fully up to speed on your situation, and Director Mayhew has authorized a generous offer should you agree to our terms. I think you'll be pleased."

Generous offer? Terms? What was she talking about? "I understand that I will be bound by the hospital's Magic Use in Patient Care policy. That shouldn't be a problem. Is there something else?"

"Let's dive in." She opened the file folder and removed the top page, turned it around, and slid it across the table toward me. I scanned it while she spoke, but what I saw was so startling, I didn't hear a word of what she said.

"This can't be right," I cut in. "This isn't my old job."

Her mouth tightened. "As I was saying, in recognition of your hard work in the ER during your previous employment and your newfound value as a practitioner, we're prepared to offer you a promotion—"

"To Lead Nurse of the Witch Emergency Response Unit? What 'Witch Emergency Response Unit?'"

"Again, if you'll let me finish . . ."

"Sorry." I wasn't sorry. I was confused, baffled, and generally unsettled. But I pressed my lips together firmly.

"In recognition of the special considerations involved in witch medical care—particularly urgent medical care—the director has authorized the creation of a new unit within the ER, the Witch Emergency Response Unit. It will be staffed by witches and tasked to oversee the safe, compassionate, and thorough medical care of practitioners who visit the ER. He's hand-picked you for the Lead Nurse position and would like for you to be involved in the interview and hiring process for your team. Several witch doctors will also be hired and attached to the unit, but they would not be under you. You would receive a twenty percent salary bump as compensation and retain your seven years of service for length-of-employment benefit calculations. This is also a salaried position, so the hours are flexible, but you'll be expected to average forty hours a week."

When she finished, I looked down at the paper in front of me again, speechless. The words on the page backed up what Lindsey had said, from the job title to the salary to the benefits. The implications were staggering. Emergency medical care for witches, by witches.

"Do you have any questions, Emily? I'm finished for now."

Only one sprang to mind. "Why doesn't this already exist?"

"I won't speculate on that. But doesn't that just make it all the more imperative that it should exist now? St. Vincent's will be the only hospital in the state with such a unit. A pioneer."

I traced the edge of the crisp white paper with a fingertip. I'd failed to answer the call to fight for witch rights by dodging that lawsuit. But maybe there was more than one way to fight for witch rights, and witches definitely deserved medical care that catered to their special needs and abilities —even if I suspected no small part of the unit's creation had to do with liability concerns. After all, who better to handle practitioners lashing out with magic than other practitioners? The WERU's nurses would need to be as skilled in bindings and counterspells as they were in starting IVs and bedside manner.

I couldn't dismiss the appeal. What if witch doctors were authorized to use healing magic—with consent, of course— on witch patients? Healing spells were strictly forbidden under the current policy. Again, a liability issue. But there were so many what-ifs involved in this that my mind spun trying to consider them all at once. And being salaried . . . the flexibility could be a godsend. Except I was still expected to put in the same number of hours, and no matter what this lawyer said about flexible hours, as a charge nurse I would be expected to keep regular hours. It's hard to ask people to keep to the schedule you set if you're not keeping one yourself.

"It's a lot to take in, I'm sure. Take your time," Lindsey said, though that she'd spoken at all was a reminder that she was waiting.

"What if I say no?"

Lindsey blinked. "Sorry?"

"If I turn down the promotion, will plans for the unit go forward?"

She looked at me like I was crazy. Maybe I was. "Yes. Or at least I hope so. I worked through the weekend on the paperwork. Are you saying you don't want the promotion?"

"Oh, I want it." I did. I really did. But I kept coming back to what Mike had said about burning the candle at both ends. And while this opportunity was amazing, it didn't make me want to work in Magic Crimes any less. "I just don't think it's a good idea for me to take on that level of responsibility. Honestly, it might be better if I come back to the ER part-time instead of full-time. But this plan is beyond exciting. I'd love to be part of it."

"You want to come back . . . part-time."

"Yeah, maybe twenty, twenty-five hours a week. Up to thirty in a pinch. I know staffing needs fluctuate, and I can be flexible. Would that be okay? I know I won't be eligible for full-time benefits anymore. Is medical coverage available for part-time employees?"

"Yes. About the medical benefits. As for the other, I'm not authorized to make that call. The director did authorize me to offer your old job as-is if you declined, but anything else I'd have to ask about."

I gave the offer letter one last long look, then slid it back across the table. "Okay. Please ask, then."

Lindsey tucked the document back into the folder and

stood with it in hand, collecting her tablet as well. "This may be a few minutes. Would you like something to drink while you wait?"

"I'm fine, thanks."

I second-guessed my decision as soon as the door closed behind her, but rather than make a fool of myself chasing her down, I whipped out my phone to call Mike with shaking hands. Naturally, it went to voicemail, so I called Matt and let him talk me off the ledge. When the conference room door opened twenty minutes later, he was extolling the virtues of the latest guy he wanted to set me up with. I'd never been more grateful to see a lawyer.

"Gotta-go-love-you-bye." I tapped the red button on the screen and set the phone face down on the table.

The folder hit the table with a quiet slap. "Sorry to keep you waiting," Lindsey said as she re-settled across the table. Her expression betrayed nothing. I took mental notes for the poker night Tracy wanted me to host for Dan's upcoming first weekend off from the academy.

"It's fine. I know I'm asking a lot."

She opened the folder and removed the top two sheets and placed them in front of me, side by side. On one side was an offer of part-time employment at the same hourly rate as my original position. On the other side was the promotion offer with its appealing salary bump. The number was larger than it had been before, too.

"The director requested I make one more appeal to you to accept the Lead Nurse position. As you can see, the offer has been raised."

If only it were about the money. I could get by on half my original salary plus my consultant fee from the police department. Finances would be a little tighter than they had been before, but I'd run the numbers with Matt and knew I could make it work. "What about the WERU? Can I be assigned to it?"

"That will be up to the Lead Nurse, once a candidate is selected. The director said he can guarantee you an interview, but it's up to you to make your case as a candidate from there."

I glanced between the two pages, worrying my lower lip between my teeth. "Do you have a pen?"

Lindsey slid one across the table. I picked it up and closed my eyes, making one final gut check before drawing the part-time offer closer and scrawling my signature at the bottom. As soon as it was done, I felt a little lighter. Lindsey collected both pages and signed the witness line on the signed offer, then ripped the other one in half before setting them both aside and picking up the first document on the inch-high stack that remained.

"Okay," she said. "Now for the rest of the paperwork."

33

I walked out of the hospital with a hand cramp from filling out and signing all the forms and other assorted paperwork involved in my re-hire. Among them was a document that waived my rights to sue them over the original termination. Considering I had gotten what I asked for in the end, I wasn't inclined to make any further fuss about it. That meant I had to call Gordon McAllister, though, and let him know I wouldn't be taking the AWL up on their offer of representation.

Though the itch to procrastinate was present, I made myself do it when I got back to the car. He took the derailment of his aspiring crusade about as well as I could have expected, though there was a tightness to his voice that suggested anger more than disappointment by the time he hung up on me with a terse goodbye.

I wasn't sure how long it would take Wendy to put me back on the schedule, so I took advantage of having the afternoon off to head to the station. Mike had called me back during the great paperwork marathon and left a message about a shoplifting teenager being why he'd missed my call. I was kind of glad that our casework was back to things like petty theft rather than felony narcotics.

I spent a few hours doing casework with Mike, but he cut me loose around three-thirty because he had to meet a contractor about drywall repair. Over the course of the last couple of days, we did at least get a tip that it had been a couple of Big G's guys who'd broken into his house and wrecked the place. The why was still fuzzy. A scare tactic or retaliation, perhaps. We'd find them eventually and get some answers.

When I got home, I decided to treat myself to a bath. I'd just settled into the suds when my phone began bouncing on the toilet seat lid. I almost let it go to voicemail but decided at the last minute to sit up and snag my phone before it vibrated its way off the toilet seat. John's name was on the screen when I thumbed the answer button and—mindful of the last ill-fated phone call I'd taken in the tub—gripped the edges of the case firmly with my still-dry hand.

"Hey, John, what's up?"

"Hi, Emily. I hope this isn't a bad time."

I glanced down at the expanse of lavender-scented water covering me from my chest down. Good thing this wasn't a video call. Making a mental note not to splish-splash and give the game away, I replied, "Not at all, I was just relaxing."

"Oh, good. I was just wondering—well, Kassidy and I were wondering—if you'd found whoever was behind that magic-imbued drug."

"I did, yeah. He's being tight-lipped about how he made it and who paid him to do it, but he's not going to be making any more of it anytime soon if the DA has anything to say about it." What was that strange feeling in my chest? Was that disappointment that the only reason he'd called was to ask about the case?

"That's great, I'm glad to hear that. I'll let Kassidy know. Or you could tell her yourself, I suppose. She's rather eager for you to return."

Oh right. The favor. The favor that involved John too. "Hmm. I admit I'm curious about what this favor of hers entails. Has she said anything to you about it?"

"No. I asked, but she said she wants to talk to both of us together. She can be quite stubborn when she puts her mind to it."

"Why do I get the feeling that's pretty much any day ending in Y?"

He chuckled. "Pretty much."

"Anyway, yeah. I'm going back to work at the hospital soon, but—"

"That's great news! Congratulations!"

The warmth and enthusiasm in his voice brought a smile to my lips. "Thanks. It's part-time, which is going to work out much better with my consulting gig. I don't know when I'm starting just yet, or what hours I'll be working. But I should be able to make it out to the Pueblo soon." I wondered if Kassidy's archive had anything about magic fluctuations in unborn babies and made a note to ask while I was there. Sure, Suzi had that appointment coming up with the witch OB, but it couldn't hurt to double up. "When would be a good time for you?"

"I'm off today and tomorrow, then I'm on for twenty-four."

"Ouch. Firefighter hours are even worse than nursing. Noted. How about tomorrow morning? I've got an appointment to interview a coven with Tracy at two, but I'm free until then. I'll bring donuts. I have a feeling this is the sort of conversation sugar will make easier."

"Sure, that works for me. What time?"

"Nine or so?"

"I'll tell Gus. He'll be excited to see you again."

"Ohh, I see. Any particular flavor of donut I should bring for him? I'm not sure they have steak-flavored ones. He seems pretty traditional. Plain cake?"

He chuckled. "No donuts for him, unless it's one of those places that has the doggie donuts. He's got to watch his waistline."

"You take that back. He's not fat, he's just big-boned." Though, truly, I'm not sure there was an ounce of fat on the dog's massive body. I couldn't say the same for mine, but I extended a leg from the water and examined it with a forgiving eye. There was something to be said for not having skin-and-bone chicken legs. As long as I was a healthy weight, I was content.

"Aren't you going to ask what kind of donuts *I* like?"

I leaned my head back against the towel I'd set on the edge of the tub as a pillow, smiling up at the ceiling. "Why, are you picky?"

"Not terribly. I'm just hurt you care more about my dog's donut preferences than mine."

"I'll make it up to you somehow. Maybe with a . . . chocolate glazed donut?"

His warm laughter rolled across the line and sent a tingle down my spine. Or maybe that was just a drop of water down my neck. "Now you're just fishing."

"Sprinkles or no sprinkles?"

"Have dinner with me."

"Er, what?" Did I hear that right? Did he just ask me out to dinner in the middle of an important donut-related conversation?

"Let me take you to dinner—to celebrate your re-employment. Or to appease your guilty conscience."

A laugh bubbled from my chest. "Did you just ask me for a pity date?"

"Hmm. I guess I did. What do you say?"

I bit my lip, a reflexive no on the tip of my tongue. I didn't date witches as a general rule. But that decision, like so many others in my life, was made under a faulty premise. I'd had to re-evaluate a lot of things to accept my justifications for calling myself a witch. Maybe this was something else I needed to re-evaluate. I certainly found John attractive, and he seemed like a nice guy. Easy to talk to. Good sense of humor. Plus, he already knew I wasn't a "normal" witch. He knew how hectic my life was, not to mention how dangerous my work could be. Heck, he wouldn't be able to throw stones in that regard anyway. He ran into burning buildings for a living.

"Emily? Are you still there?"

"Yes." My heart beat a little faster as I answered both questions at once.

"Oh, okay. If you don't want to, that's fine . . ."

"No, I mean yes. Yes, I'm here and yes, I'll have dinner with you."

"Oh! Great, then. I'll pick you up at seven?"

"Sounds good. Is this a wine-and-charcuterie-board sort of place or a tequila and nachos kind of place?"

"Which would you prefer?"

"Tequila and nachos," I said without hesitation.

"A woman after my own heart. Consider it done. Enjoy your bath, and I'll see you soon."

My mouth dropped open and my cheeks heated, but my phone beeped as the call disconnected before I could figure out whether to confirm or deny it. In the end, I laughed and dropped the phone on the floor beside the tub, spooking Barrington who'd wandered in while I was on the phone.

"Oops, sorry, buddy."

The cat hopped up on the edge of the tub and fixed extremely judgy eyes on me for having the unfathomable audacity to submerge myself in weird-smelling water on a regular basis. I scooped up a handful of bubbles and blew them at him. He vanished so quickly that if he'd been a cartoon roadrunner, he would've left a puff of smoke behind.

I had plenty of time for a soak before I had to get ready to go, so I slumped down farther in the water and closed my eyes, letting my mind drift. For once in a good while, things finally seemed to be going my way. I had stable full-time employment again, my apartment to myself, the Circle off my back, and a date with a handsome man to look forward to. And though the specter of Kassidy's favor loomed on the horizon, there was no sense in fretting over it when I didn't know what it was. I just hoped it wasn't illegal.

I had told her I wouldn't do anything illegal, hadn't I?

AUTHOR'S NOTE

What a wild ride this has been! The seeds of this book were sewn back in chapter one of book one, and it's always fun to nurture a plot and watch it grow over the course of a series. And as you might have noticed, there's more to this one yet!

Emily's magical, crime-solving adventures will continue in 2022. In the meantime, I invite you to visit my website and sign up for my newsletter for release dates, recipes, sneak peeks, bonus content, free reads, and more.

www.loridrakeauthor.com

ABOUT THE AUTHOR

 Disenchanted with her mundane human existence, Lori loves spinning tales of magic and creatures of myth & legend existing in the modern world. When not indulging in these flights of fancy, she enjoys cooking, crafting, gaming, and (of course) reading. She's also a bit of a weather geek and would like to go storm chasing one day.

Lori lives in Austin, Texas with her husband and three adorable kitties that don't understand why mommy doesn't like them climbing on her laptop and batting at the screen.

The kitties, that is. It'd be really strange if her husband did that.

www.loridrakeauthor.com
lori@loridrakeauthor.com

f facebook.com/loridrakeauthor
BB bookbub.com/authors/lori-drake

Printed in Great Britain
by Amazon